DOCTOR WHO

TRADING FUTURES

LANCE PARKIN

BBC

Published by BBC Worldwide Ltd
Woodlands, 80 Wood Lane
London W12 0TT

First published 2002
Copyright © Lance Parkin 2002
The moral right of the author has been asserted

Original series broadcast on the BBC
Format © BBC 1963
Doctor Who and TARDIS are trademarks of the BBC

ISBN 0 563 53848 1
Imaging by Black Sheep, copyright © BBC 2002

Printed and bound in Great Britain by Mackays of
Chatham
Cover printed by Belmont Press Ltd, Northampton

Prologue
The Banquo Legacy

Now Baskerville mentioned it, the night was getting cold.

They stood at the side of the road. Cosgrove took in the scene, savoured it like an '07 Tattinger. The water in the loch was glittering, almost purple. The scent of heather filled the air. It was so quiet – no cars and lorries trundling in the distance, no aircraft scoring a line through the sky. Everything was so sharp, so well-defined. He didn't know what he was expecting, but this felt almost more than real. Hyper-real.

Baskerville looked distinctly bored. He was leaning against a tree, checking his nails. He was the younger man here, in his sixties, with thin white hair. He had an aquiline nose, a high forehead. Cosgrove studied the face, for future reference.

'Have you seen enough yet, Mr Cosgrove?' Baskerville asked.

'Don't use my name,' he snapped. They'd agreed that from the start. No names.

'My dear Cosgrove, no one is listening in.'

It was a liberating thought. When was the last time Cosgrove had known for certain that he was having a private conversation? He'd almost forgotten what it felt like to speak without assuming that someone, somewhere, was recording it and filing it away. No concealed microphones, or phone or data taps, no lasers on his windows, registering every vibration in the air. He was in unmonitored territory here, for the first time in years.

There was more, though. He was beyond the law here. He could kill Baskerville where he stood, leave him lying at the side of the road. And no one would ever know. The thought of killing someone without having to do any paperwork was a refreshing one.

'Can I walk around?' Cosgrove asked, looking back at the loch.

'You can do what you want. How about you walk towards the forest, there?'

He hadn't noticed the forest. Cosgrove found himself nodding, then decided against it, in case it was a trick. 'No – the other way.'

Baskerville smiled. Of course. Lead on.'

Cosgrove stepped back up on to the road. 'And this is the year…?'

'1040, as requested.'

'You can prove that?'

'I'm not sure I can. Look around, though, there could be some evidence. Judging by the hoof prints, this road is a busy one.'

Cosgrove found something after a few minutes. An arrowhead, dropped in the mud. He examined it.

'Keep it,' Baskerville suggested. 'Give it to your people for analysis. That should be your proof. Wait! Can you hear the horses?'

He could, but only just. Baskerville had keen senses.

'Do you think it's them?'

'Yes. We're in the right time and place. It's why we are here, after all.'

'But the witches should be here –'

'They aren't. You remember what the witches said?'

'Of course. Don't you?'

'I don't have the benefit of a classical education. If you remember what was said, then say it.'

'But we're not witches. There aren't even three of us.'

'My dear fellow, Shakespeare was a writer, a maker of fictions. You don't think he let his research get in the way of a good story, do you? You think when he said a man "takes off his helmet" that he'd have found an old book and thought, "yes, the helmet would be similar to those of Norman design, but with a nasal reinforce bar integral with the skull, cheek plates, and a nape plate"?'

'No.'

'No – he thought of a nice dramatic opening, something to intrigue his audience. Nothing like this. I suggest that there are no witches here because there's no such thing as witches. So it falls to you to understudy.'

There were two of them, they were exactly how Cosgrove pictured them.

'Terrible weather,' the taller of the two said, in an accent so thick it was practically another language.

'How far is it, now? Wait! Who are you?'

Cosgrove took a deep breath.

'Speak, if you can.'

'All hail Macbeth, hail to thee, Thane of Glamis! All hail Macbeth, hail to thee, Thane of Cawdor! All hail, Macbeth, that shalt be King hereafter.'

The smaller man pushed his way forward while his master absorbed that announcement.

'You have the sight? You can see the seeds of the future in the here and now? You've told mac-Bethad. Now tell me my fate.'

'Lesser than Macbeth, and greater. Not so happy, yet much happier. Thou shall get kings, though thou be none. Banquo and Macbeth all hail!'

The two men leant in to confer.

Baskerville took a step towards Cosgrove. 'Excellent. Now, I suggest we get going, before there are too many awkward supplementary questions.'

Cosgrove clutched the arrowhead.

'I think you've made your case, Baskerville. But next time, I want to bring a scientist to look at the machine.'

The mists were growing thick. Reality was swirling away. Baskerville's voice persisted, seemed to echo.

'Very well. But no more than two of you, unarmed, no recording devices or communications equipment. I'll arrange the meeting. You know my price. Tell your masters that it is non-negotiable, tell them that they must decide quickly. And tell them that it is no exaggeration to say that if they don't listen to my warnings, then this whole planet will be destroyed.'

Chapter One
Friendly Fire

The hydrofoil was something secret, something not of the everyday world. Its design embodied a contradiction, revelled in it.

The boat was invisible, with camouflage that went far deeper than its black paintwork. The hull was coated in rounded and smoothed thermoplastic, so radar beams just slid off it. The hydroplanes themselves were designed so that the boat barely disturbed the water it was slicing through. The motors were electric, all but silent, but were muffled anyway. On a night like this, you could stand twenty feet from the hydrofoil as it passed you and you couldn't be sure that it had.

Despite being invisible, it was also evil-looking. That was the contradiction. It glistened, it looked more like an ocean predator such as a ray or a shark than a piece of military hardware. The fact that the gun ports and missile tubes were hidden behind radar shielding just made it look more sinister – who knew what weapons it had, where they were concealed? If you did happen to see it, you'd rather wish you hadn't.

The incursion began at 23:11.

Unaware of it for the moment, Cosgrove sat at the back of the cabin. It was three hours since he'd left Baskerville. He still felt dizzy – a little lagged from his journey. He refused to believe it was his age: he was as fit as most men half as old. He felt excited, too – a thrill and anticipation that he'd not felt for far too long. That may have been because he was out here in the field again. He'd missed this. It had been too long, he'd begun to grow soft. Out here anything could happen. The boat could be in someone's sights, there could be a bomb on board.

At least he could trust the two others here, they were both men he'd hand-picked. Even so, they didn't know why he was here, they thought they were taking him to a rendezvous, not away from one. For the moment, all three of them sat in comfortable padded seats, facing forward. The boat didn't have a windscreen or portholes, although there was a plasma screen pasted round the front bulkhead which simulated one. The picture enhanced the available light, extrapolated colour, made it look like midday outside.

The soldier, King, was alert, the pilot was busy managing her navigation software. Neither spoke, or had brought anything to read. Cosgrove found himself growing steadily more bored. The briefcase was heavy on his lap. There was little engine noise, barely a hum.

Cosgrove took two painkillers. There had been a time when he'd had nothing to do with them. They dull the senses, as well as the pain. They blunt a man's edge. But the nagging headache, the one that hadn't gone away for weeks, the dizziness, the ache in his shoulder that was there all the time, now... the edge was already a little blunt. He remembered the words of Churchill's doctor – he'd inherited good health, but by now much of that was spent.

They all heard something drop on to the deck, then footsteps above them.

King looked up, puzzled.

'What is it?'

'A wave?'

'The sea's flat.'

'Go and check,' Cosgrove ordered King.

'It's nothing.'

'Go and check.'

There was a man standing on the deck. He watched King clamber out through the hatch with nothing more than mild curiosity.

King raised his gun, aimed a shot at him, but the pistol's software overrode him. The man was unarmed, and tagged as a civilian. You couldn't shoot civilians without special orders.

'Could you help me with this?' the man asked. He was holding a great bundle of white material – a parachute, King realised.

'Wait, I…'

'Here,' the man said, pushing the parachute into his arms.

'You can't…'

The man yanked the material up, until it was a hood over the soldier's head.

The heads-up display in King's helmet was flashing a number of warnings now. One advised that the civilian had been reclassified as a threat. The second warned him not to take another step back. The last told him of an imminent physical contact. It came moments before he was gently tipped over the rail that ran along the side of the boat.

His life jacket automatically inflated on contact with the water, restricting his arms and legs, swathing him in bullet-proof fabric. His pistol was floating just out of reach.

By the time King had pulled himself free of the parachute, and he'd splashed around to face the boat, it was several hundred yards away. There was no sign of the civilian, and the hatch had been shut.

Cosgrove had put his helmet on, and it had already told him about the intruder.

The briefcase remained cuffed to his wrist. It was an obvious encumbrance, so Cosgrove opted for the element of surprise. He took his position behind the hatch, lodged in place, waiting until the intruder was on board. The intruder took his time. Cosgrove got a good look at him. He was a Caucasian male, about forty, not moving like he was combat trained. Not moving with any urgency at all.

He had something in his hand. A grenade? No, a rubber ball.

The pilot turned in her chair, covered the intruder with her pistol.

6

'Hello there,' the intruder said.

'Drop that,' the pilot ordered.

The ball slipped from his hand, bounced and hit the control panel.

The roof blew off, and the pilot's ejector seat fired. The idiot squealed as she flew off, up and over the boat. The boat was already powering down.

'As a security precaution, the auto destruct sequence has been engaged. Sixty seconds.' The voice was synthesised, disjointed. Cosgrove could override it, but he'd need to get to the controls.

It didn't trouble the intruder, who retrieved the rubber ball, before stopping at the water cooler that sat opposite the hatch and pouring himself a drink of water. His hair flapped in the breeze.

There was plenty of time for Cosgrove to target him - the crosshairs in the helmet display narrowed over the intruder's back. One through the heart.

'Stay where you are,' Cosgrove ordered.

The intruder did as he was told.

'Are you armed?' The helmet's display had already given him the answer, but he liked to hear it from the intruder himself.

'I have a glass of water. Well, not a glass. Plastic. I have a plastic of water.'

'Hardly a weapon.'

'Well… no. But it's enough to overpower you. If that's all right.'

Cosgrove laughed. 'Turn around.'

The civilian did as he said.

'If you're going to overpower me, you have –'

'Forty seconds,' the computer supplied.

'Forty seconds. You'd better hurry.'

The civilian smiled. 'I thought you'd never ask.'

He tipped the water over Cosgrove's shoulder, and ducked out the way as the lifejacket automatically inflated, splaying his arms, lodging him in the doorway.

'Who sent you?' Cosgrove shouted, trying to wriggle free.

The intruder looked at him thoughtfully, slipping some sort of tool from his pocket. 'Who do you think?'

'How did –' he asked as the handcuff fell away from the briefcase handle.

The control panel started buzzing. The intruder stepped over to it, sat down in one of the remaining chairs, rested the briefcase in his lap.

'Appalling layout,' he said. 'Nothing's where you need it to be.'

'You have to deactivate the self-destruct. We'll be killed.'

'You'll be safe in that lifejacket of yours.'

'You won't. You'll be killed.'

The intruder shook his head.

He tugged at the control that fired his ejector seat, and launched into the night sky.

And he was waving goodbye, with a grin on his face, as he went.

A couple of grey-haired lesbians were telling the people on the next table that they'd come to San Antonio every year since they were teenagers back in the nineties. An hour before, the cabaret singer had started singing *Smack My Bitch Up* and the other diners started cooing about the golden oldies and asking if anyone else remembered Compact Discs.

Welcome to the future, Anji Kapoor.

Before she had met the Doctor and she'd become a time traveller, Anji had been starting to feel a little old – she was twenty-seven, she had a real career, her student loan was all but paid off, she was in a steady relationship, and Friday nights had come to mean *Changing Rooms* and *Frasier*. Now she was surrounded by people pushing pensionable age who she could have been to school with. People who still came to Ibiza on holiday, but who only popped vitamin pills. Or would do, if the EZ hadn't banned them. Ecstasy, on the other hand, wasn't just legal, it was on the restaurant's dessert menu.

Before, when they'd landed in the future, it had almost always been the far future – on space colonies with flying cars and cyborgs. That was easy to cope with, it was just like being a character in a science-fiction novel. But this was weird – she just had no idea if she was meant to feel very, very old or very, very young.

It was strange to think that her dinner companion was only a couple of years older than her, but also almost too old to be her dad. Fitz had been born before the Second World War, and the Doctor had picked him up in the nineteen-sixties. His sense of time lag must be even more acute, he must find this place even more disturbing.

Anji looked up to see Fitz giggling at the menu.

Three hours or so ago, Anji had been impressed, too. After sitting them down, the waiter had handed them both what looked like a small piece of laminated card, but which had turned out to be some sort of liquid crystal screen with an interactive menu. If you tapped at it, it showed you pictures of the dishes, it gave you a detailed description, it showed you the ingredients and nutritional information, it even gave you a restaurant critic's opinion. You could scroll off in any direction, and it never seemed to end.

A logical extension of technology. Anji was starting to piece together a bit of future history. She was a futures trader. It had been – still was? – her job to spot trends, see patterns. So, this menu was a step up from the Psion organiser in her bag, the one she'd been so impressed with in the shop, but centuries less advanced than the library she'd seen on Hitchemus, which was positively Neanderthal compared with the technology Silver had operated in Hope.

The menu was guilty of all the worst sins of bad website design back home – doing things simply because it could, piling information on information, it was designed to actively – interactively – get in the way of simply ordering a meal.

Fitz had insisted on keeping the menu even after they'd ordered, and had played with it through each of the four courses, leaving Anji to play with her food.

The view was spectacular. The Mediterranean, on a beautiful summer's evening, now a beautiful summer's night. There were flaming torches on the beach, and some sort of party going on down there. Anji's fellow diners glanced out every so often, but now the singer had gone, most were looking at the vast wall-mounted TV screens. A soccer game between the Eurozone national team and Brazil was getting underway. Every few minutes play would stop for an ad break, which ended with a short news bulletin.

There was trouble in North Africa – Anji tried to get the context from the tiny snatches of news and a few images – gleaming tanks with EZ flags nudging past bemused Arab onlookers. The tanks were chrome, the shape of tortoiseshells. Sci-fi weapons. Cut to a White House spokesman in jeans and T-shirt, with the anchorwoman talking over him, saying class twos had been deployed, purely in a peacekeeping capacity. Hyperlinks swarmed uselessly around the pictures.

Then back to the soccer game. The referee started the second ninth as soon it was clear the ad break was over.

'Where is he?' she asked.

Fitz looked up. 'The Doctor? He said wait here. He'll be here.'

'Have you any idea how we're meant to pay for this meal?'

'It says they take any IFEC card.'

'And do you have an IFEC card?'

'No.'

'Do you even know what one is?'

'Back in my day,' Fitz said, changing the subject, 'if you couldn't pay, you had to do the washing up. I suppose they've got robots to do all that now.'

'I'm sure the waiter's giving us a funny look.'

'Relax. We're the customers. Just keep ordering coffee. They've got different types, you can mix and match. Look. Decaffaraspberchino.' He waved the menu at her, before returning his attention to it. 'You can get it to do different languages. What do your lot speak?'

'English.'

'No... ah, there we go. Hindu.'

'Hindi.'

'Look at it.'

'I know what a cup of coffee looks like.'

'This is coffee of the future. Look, the last couple of places we've been, the coffee wasn't up to much. Enjoy it while you can.'

There was an explosion out at sea. Just a flash of orange light. The other diners, and the waiters, hurried over to the window. Which was almost certainly exactly the wrong thing to do in the circumstances. Anji remembered when a few IRA bombs had gone off in the City. There had been an email circulated about it – if a bomb goes off, stay away from the windows. Glass shatters. Shattered glass does nasty things to your eyes if it gets into them.

'Could it be terrorists?' one of the tourists said.

'There aren't terrorists,' the other one reminded her. 'Not any more.'

'But this might be some sort of comeback. There was an article about neo-terrorism last week and –'

Fitz looked up from his menu.

There was something burning on the horizon. A black shape, surrounded with flame. So how far was that? A mile? No, more than that.

'It could be nothing. A coincidence,' Anji suggested.

'Yeah, right. Coincidence. Like every single time we land somewhere there's a big coincidence. Before you met the Doctor, did things ever explode?'

'As a matter of fact –'

'Hey, look at that,' Fitz was saying.

She realised, with a start, that they'd interrupted the soccer match on TV to report the explosion. An aerial shot – some news channel's helicopter, already on the scene.

Anji was more interested in the man who'd just walked in through the door. He was in his early forties, apparently at least, and wore a long black coat.

'Doctor!'

'Hello there.'

Fitz turned at the sound of the familiar voice.

He was carrying a briefcase, a small, silver one. Very expensive. His hair was wet.

'You have a fish in your pocket,' Fitz observed.

The Doctor handed it over to him. 'So I do. Have you eaten?'

Chapter Two
A Case for the Doctor

The jet-black Saab had abandoned any pretence that it was just happening to be passing along the same mountain road. Now it was in pursuit.

Malady pulled her Ford Panther down a gear and squeezed another ten kilometres an hour from it. From a few glances in her mirror over the last few minutes, she'd worked out there were two men in the car, both of them made from the same mould – heavy-set, unsmiling, straight from central casting.

Her passenger, Garvin, was looking nervous, he was clutching his laptop. 'They're on to us,' he whispered.

'Don't worry, that's what I'm here for. You concentrate on enhancing that image.'

The driver of the Saab was good, though, and she was surprised the EZ could still make cars like that. Perhaps it was just prejudice, but she thought a generation of safety legislation had emasculated European cars, made them into little more than shopping trolleys with lawnmower engines.

'How did the EZ know we were watching them? How did they get a car out here so fast? They probably think we sunk that Manta.'

'They aren't the EZ. The Union are more efficient than this.'

There were a lot of talented people in the Union, and they'd always been careful to have enough 'hotspots' to act as training grounds for their military. If she'd been marked by the EZ, she'd have been picked off by some Kosovan sniper, or some Frenchman or Irishman would have stuck a bomb under her car. Was it one of the various Mafias? The Russians were keeping their gangs out of the EZ at the moment. The Italians were meant to be too busy fighting each other.

'So who is it?'

'It could be any number of people. It could even someone on our side who doesn't realise we're the good guys. I'm not going to stop to ask.'

The Saab was lurching forwards.

'They're making their move.'

It was inches away from her rear bumper.

She picked up speed. Her car ought to be faster, and she was confident she was the better driver.

Her eyephones were ringing. She used one hand to take them out of her shirt pocket and slip them on, keeping the other hand clamped to the steering wheel.

There was a click from inside the arm, and the retinal scanner whirred into life. She let it read her.

The CIA seal flickered up, only partially blocking the view of the curve in the road ahead. She had both hands back on the wheel, but the distraction had cost her a little time.

'Go ahead,' said a computerised voice, an autosec by the sound of it.

The man at the other end of the line didn't waste any time. 'CNN are reporting an EZ patrol boat just exploded five miles from your position, Malady.'

'It wasn't a patrol boat, it was a Manta. And it was nothing to do with me, Control.'

'No? I'm tempted to ask why not.'

'Jonah Cosgrove was in the boat, sir.'

A pause.

'And is my opposite number…' He was clearly struggling for the euphemism. You'd think they'd come more easily. '…inoperative?'

'I don't know, sir. They had a man overboard, then the pilot ejected, then the boat self-destructed. No sign of Cosgrove. They were attacked.'

Another pause. 'Not by us.'

'Sir, if it was us, we probably just started World War –'

'Not by us,' Control repeated firmly. 'You and Garvin are the only two people on the island.'

Hard left. The Saab was still almost on top of them.

'Have you been able to track their course?'

'Of course not.'

'Find Cosgrove. Find out what he was doing here. He's not left his desk in London for nearly twenty years. Jonah is one of the most shadowy of the European shadow government. He's involved in something big. Find out what, Malady.'

'Understood.'

The eyephone screen faded.

'Problem?' Garvin asked.

'Not the sort of thing a techie can deal with. How's that image?'

'It's kinda difficult to concentrate.'

The back axle buckled.

It had been hit, Malady realised. As she struggled with the wheel, she could tell the axle had been sliced apart. She couldn't think of a weapon that could do that, and she was damn sure it wasn't something she'd hit on the road.

She also knew that she had other priorities.

She quickly brought the car under control, slowing it, managing to swerve it so that the rear driver door was facing the Saab. There wasn't time to get out, though.

Malady braced herself, turned to watch the Saab hit her. The driver and passenger sat impassive, letting it happen.

Her car was shunted along, spun a couple of degrees.

Garvin had hit his head on the dashboard. He was unconscious, possibly worse.

Malady grabbed his laptop, and was out of the driver's door. She kept low, using the car as cover. The computer was the important thing here.

She heard the Saab's doors open. Both doors – she'd hoped one of them would have been incapacitated, or at least trapped in the car.

One of them pulled open the passenger door, she heard him moving in to get a look at Garvin.

Her pistol was in her hand. She popped up, fired two shots, dropped back to a crouch. The larger man fell, blood sprayed from his head, he twisted slightly, looked surprised.

And then there was the light.

A pencil-thin beam of light sizzled past her. A thin white line, perfectly straight.

The other one was firing some sort of ray gun.

She barely registered the sound of the felled tree behind her. The second beam was even closer, it scored a line in the tarmac of the road.

Her side had nothing like that – nothing handheld, anyway.

A cutting beam. Something that could slice through anything. It must have been what had smashed her axle. A deadly weapon.

But it had a disadvantage. With a bullet, you could get only a rough bearing on the man firing on you from the sound, or you might spot the muzzle flashing. This weapon drew a straight line back to the person holding it, and even lit up the surroundings. Every time he fired, it was as if he was pointing a giant luminous arrow at himself.

Malady stood, fired three shots, watched one of them catch his shoulder, one catch his chest, the last catch the gun itself.

He didn't make a sound.

The gun exploded, a burst of white light, like it had been loaded full of rays. She saw him in silhouette, pure black against pure white. The blast took his arm off, at the elbow. As he fell, he seemed to grow larger, became twisted. His head seemed to grow longer.

He grew horns.

Malady watched, as he fell apart.

A moment later, it was dark again. And there was no sign of either of the bodies.

Malady picked up the laptop, silently scolding herself for dropping it in the first place. She stepped back over to the cars. The men had disintegrated, there was no trace of them.

And so had their Saab. There was the wreck of her Panther, Garvin was dead, but there was no sign of the car that had hit it.

Those people weren't EZ.

Malady wasn't convinced they'd been people.

The laptop bleeped at her. She looked at the display. The computer had finished enhancing the image of the man who'd blown up the EZ Manta, and possibly assassinated the head of the EZ secret service.

His long face was oval, with an aristocratic nose and a full mouth. He had a high forehead, framed with long brown hair. He wore a long, dark coat. He had blue eyes, with traces of crow's-feet around them.

Malady had no idea who he was, but he'd triggered a diplomatic incident, possibly a World War.

She couldn't wait to meet him.

The morning before, it had become obvious that the TARDIS was up to something.

The air was full of bad mood. At first, Fitz assumed the Doctor and Anji had had a row. He'd heard them together in the control room, discussing something, and had stayed out of their way for an hour or two. In the end, he'd gone in – and was bemused to find them smiling, puzzling over some problem. The Doctor was standing over the control console, tapping his lip thoughtfully. Anji stood opposite, studying his expression. Neither of them had noticed Fitz arrive.

'Look!' the Doctor said suddenly, waving a finger at one of the displays.

'It's moving again.'

'Yes.'

'And you didn't touch it?'

'No. You were watching me. We've changed course again.'

'Could you have started a pre-set sequence running or something like that? Like a washing machine?'

The Doctor scowled at her. 'A washing machine? You're comparing the TARDIS to a washing machine?'

'Yes,' Anji insisted. 'Look, it's possible, isn't it? You could have switched on the autopilot, or the cruise control, or accidentally programmed it to do whatever it's doing at a set time. I mean you don't really understand how the TARDIS –'

A glare from the Doctor had shut her up. He didn't like to admit that his piloting of his time machine was essentially a series of educated guesses. And Fitz and Anji certainly didn't like to think about that. So there was an unspoken pact that no one ever said it out loud.

The Doctor turned to see Fitz, noticing him for the first time. 'You've not touched the controls?'

'No,' Fitz told them.

'Neither have I,' the Doctor said thoughtfully.

'So where are we heading now?' Fitz asked.

The Doctor studied the readings, appeared to do some mental arithmetic. 'We're heading out,' he said.

'Out?'

'The far future?' Anji asked. 'Or out of the galaxy?'

'Both,' the Doctor said, after a moment's consideration. 'I'm sorry Anji, but I won't be taking you home to the twenty-first century today. We are travelling into unknown realms. We have already left the universe with which we are familiar. The journey will be a long one. Hours at least, maybe days. We should all get some sleep while we have the chance.'

The TARDIS had landed on a beach full of sunbathing tourists before they'd reached their bedrooms.

The Doctor had spent a little while insisting that this was merely a simulacrum of Earth, like EarthWorld had been. He stayed in the TARDIS to calibrate the instruments, to work out their exact location in time and space. Fitz and Anji had popped out to buy ice creams.

They'd worked out roughly where and when they were almost before they'd stepped from the ship. The hotels and shops were in familiar styles, give or take, but the fashions – what there were of them on the beach – the electric buses and the animated billboards all provided evidence that they were a few years after Anji's time.

When they'd got back to the TARDIS, they handed the Doctor a copy of *The Times*, with the date on it, which they'd found at a small newsstand. The Doctor had held up his notebook, and told them that the equations he'd scrawled down led him to the exact same conclusion, although he'd flipped it closed when Anji asked to see that for herself. The Doctor had gone on to say that there was a time machine in operation in the area. He produced some sort of portable oscilloscope as evidence. He'd seen the same patterns before, and it meant displacement in the time field, which, in his experience, invariably meant trouble.

The Doctor headed for the door, suggesting they explore and try to find the time machine. His plans didn't extend past that. Anji had tried to pin him down, to focus a bit more on specific objectives. She'd got it into her head that there was a pattern to their travels, that there was a bigger picture they were all missing. She didn't go on about it this time, but she'd mentioned her theory to Fitz a few times, and from the glazed look in the Doctor's eye, he'd copped for the same conversation, too.

Fitz had his own theory, and he was the last to leave.

Something was nagging at him.

He told the others he'd left his red suede jacket in his room. Once he was sure he was alone, he went to the back of the TARDIS, the point furthest from the door. It was through a couple of doors, at the end of the corridor that didn't lead anywhere.

He'd heard something scratching against the other side of this wall once, like a wild animal trying to get out. The TARDIS had once been bigger than this. Infinite, according to the Doctor. Perhaps the rest of the ship was still there, trapped behind doorless walls. Perhaps there were other things trapped there, too.

'*They* didn't like people time travelling, did they?' he asked the wall.

No answer.

'The people that created you? The Doctor's people? I... think I remember what happened to them. If it ever happened. It happened to me, it happened to the Doctor. So it's got to count. Hasn't it? Just because I don't remember all of it doesn't mean it doesn't count.'

No answer.

'They didn't like other people time travelling. They tracked them down, punished them. Probably for all the right reasons, don't get me wrong. I do get it, you know – I do understand that if those... laws... hadn't been enforced, then everything we know could have come crashing down. There would be anarchy. We got a glimpse of it, remember. It was madness. But now *they*'ve gone. Everything they stood for is gone. Their time has passed. You do know that? There's no law, no order, not now. You're a police box, but there aren't any policemen left.'

There was a rumble, something echoing deep, deep below his feet.

'I wish that I was wrong,' Fitz said softly. 'But I'm not. It's just us, now.'

Fitz had left the ship to consider that, emerging into the sunshine and joining his friends.

Twenty four hours later, they were back on the beach. The TARDIS stood there as if it always had. The Doctor, Fitz and Anji sat nearby.

'Aren't you hot in that coat?'

Anji was hot in her bikini, even covered in the cooling suncream she'd bought ('Now with telomere fray protection', according to the bottle). The Doctor hadn't even taken off his jacket. The three of them sat on a large beach towel in the shade of the TARDIS, the Doctor intently examining the briefcase, Anji watching the Doctor, Fitz trying so hard not to look like he was ogling the sunbathing women.

'I suppose you're just trying to blend in. All the teenagers are wearing suits.'

'So?' Fitz and the Doctor asked.

'It's just odd.'

'Not particularly. Teddy boys wore suits, the mods wore suits,' Fitz reminded her. Anji hadn't really thought of it like that, but it was true. The ska bands, or whatever they'd been called, wore suits, too. It was one of those things that came around.

'The Beatles started off in suits,' she said.

'Well, they didn't start off like that,' the Doctor said, taking a small black box out of his pocket. 'But they took the suggestion well, I have to say.'

The fashion seemed to be unisex, and it was almost an eighties look – baggy and with shoulder pads. None of the natives, men or women, were wearing anything underneath their jackets, but they were wearing ties. Most had a metal lapel badge, a stylised monogram – R:C.

'Rebel: Conform,' the Doctor said. 'The children of this generation realised that the best way to worry their parents was to pass exams, become teetotal and settle down in a steady job.'

'It doesn't sound much fun.'

'Precisely. Their parents, who are your generation, after all, don't understand it, so it really worries them.'

Anji wondered how someone who'd lived for over a hundred years could make her feel so old.

'You still look worried, Anji,' the Doctor noticed.

'You're waving a Geiger counter around. If you're doing it to reassure me, then there are better ways.'

21

'This?' The Doctor passed her the device, a featureless black box the size of a audio cassette. 'This registers disturbances on the Bocca Scale.'

'And that means?'

'It can tell whether an object has passed through different time fields. Here –' He pointed the device at her, it squawked, then started bleeping excitedly. Then passed it over the sand, and it almost stopped bleeping. He pointed it at himself, and the bleeping quickly became a constant high-pitched tone. Finally, he aimed the device at the briefcase. The reading settled to a new rhythm – bleeping more than it had for the beach, less than it had for her.

'You're saying the case has travelled through time?'

The Doctor hesitated. 'Well… it might have done. I think, to be honest, that I might have contaminated the case by touching it.'

Anji rolled her eyes.

He handed Anji the detector. She slipped it into her bag. At least it would be at home there with her PDA with its almost flat battery and a mobile phone which she kept on, even though it was ten years away from the nearest person likely to call it.

'I'll have to open it,' the Doctor decided, tapping the case.

'It could be booby-trapped.'

The Doctor drummed his lip. 'True. Still – think of it as a challenge.'

'Is there anything I can do?' Fitz asked.

The Doctor shook his head.

'Well, seeing as it's a nice day, could I…?' He didn't quite have the nerve to ask.

The Doctor was peering at the case, as if he could open it by staring at it.

'Doctor?' Fitz asked.

'He wants a day off, boss,' Anji prompted.

'Not a day. Just an hour or two, really.'

'Go on, then.'

Fitz was already on his feet. 'Coming, Anji?'

She looked over. 'No. I think I'll help here.'

'Anji, there's a beach, there's the... er... it's the Mediterranean, isn't it?'

'It's the Mediterranean.'

'Thought so. You'd rather be sat there than exploring?'

'You go and enjoy yourself,' Anji assured him.

'Have a nice time, Fitz,' the Doctor echoed. 'Oh, and watch out for the owners of the case.'

Fitz and Anji looked at him.

'Well, I imagine they want it back, don't you?' The Doctor asked, searching his pockets for something.

'And who are they?'

'The human military of this era.'

'All of them?'

'The British, from what I gathered last night. Or the EZ. It's all much of a muchness now. Special forces, with state of the art equipment and weapons.' He was holding the sonic screwdriver, made a show of adjusting some of the settings.

'Well, I suppose a bunch of blokes in balaclavas will stand out here.'

'I imagine they're skilled in covert operations. The three of them on the hydrofoil saw my face, so they'll be looking for me.'

'Then why are we sat out here in the open?'

'You said it yourself: it's a nice day, it would be a shame to be inside.'

'They won't know me, though? I'll be safe?' Fitz looked over at Anji. 'I mean me and Anji, obviously.'

'They've probably got access to CCTV footage of the three of us together,' the Doctor murmured. 'We were together the whole of yesterday, and at the restaurant and hotel last night. So, enjoy yourself, but –'

'Enjoy myself but watch out for the SAS trying to slit my throat?'

The Doctor grinned. 'That's the one.'

Chapter Three
A Pretty Girl is Like a Malady

Fitz left the Doctor and Anji behind, and wandered up to the road, a pedestrianised boardwalk. Most of the people here were middle-aged, but this was a holiday resort, there was bound to be some sort of entertainment. He decided to cross the street to an amusement arcade he'd spotted.

Maybe he'd even learn the name of the island at some point. Yeah – he'd make that the mission for the morning. He'd been here more than a day now, so he felt a bit embarrassed asking Anji or the Doctor.

The amusement arcade was full of noise and light – but it was also air-conditioned, so it was an easy decision to go in. There were rows and rows of games, all with a huddle of people around them. Kids mainly – everyone was at least half his age, from the look of them. The games were just space-age fruit machines and pinball, as far as Fitz was concerned. He recognised the intense concentration, the frantic slapping of buttons, the lights and sounds.

Right at the back of the place was something more substantial.

RealWar.

There were six booths, taking up most of the back wall. Despite the number of machines, there was a short queue, and it seemed to be attracting an older crowd – people in their twenties. There was a man dressed as a soldier standing at the front, acting like an usher, working through the line, checking people's identity cards. The screens were vast, letting everyone take a look – the quality of the images was completely realistic: a forest in midwinter, from the viewpoint of some vehicle or other. That was it – as he

24

watched, Fitz saw that all six pictures were of the same forest, from slightly different angles. The players were all part of some military patrol, on some sort of co-ordinated search. So it was a team game of some kind.

The players didn't seem to be enjoying themselves much, it had to be said. Perhaps this depiction of war was a little *too* real – a bit too much of the waiting for something to happen, not enough of the action.

Fitz would probably have drifted off to find something else, if he hadn't seen the woman watching the players.

She was Chinese, and the only person his age in the place – well, the only good-looking woman, which was the same thing. She was short, dressed in tight black leather trousers and a college sweatshirt. She smiled back at him, briefly, which was more than enough for Fitz to file her under 'Possible'.

Fitz could speak Chinese – a long story – and wondered if a quick *ni hao* would impress her. He decided against it.

'Not playing?'

She shook her head. 'Spotting talent.'

An American accent – not just the sort she'd have picked up from watching Hollywood movies, either. Fitz was useless at pinning down exactly which part of America accents were from. A shame really, because a quick 'so, you're from Philadelphia', or whatever, would have come in handy to get the conversation going.

He tried to think of something.

'You're American?'

She was still staring over at the screens, she'd not looked at him. 'Well done. You're from the land of Sherlock Holmes after all. What gave it away? The accent, the Berkeley T-shirt, or just the fact everyone here is staring at me like I'm about to break the cease-fire?'

'Mainly it was the accent,' Fitz deadpanned. 'Calm down, we're all on the same side.'

She chuckled at that, and looked at him properly for the first time. 'Very good.'

The soldier tapped him on the shoulder.

'Are you Sutcliffe, J?'

'No.'

'You know him?'

'No.'

'You're an EZ citizen?'

'Er… what's aneasy?'

'Where are you from?'

'London. Originally.'

'Then you're drafted. Sutcliffe hasn't shown up.'

Fitz glanced over at the Chinese girl. 'Time to do my bit for Queen and Country.'

He stepped up to the control panel. It seemed straightforward enough.

'You've driven a class two before?'

'Oh yes,' Fitz bluffed, grabbing the control stick and placing his hands resolutely on the control panel. 'So, where's this set?'

'The disputed Siberian territories.'

'And who am I shooting?'

'Whoever the computer tells you to.'

'Gotcha. And do I pay you now, or…'

'You get your pay in twenty minutes.'

'Oh. Right.' He must have misheard.

The soldier handed Fitz some goggles. Putting them on was like wearing a pair of glasses someone had scribbled on with a felt tip. All sorts of information ran past, flashed up or moved around the screen. What with the movement of the tank, it made him a bit travel sick. The one constant was a countdown in the lower right hand side – currently at 19:40. That, he presumed from the 'twenty minutes' comment, was the game time remaining.

'Sutcliffe, you with us?' a voice from somewhere in his goggles asked.

'It's not Sutcliffe, it's –'

'You're with us?'

'Yes.'

'Yes, *sir*.'

'Yes, sir.'

'You're left flank. Keep an eye out for drilling operations.'

'Sir.'

'Got them!' another voice cried out. 'Tracked vehicle, one point four kilometres away.'

'I got the logo – it's Exxon. They lodged an exploitation claim with the last but one regional government.'

Exxon, Fitz tutted, was a silly science-fiction baddy name. Too many Xs, and ending with -on to make them sound like robots, or something. It took him right out of the reality of the game, and reminded him of the B-movies.

'Alter course.'

Fitz glanced over to the bloke in the next cubicle, and copied what he did, shifting the control stick to the right.

Something streaked across the screen. There was an explosion quite a way behind him.

'Seekers,' someone called out.

A light was flashing on the control panel. Fitz pressed it. A message flashed up telling him countermeasures were online. He understood the word 'were'.

There was a gun emplacement right in front of him, a machine gun nest, surrounded by a bank of snow. He hadn't seen it until it had started firing.

He realised he didn't know how to fire his own guns back at it. Or even if he had any guns.

The machine gun was turning automatically to face him. It stood out against the snow, it was black, on a tripod. He could hear the bullets clattering against the armour of his tank. He shifted the steering column, and found himself moving towards the nest. He pushed the stick forward, and found himself accelerating. Part of the display started flashing with the message that his main and secondary guns were malfunctioning due to enemy fire.

His tank continued towards the nest. Whatever he did with the stick didn't seem to make any difference.

'What are you doing, Sutcliffe?'

'I'm – I'm doing all I can, sir.'

The tank hit the machine gun nest, and tipped over. Fitz wasn't sure which exploded first, the tank or the gun, but whichever it was, one completely destroyed the other.

The screen went dead, the only thing remaining on the display on the goggles was the clock – showing 19:10.

The usher came over. 'Unorthodox, but you got rid of that nest. Here.'

He handed Fitz a five hundred Euro chip.

'Er, thanks. Is that it?'

'Until they drop another tank in the area. Report back on,' he checked his list, 'Friday at two.'

The Chinese girl was smiling. Fitz went over to her.

'Another great day for democracy and freedom.'

'I try to do my bit. I'm Fitz Kreiner.'

'You're German-English?'

'Er, I suppose so. I don't really think of myself like that.'

The woman smiled forgivingly, and Fitz wasn't sure why. Did she think he was a simpleton?

'I mean – my parents were German. But I was born in Britain. Went to school in Britain. I think in English. I think.'

Fitz caught himself wondering what language the Doctor thought in.

'Everyone thinks in English these days,' the woman assured him, 'it was easier teaching the rest of the world English than trying to teach American or British kids other languages.'

'Er, right. Can I, er, get you a coffee or something? My shout?'

She checked her watch. 'Nine-fifty. I've got ten minutes to kill, so why not?'

* * *

Ever since the Doctor had warned Fitz about the soldiers, Anji had been on the lookout.

They were surrounded by people, any of whom might be secret service types. She looked around. Well – she could probably rule out the young family immediately adjacent to them. And the pensioners in front of them.

Or perhaps that's what they wanted her to think.

The Doctor had twisted the catches on the briefcase, claiming that was what James Bond did. She'd seen the film, and found herself flinching, expecting the case to explode in his face.

This was not a normal reaction to have, when faced with a briefcase.

'You were reading the *Financial Times* earlier,' the Doctor said quietly.

'Yes. I was trying to get some context for this US/EZ situation. I watched the TV news last night and I couldn't make any sense of it.'

'And what did you find out?'

'There's a power vacuum in North Africa – a couple of the old regimes collapsed. It's right on the EZ's doorstep, so they don't want refugees coming over – or anyone setting off ABC weapons, whatever they are. The US see it as a whole new market, and strategically important. Well – it's access to Africa, the Mid East, southern Europe...'

The Doctor nodded. 'I'd gathered it was something like that. So both Zones have sent in peacekeeping forces?'

'Yeah – and both are meant to be working together, but they're actually competitors and they know it. It's not a war yet, but both sides are taking up positions. And they both know that the person who starts it will have an advantage.'

'When you finished with the paper, you put the share pages in your bag.'

'Er... yes.' She knew what he was going to say next.

'You're planning to use the knowledge when you get home.' It wasn't a question.

29

'I don't think there are any DTI regulations against it. And I don't see what harm it will do.'

'You'd use the knowledge for personal gain?'

'For the gain of MWF, I suppose. I mean, I would gain, obviously.'

The Doctor raised an eyebrow and was just about to say something when, completely of their own accord, the catches of the briefcase snapped open.

'Careful,' Anji warned, as the Doctor leaned in.

'It's all right. It was obviously on some sort of timer.' He held out his pocket watch. 'It opened at exactly ten a.m.'

He opened the case. After a quick search, all he had found was a piece of card, and a small arrowhead.

The Doctor handed Anji the arrowhead. 'Recognise it?'

Anji turned it over in her hand. 'It's old.'

'It's from eleventh-century Scotland.'

'It's in good condition.'

'Yes... yes, it is. Almost as good as new. Not what I was expecting to find. Not that I knew what I'd find.'

'So what does that card say?'

'"The bearer of this card is invited to..." and then it's in code,' the Doctor told her. 'Give me a minute or two and I'll work it out.'

He handed that over, and took the arrowhead back. Anji saw a string of numbers.

'It's a map reference,' Anji told him. 'You know, like a GPS uses. I've got a GPS database on my organiser, we can look it up.'

'What about the equation on the second line? Three, slash, seven, space, nine, colon, zero zero?'

'It's a date and time.'

'Oh yes, of course it is.'

Anji had fished her Psion organiser out of her bag and was waiting for it to boot up.

'The seventh of March.'

'More likely it's the third of July – tomorrow. So, where do we have to be?'

'Hang on.' She entered the numbers on the card.'Athens.'

'Athens? Not that far, relatively speaking.'

'So, I'm Fitz.'

'Malady Chang.'

'Is that Chinese?'

'It's English. It means "disease". I'm not sure my parents knew that. Do you think your parents knew what "Fitz" meant?'

Not knowing what her name meant made him look dim, but not knowing what his meant would make him look like a complete idiot. Fitz settled for offering her a cigarette.

'You still smoke tobacco?'

Fitz was holding out a cigarette.'Well, yeah.'

'I'm amazed. I suppose if anyone asks, you tell them it's hash.'

'Yeah, that's the one,' Fitz said. Long experience of time-travelling had taught him that you answered questions by politely agreeing with the person asking them. Anji had said once that she never asked a question she didn't know the answer to. It hadn't occurred to Fitz until then, but most people followed that rule. So, on his travels, when people asked 'do you know this is a restricted area?' or 'what shall we do with you, rebel scum?' or the like, he'd learned to shrug and let them carry on with whatever they were going to do anyway.

'Are you sure you wouldn't prefer a nicopill?'

'A what?'

She handed him a small bottle of yellow pills.

'Nicotine oil capsules. Gets rid of the craving, doesn't leave you with bad breath. Or cancer.'

'What do they taste like?'

'Nothing.'

'Nothing?'

He popped one of the pills, swallowed it. And then realised he didn't want the cigarette he had in his other hand any more.

'Not much fun.'

31

'Ten years ago they marketed them as a way to help people give up smoking. But people got addicted to them instead. There wasn't tax on them – not at first. And you can use them in restaurants.'

'Can I have another?'

'Be my guest.'

'They're very more-ish.'

'That's kind of the point. It's an addiction, but it's not an anti-social one.'

'When I smoke, it relaxes me. And I like the taste. These pills – they're killing the craving, but they don't do anything else.'

'That's right.'

'It's a product that serves no purpose?'

'It does what all products should do – it makes you want to buy it again. It just doesn't do anything else. It's capitalism in its purest form. Create a need, then exploit it.'

She checked her watch.

'Do you want these back?'

'No, you have them. You don't think I take them, do you?'

'Then what…?'

'Helping the US export drive.'

'Ah, what if I buy British?'

'That pack in your hand is Region One. You'll only want to add to the US balance of trade from now on.'

Fitz glared at her, then popped another pill.

'Do you see those men over there?' she asked.

Fitz looked round.

Two heavyset men in trenchcoats. They looked so much like secret policemen that they couldn't possibly be.

Fitz kept his eye on them. The men hadn't seen them. 'Who are they?'

'I don't know. What I do know is that I killed them last night. Blew the arm off the one on the left.'

'Then, er, the obvious question is…' he turned back to Malady.

She wasn't there.

A couple of seconds later, it occurred to Fitz that vanishing into thin air was a pretty good idea.

The police station was little more than a small hut, just off the beach.

The Doctor entered, smiled at the duty sergeant. There was another officer, filing some screenwork. He didn't look Mediterranean. He looked more like a soldier than a policeman.

'There was something on television about a briefcase?'

The duty sergeant and the soldier made an effort not to look at each other.

The Doctor plonked the silver briefcase on the counter.

'There was a reward, wasn't there? The television said something about 10,000 Euros? What's that in pounds, please?'

The soldier stood. 'You're English?'

'Not exactly,' the Doctor replied, carefully.

'We're all Europeans now,' the policeman reminded his colleague.

The Doctor kept quiet.

The soldier was running some sort of scanner over the case.

'Where did you find it?'

'I was on the beach with some friends, it just washed up.'

'It doesn't look dirty.'

'Well, it's just been in the sea.'

'It doesn't look particularly wet.'

'It was when we found it. It must have dried off in the sun.'

'You're in the habit of picking up strange briefcases?'

'If there's a reward.'

The soldier had put his scanner away and was taking out a wallet. 'We'll need a name and ID.'

The Doctor handed over his passport. Well, *a* passport.

The soldier had lost interest in him, now. The policeman gave the picture something that barely qualified as a glance, then handed it back.

'Thank you,' the soldier said, although he clearly meant to tell him to get lost.

The Doctor was happy to do so.

Chapter Four
Never Say Neverland Again

Two hours later, the briefcase had arrived in London. An hour after that, the forensics people handed Cosgrove back his case and told him there wasn't any evidence that it had been tampered with. That might have sounded reassuring, but it only meant what it said. The case could very well have been opened, by someone expert enough to leave no trace that he'd done so. Another team of experts told him that as the arrowhead was metal, it was impossible to carbon date it, but it was consistent with an eleventh-century Scottish design.

Still, he had his case back now.

Cosgrove took it back to his office, laid it on the desk and opened it, with some difficulty. His left arm was still badly bruised.

He reached for the bottle of painkillers in his jacket pocket.

The plan was to take a scientist along for the next meeting with Baskerville. There weren't exactly many people who specialised in the necessary field. He needed someone broad-minded.

He smiled. Professor Lik. Penelope Lik, the daughter of Korean immigrants, who'd joined the Service straight after completing her thesis. An imaginative young woman, and quite a travelling companion. But where were they travelling to?

He checked the case. The arrowhead was there, along with a handwritten invitation – GPS co-ordinates and a time to be there. He checked the co-ordinates in the atlas he kept on his desk. Even here, he couldn't be sure that his computers weren't being monitored or hacked. The atlas, complete with its sigil on the cover, was more secure than any piece of electronic equipment on the planet.

The leather-bound book was an anachronism. Books weren't, of course – in this day and age, the printed word was the only form of entertainment that wasn't easily pirated. Even theatre productions and operas could be covertly recorded and turned into vrooms. The entertainment corporations either factored piracy into their costings, or paid for a pinpoint smart missile strike on known pirate factories. Books and comics thrived. Magazines, of course, were ractive now.

No, the atlas was an anachronism because of its contents. All the countries, fitting together like colourful jigsaw pieces. Clearly defined boundaries. Individual states. Countries grouped together geographically, rather than economically, or by travel times.

The world just didn't work like that any more.

Cosgrove wasn't sure the world worked at all.

The meeting was going to be in the United States.

California.

Enemy territory.

Cosgrove wondered if it was Baskerville's joke at his expense.

He had twelve hours to get there with his scientist – if he was going to travel by commercial airline, as was the usual practice, then he would barely make it. Even travelling hypersonic, he'd have to get a move on.

He told his autosec to ready the royal airliner, but the autosec complained that it wasn't authorised to do that. So Cosgrove had to make the phone calls himself. Convincing the people he needed to convince took almost as long as the trans-Atlantic flight would. By then, Penny Lik was downstairs in his car, with a packed suitcase.

There were formalities before he left. Cosgrove didn't believe in ritual blessings, but it was procedure, a tradition dating back to the late eighteenth century, and these things were audited. He pricked his thumb, let a drop of blood fall on to the map, then drew a sign of power over Los Olivos. That done, he wiped the blood off the page, before it had a chance to congeal.

The secret signs of power, as determined by the men in secret societies, who thought they were the secret masters of the world. That's what the sigil on the front of the Atlas was meant to mean. 'Ours.' The conspiracy theorists had been saying it for decades – there was a group of people, small enough to fit around one table, who controlled the flow of capital, who manipulated the economies of the world.

Cosgrove knew of at least nine organisations, six of which were still active, who thought they were the ones in charge, that they were the secret masters of the world.

Only one of them needed to be right, of course. But Cosgrove had thought for years that if there had been a small cabal of people running the world then it would be a lot better run than it actually was.

He had been in the Secret Service for sixty years. He knew a lot of secrets. There were things out there, beyond the normal, human, world. The truly ancient, the ones for whom this mere world would not be enough. There was a grand scheme of things. If there was a master of the world, he wouldn't waste his time with mere national economies, or local stock markets.

An instinct, and he realised that this was what he was dealing with. Something not of this Earth, not of this time. Something alien to humanity. Something that had to be fought.

He headed downstairs, to Professor Lik, and his car.

Anji came back into the control room, buttoning up the silk shirt she'd found in the TARDIS wardrobe. It might not be the height of fashion where they were going, but it suited her. It felt odd to be wearing her bikini underneath instead of proper underwear. It felt more odd than being in a time machine en route to Athens airport some years in her future.

She was sure that should have told her something very profound about her psychology and lifestyle, but wasn't quite sure what. She remembered that Fitz had warned her about that, told her that you get swept up in all the weirdness, that the ordinary stuff would start to feel odd.

'Where's Fitz?' she asked.

'The invitation to Athens was for two people – a scientist and his assistant. So I've sent Fitz on an errand. I've just dropped him off at Neverland.'

'Neverland?'

'That's right.'

The Doctor was leaning over the console, looking relaxed.

'You're not going to explain, are you? Are you going to explain why you can fly the TARDIS to, er, Neverland and Athens, but you won't take me home?'

'We're not going to Athens. We're on the way to London. It's important we take a flight from Heathrow.'

'I've never been to Athens,' Anji noted. 'You have, I suppose?'

'I would have thought so. Yes... yes. I remember attending the Olympics.' He hesitated for a moment, relaxed, let the memory wash over him. 'All the athletes were naked.'

'Oh, right – I remember reading about that. In Ancient Greece all the competitors went naked.'

The Doctor frowned. 'No, I think this was the future. Something to do with flagging TV ratings, I believe.'

Anji had spotted a scrap piece of paper – the Doctor had written down some plans.

'"Lax security",' she read.

'What? No – LAX. Los Angeles... er... X. Airport. I was wondering how Fitz would get back from the West Coast of America without the money for a ticket.'

'And without a valid passport.'

The Doctor nodded.

'And the answer?'

The Doctor shrugged. 'You've not asked me why I gave the case back to its original owner.'

He waited for her to do just that, until it became obvious he would have to skip that bit and just go straight to answering his own question. He took a small card out of his jacket pocket. 'This is the invitation to Athens. I wrote out an invitation of my own which has just sent its rightful owner off somewhere else.'

'Where?'

'Out of harm's way.'

'The implication being that we're going to be *in* harm's way.'

The Doctor nodded happily.

Anji had taken the note from him. 'It's a very roundabout way to pass on a message, isn't it? Why not just send an email?'

'Because the message is too important. It's the only explanation. And it's got something to do with those time particles. There's a larger picture. We're being shown tiny bits of it.'

'Like that Chinese girl.'

'Ms Chang was American.'

'Fitz said...'

'I know what he said. Her ethnic origin is Chinese, but she was American. And that note was meant for a European. The man I took it from had a Scottish accent.'

'You think it's got something to do with the war that's brewing?'

The Doctor looked up, puzzled. 'No. Do you?'

'Well, it's part of the larger picture, isn't it? If there's rivalry between the EZ and the Americans, and the EZ are doing something secret that the Americans are interested in, then that's got to be significant, hasn't it?'

The Doctor nodded, conceding the point. 'I wonder how much the two sides know.'

'I already feel like I ought to be taking notes.' She tried to keep track. 'The American woman, Malady... is she going to show up in Athens?'

The Doctor checked his watch, surely nothing more than an affectation. Anji's own watch was set to... well, she wasn't sure any more. She set it to 6.30 every time she woke up, because she always woke up at six-thirty. That seemed like circular logic, but

39

it meant she had some idea of how long it would be before she'd want to eat and sleep.

'We have to assume that she'll be on the way.'

'And she might have backup there?'

The Doctor looked a little uncomfortable. 'Well, yes, I hadn't thought of that.'

'We can't outrun a phone call, can we?'

'No.' His mouth dropped. 'Well, we could always set the…' he stopped. 'No. No, we can't outrun a phone call.'

Anji was sure she hadn't had the answer to one of her questions, but she couldn't remember which one.

'Where's Neverland?' Anji asked finally.

'Oh come on, Anji, you must know. You must have heard of him.' The Doctor smiled.

Well, Fitz had never heard of him.

'The greatest musical entertainer of the twentieth century'? Fitz doubted it. Granted, his knowledge of the twentieth century fizzled out a bit past the late sixties. But he'd heard some of the music of the eighties and nineties. Half of it seemed to be cover versions of stuff from his day. But, y'know, live and learn. This guy could be good. Seeing as the tour of the house took six hours and covered two thousand seven hundred acres, presumably he'd made enough money from selling records.

Too much money. The first thing the coach passed, once it was through the gates, was a twenty-foot marble statue of a chimpanzee. In the distance, past the lake full of swans, where giraffes were sipping at the water, he could see what looked like a fairground. The gravel path there was lined with statues of all sizes and shapes. Children, monkeys, fairyland creatures, all playing musical instruments or playing with toys.

Fitz was sat at the back of the coach. The kiddies here – about half the passengers – were lapping it up. If Fitz had had millions of quid to spend on a house, it wouldn't look anything like this.

But it was exactly what those kids would do with the cash.

All this wholesomeness was beginning to nag at him. He fished out the packet of nicopills, and discovered he'd already had the last one.

'Er, miss?' he asked the tour guide, who hurried up the coach. He'd found out on the way over from the airport that her name was Barbara Millicent Roberts, that she'd been a guide at Neverland for over a year, and discerned that he have more chance of getting a shag at a Cliff Richard concert.

'Yes, sir?'

'I don't suppose there's anywhere here where I can buy nicopills? Or ciggies? Ciggies would be better.'

She looked like he'd just asked if he could strangle her pet hamster.

'No, sir. That would go against the whole spirit of Neverland. Before he left this Earth –'

'Left the Earth?' Fitz asked.

'He now lives in a mansion in the grounds of LunarDisney, sir,' she told him, as if explaining that the sky was blue and the sea was wet. 'Even on Earth, the founder of Neverland never smoked or took drugs.'

'It's not really a drug,' Fitz squirmed.

'– he didn't drink alcohol or caffeine. There's a very strict policy of enforcing those rules throughout the whole Neverland complex,' she completed.

She went back to the front of the coach.

Fitz wasn't feeling very well disposed. He shook the packet, wondering if one of the nicopills had got loose.

He was surprised when a small metallic disc fell out. He turned it over in the palm of his hand. It looked for all the world like a little microphone.

Malady had given him the packet. She must have known where he was and what he was doing since he'd met her. In that time, he'd gone back to the Doctor, they'd discussed plans. She'd know

41

all about Athens and Neverland, and the briefcase.

Best not to mention this little debacle to the Doctor, next time they met up, Fitz concluded. Least said, soonest mended.

He squished the microphone with his thumb.

Malady's eyephones beeped to warn her that the microphone had been destroyed.

She'd always known it was going to be found, and she'd got all the information she needed, anyway. She wasn't sure she could stand any more of Fitz humming to himself. Although she was impressed he could hum *Revolution 9* – she'd have thought that was physically impossible.

Fitz stayed true to form. Seeing him at first, Malady had wondered if the bewildered expression and casual attitude was a mask, whether he was one of Cosgrove's men. After two minutes, knowing there was probably someone following him, he'd just walked back to a couple of friends on the beach. A pretty Anglo-Indian woman, about Malady's age, and a slightly older man in an absurdly heavy coat.

Malady was heading for Athens, on the only scheduled flight of the day from the island. Fitz's associates – 'the Doctor' and 'Anji' – ought to be on the plane, unless they had their own transport. She hadn't been clear on that. The Doctor had mentioned something about 'taking the TARDIS', but she wasn't familiar with the term (and it wasn't on her database). Was that a plane, or some sort of weapon? Whatever it was, the signal had broken up for a couple of minutes, then Fitz had been in an airport. Then it hadn't made much sense – from the things he was saying, he seemed to think he was already in America.

Fitz had struck Malady as a little confused, generally.

The Doctor and Anji, though, from what she could gather from the short time she was able to listen in to them, were operators – professional, focused, organised. Malady instinctively knew she'd have to stick close, and lie low.

The two of them weren't on the plane. She'd checked, discreetly, first by hacking the unhackable airline security and checking the photos on the boarding passes, then with a quick physical search of the small plane, on the pretext of trying to find a glass of water.

During the flight, she'd had a call: new instructions from the Octagon. Control had conferred with the President himself. She was to discover what was being offered to the EZ, and to either acquire it or destroy it. A simple enough order to give, but the Doctor and his companions were her only lead, and she didn't feel happy about that. Whoever they were, they weren't working for the EZ. Neither were the goons who'd forced her off the road and killed Garvin. There was a lot of interest.

Ah yes, the goons.

Athens was only a few hours away, which gave her a little time for some counterespionage before catching this flight. She'd doubled back, watched the goons follow Fitz and the briefcase. There had never been any doubt that they were the two men who'd chased her off the road and killed Garvin. Except, of course, that she'd shot and killed one of them, then blown the arm off the other one and watched him burn to death.

Twin brothers? It seemed unlikely. Clones? They were in their late thirties, so too old to be clones. Why copy security people, anyway, when you could hire new ones for a fraction of the cost?

They must be the same people. She must have been wrong – it had been a dark night. The first guy was wearing a vest. *The larger man fell, blood sprayed from his head, he twisted slightly, looked surprised.* The flames must have confused her – she saw twisted shadows, not the man himself. *But the flames were only there because his gun exploded. His ray gun.*

Whoever they were, wherever they'd come from, however they'd survived, they weren't that bright. There were two of them, and both of them followed Fitz. One of them ought to have gone after Fitz, the other one should have looked for her.

If they'd been looking for her, they'd have seen her no more than fifty yards behind them at any time.

Eventually, though, she lost their trail. Annoying, but only just before she had to catch her plane to Athens. The goons weren't on the plane, either.

Malady hoped to hell she could find the Doctor in Athens.

Anji lay back in her chair. The hologram display on her armrest told her that she was about half an hour from Athens.

It would take her half an hour to work out the interactive menu that picked her movie or choice of music. After checking the news, which was dominated by the sudden death of a young actress, Bermuda Atkins (who, of course, had still been in nappies back in Anji's day), she decided to dial up a tourist guide to Athens instead and sip some free champagne.

Anji was enjoying herself in First Class. She'd only flown First Class once before, and that was because she'd been upgraded for being outrageously late. A business trip with the bank to Hong Kong – not that she'd had any time to take in the sights.

'This is the way to travel,' she concluded.

The Doctor was lying back with his eyemask on. 'It's not exactly the TARDIS, is it?'

Precisely, thought Anji, but knew better than to say it.

'And the TARDIS will be safe in the long stay car park at Heathrow?'

'Oh yes. It's got a ticket in the window.'

Travelling with the Doctor wasn't without its occasional discomfort or life-threatening moment, but... well, she'd always regretted not taking a year out to go backpacking before or after university. See different places, walk paths no other Westerner had ever walked (except for the other backpackers, of course). She'd certainly done that now. Gone where no one had gone before, and all that. She enjoyed travelling with the Doctor. The way time travel worked wasn't like being abroad: she didn't even have to worry too much about where her friends and family thought she

44

was, or how it all looked. Until she'd realised that, she'd felt all sorts of things – guilty she wasn't in contact with her parents, or Dave's parents, vaguely concerned she ought to be at work, and that she'd be completely out of touch if she ever got back. It had even occurred to her that the police might think she'd been murdered – or had murdered Dave and gone on the run.

But none of that mattered – that would all sort itself out, the Doctor had assured her of that. She could sit back and enjoy the ride.

'What do we do in Athens?'

'We're expected, remember? We turn up at the right place and the right time, and see what happens from there.'

'What do you think is going on?'

'Something to do with time travel,' the Doctor said. 'Quite what, I'm not sure. But whatever it is, we'll stop it.'

Chapter Five
Baskerville

Malady passed through airport security without a hitch, despite the two guns, the knives, the explosives and the hunter/killer software that were either on her or in her luggage. As ever, that left her feeling both smug and unsettled.

She only had hand luggage, and had been to Athens airport before, so was confident she'd be out of the terminal building in a matter of minutes.

That was until she strode straight into the first target, the Englishman in the long coat, the Doctor. He had also been striding along the main concourse, when he suddenly stopped to tie his shoelaces.

She tripped over him, rolled over his back and landed uncomfortably on his other side.

'I'm so terribly sorry,' he said. After doing up his lace, he held out his hand, helped her up. 'I'm the Doctor.'

'I'm Malady Chang.' She was too busy looking for 'Anji' to bother with an alias. The Asian girl was behind them, struggling to keep up with the Doctor.

'An unusual name.'

'My parents didn't know what it meant. They liked *The Three Musketeers*, and there's a "M'Lady" in that. I think they wanted me to be a lady.'

'I suppose my parents must have wanted me to be a definite article,' the Doctor said, smiling.

Malady picked up her bag. 'Are you here on business?'

'I am. And it looks like our... ah... business associate is here.'

A Teutonic-looking man in a dark suit was introducing himself to Anji, who had passed over a small piece of card. He wasn't particularly heavily built, but moved as though he was trying not to look combat trained. Malady smirked – hopefully she was better at that than he was.

'Doctor?' he came over and asked.

The Doctor nodded happily.

'If you'll excuse me?' he asked Malady, before walking off with the man.

At least she'd slipped a buglet into his… she glanced down, and saw the surveillance device lying on the concourse floor.

Malady waited a moment before hurrying after them. Outside, the Doctor and his companion were just getting into a silver limousine.

Malady crossed over to the taxi rank, and told the driver (who seemed surprised by her fluent Greek), to follow the Doctor's car. The taxi driver was pleased to, telling her he'd seen people say that in the movies, but in ten years of being a taxi driver no one had ever asked him to follow a car before.

Malady stayed alert. 'Any idea where they're heading?' she asked. Her training called this technique 'gathering data from a local soft asset'.

'Towards the docks?' the driver guessed. 'Ten minutes or so, even in this traffic.'

'OK.' She kept her eyes on the car in front – she wanted to stay ready for anything. The car didn't have tinted windows or privacy LCD – she could see the Doctor and Anji sitting primly in the back seat.

The taxi driver was wrong – the limousine was now heading away from the docks.

'Ah, business district,' the driver told her.

There were more modern buildings here – it must be some new development. Still a bit of a ghost town. Most of the new office blocks looked empty.

'We couldn't build this tall until the last few years,' the driver

47

explained. 'Earthquakes.'

'Yeah, I'm from California, and it's the same.'

They were heading towards one of the tallest. The limousine drew up outside it.

'Who owns that building?'

'No idea, ma'am. Drop you here?'

Malady nodded, passing over the fare and a generous tip. 'You look after yourself,' she told him.

She got out of the cab, putting on her eyephones. They could detect most forms of surveillance, and warn her if she'd been spotted. The idea was to avoid being seen in the first place, of course.

She was *pinged* almost immediately, but not from the office block. She checked the display. From behind – there were two of them on the roof of the building opposite. A man and a woman in purple uniforms. Who were *they*?

The picture shifted, automatically following the man in the long coat as he entered the office block.

'I can't believe it's him,' Roja said.

'Both he and the girl are showing an anomalous temp-trace. I'm running ident software to be sure. There: the identification computer says there's no doubt. It's the Doctor.'

'He's involved in this?'

That earned a withering look. 'You can see he's involved.'

'You think he's behind all this, Madame Jaxa?'

'He interferes. Records from my time show that this is a critical point in the ancient history of the Earth. He probably thinks he's helping.'

'All rogue time elements think they're helping.'

'Indeed,' Jaxa said, rewarding the boy with a smile.

'What should we do?'

'We treat him like any other time criminal – we establish his guilt, then eliminate him. We have to identify the transduction point he is using. I'll attempt to do that, while you set up a sniper position.'

'I've only killed in simulations, Jaxa.'

'Then your first blooding is overdue. Will you be able to carry out your duty?'

'Of course, Jaxa.'

'Good. Prepare.'

This really wasn't Fitz's scene.

He'd wandered up to the zoo, had a look round the reptile house, which had an enormous pair of pythons, a cobra and a pit full of rattlesnakes. The place was swarming with something far worse, too – kids. Little kids, all screeching and clapping and running around to tell each other what wonderful new thing they'd discovered.

Yuck.

The Doctor's instructions had been clear enough – buy a camera at the airport, take a photo of anyone who looked out of place.

Fitz had a good mind to hold the camera at arm's length and point it at himself. The only other people that had qualified were a pair of blokes in trenchcoats. When he'd tried to take their photo on the digital camera, the pictures came out as a blur. Fitz clearly hadn't mastered the intricacies of high technology.

Then he saw the old man and the totty with him.

Totty first: she was in her early twenties, wearing the unusual combination of tight shorts and a scientist's white coat. She was oriental, and had an incredible figure – slim, athletic. Her hair was dyed honey blonde.

He was well preserved, but in his seventies at the very least. His hair was snow white, with a buzz cut, and a neat beard. He was wearing a smart double-breasted suit. He was broad-shouldered, tall.

And he was sleeping with the girl. Not right this minute, obviously, but it was pretty clear. She was smitten. Lucky old sod.

'Could you tell me the time, Penny?' the old man asked. A commanding voice, with a slight Scots accent.

'It's ten past nine, Mr Cosgrove.'

Fitz took their photograph.

The camera was virtually silent, but Cosgrove's head snapped round as the shutter clicked.

Through the viewfinder, Fitz saw a look of rage cross the old man's face. He saw the man lurch towards him.

He didn't hang around to see what happened next.

The Doctor and Anji sat on opposite leather sofas in the reception of the office block, acutely aware there was likely to be, at the very least, a concealed microphone in the room.

The chauffeur had told them to wait here, and that someone would be coming to see them shortly.

Most importantly, they hadn't been taken outside and shot in the head, which meant their little deception hadn't been detected.

There was a computer here instead of a receptionist, and their chauffeur had gone back to whatever his other duties were. There was no sign that there was anyone else in the building. There were three doors, all of which remained resolutely closed.

After three or four minutes spent speculating about the chauffeur's accent, and which part of East Europe he came from, a woman about Anji's age came through the middle door. She was tall and slim, with long legs. Anji hated her already. She wore a trouser suit, with – as was the fashion – nothing underneath the jacket, and elegant pointed boots.

'Hello, I'm Baskerville's assistant, Dee Gordon.' It was an accent she'd bought in the best finishing school. 'You can call me Dee.'

'I was expecting to speak to Baskerville, and only Baskerville,' the Doctor said haughtily.

'You're the British scientist?'

'That's right. The Doctor. Cosgrove couldn't make it – he had a small boating accident.'

'And you're his assistant…?'

'Malady Chang,' the Doctor said quickly, stepping between Dee and Anji.

'Chang? But that's a Chinese name and you're –'

'Is that a problem? You have a problem with my skin colour?' Anji asked brusquely.

'No!' she said quickly. Then, after a moment's reflection, 'Wait here a moment.'

Ms Gordon disappeared through the door.

Anji and the Doctor stayed silent, kept up the act, but Anji was buzzing with questions. All would be revealed shortly, she assumed.

Dee came back in with neatly printed name badges, with their names – or rather the Doctor's name and Malady's – and photographs on.

'Follow me through, please.'

The Doctor stood, held out his hand, indicating that Anji could go first.

They stepped along a short corridor, into a lift, which climbed an indeterminate number of floors (there wasn't anything that indicated which floor they were on), before discharging them into a small circular room, done in the quasi-futuristic style that had gone out of fashion while Anji was still at primary school – all moulded plastic, round TV screens and primary colours.

The man sitting behind the circular desk was in his sixties, with a high forehead and aquiline nose. He indicated that they should sit down on the plastic chairs. Dee took her place, standing, behind her employer.

They were very high up here – twenty or thirty storeys, Anji guessed. The city beneath them was a stark contrast to the modern décor of the office. Anji had been a little disappointed by Athens on the way over – there was the Acropolis, of course, but other than that, the rest of the city seemed to be concrete and anonymous apartment buildings. From this vantage point, she could see she'd been a little unfair, there were older areas, there were plenty of churches. There was a lot of scaffolding, too – perhaps there was a renovation programme underway.

'This is the Doctor, and his assistant Ms Chang,' she announced. 'And this is Baskerville.'

'Lady and gentleman, thank you for coming,' he said softly.

The Doctor looked suspiciously over at him for a moment or two.

'Do you know why you are here? Have your superiors told you?' the old man asked. A refined English accent.

'Of course,' the Doctor said huffily. Anji could almost hear him regret the false bravado it as he said it – if he'd told him 'no', then perhaps Baskerville would have explained it all to them.

Baskerville nodded, smiling. 'You don't seem to have brought any equipment. I would have thought you would have brought instruments of some kind.'

Anji briefly wondered if they'd been booked to play a gig.

'I have a few tricks up my sleeve,' the Doctor assured him.

'Good. Now, as you will know, Doctor, Mr Cosgrove has had a demonstration. I take it that you require a further test, with Ms Chang –'

'– call me Malady,' Anji cut in.

'– with Malady as the test subject. Dee, could you prepare the sending chamber?'

'Of course, Baskerville.' She left the room.

'Er... "test subject"?' Anji asked, a little nervously.

'Nothing to worry about, my dear. While we wait for Dee, you might like to think about a destination.'

'Right,' Anji said, in a tone she hoped was decisive.

'Mr Baskerville,' the Doctor began.

'Just Baskerville.'

'Baskerville. Clearly we know exactly what you've got here. And it all sounds very impressive, from what we've heard, doesn't it, Malady?'

'What? Oh yes. Desperately impressive.'

'But what we don't understand, if you'll forgive us, is what is in it for you. You're offering us something that I'm sure is wonderful. Desperately impressive, to coin a phrase. But we're not sure what you want in return.'

Baskerville looked at him coldly for a moment. 'You are at a crucial point in the history of this planet,' he told them. 'Europe and America, poised on the brink of a war that would alter the course of this century, and only for the worse. Millions will die.'

'"You",' the Doctor said.

'I beg your pardon?'

'"You are at a crucial point in the history of this planet." *We*, surely? We're all in the same boat, aren't we?'

The old man smiled. 'Yes. Well done. You have uncovered my little secret. While I have presented myself as a reclusive scientist, I am in fact –'

'– a time traveller,' Anji finished for him.

His smile flickered, he clearly didn't like having his big surprise spoiled.

'Indeed. I should have known not to underestimate the people of this time zone.'

'So the –' Anji realised she was going out on a limb, '– time machine you have is the product of a future technology. You are from the future?'

'Indeed. Over ten thousand years in your future.'

The Doctor looked over at Anji and grinned, like she'd just won a round of charades.

'A dangerous time to be here,' the Doctor suggested. 'You said yourself that the world's on the brink of war.'

'The war will be averted,' Baskerville said simply. 'Historians aren't clear how, but I think I know.'

'Care to share?' Anji asked lightly.

'I think I prevent it. I think I prevent it by reaching a deal with the European Zone that sees them acquire a working time machine. From that, the elite of the EZ become the Lords of Time, and usher in a new age of peace, prosperity and social and scientific progress. That is what I am offering.'

The Doctor opened his mouth to ask the next question, but Dee had come back in. 'The sending chamber is ready,' she announced.

Dee led Anji and Baskerville to an airlock with solid metal doors.

'Dangerous, is it?' Anji asked, a little nervously.

'Not for the subjects,' Baskerville said quietly.

The airlock door slid open. Anji and Baskerville stepped through, waited while the door slid closed behind them, some fans whirred, then the door in front of them opened. The room beyond the airlock was bare, with plain white walls. A stainless steel device sat incongruously in one corner. Anji quickly worked out why the room smelled of coffee once she realised it was a coffee machine.

Dee and the Doctor watched her through a thick glass window.

'This is the time machine?' Anji asked.

'This is the sending area.' Baskerville told her.

'Have some coffee while I prepare the process,' Dee suggested, her voice echoing slightly over the PA system.

Anji went over and poured herself a cup but she wasn't impressed – too bitter. She glanced back up at Dee, who was adjusting dials and pressing buttons behind the plate glass.

'Where would you like this demonstration to take you?' Baskerville asked. 'There's an effective range of about two thousand years – it's past-facing, but can reach any point on Earth.'

On the other side of the thick glass, the Doctor was bending over a control panel, trying to figure out the controls and displays. There were some very thick cables coming up through the floor, all connected to a central box about the size of a fridge-freezer. There were switches and displays all along that box.

'That's the time-path indicator, I take it?' he asked, pointing out one of the displays.

Dee gently moved him aside. 'If you don't mind, sir, this is quite a delicate stage of the operation.'

'What's the power source?'

'I'll explain later.'

The Doctor nodded. 'I see. And it only has a range of two thousand years.'

'Only?'

The Doctor's smile flickered. 'Well, I admit that two thousand years is very impressive.' A thought struck him. 'If it can only take someone back two thousand years, and Baskerville is from more than two thousand years in the future, then how could he use it to get here?'

Dee frowned. 'That's something you'd have to ask him.'

'Could he have made a lot of little two-thousand-year hops? Does it work like that?'

'You'll really have to ask him.'

'So, Ms Gordon, you're not from the future?'

'No. I'm from this time zone.'

'So how did you and Baskerville meet?'

'He contacted me when he arrived in this time. He had access to historical records, and he knew from them that we were destined to meet.'

'That must be quite reassuring.'

She cocked her head. 'How so?'

'To know you make your mark in history. Did he tell you how your adventures together ended?'

'No.' She hesitated. 'The records are fragmentary, and history can be changed.'

'I see.'

She turned her attention back to the control box. 'We're ready for the demonstration.'

Anji mulled it over. With the whole of history to choose from, where would you go? She'd had this conversation before, back at school, then at university. Then again with Dave. Her boyfriend had wanted to go a few years in the future, but when pressed why, he'd mumbled something about wanting to buy all six *Star Wars* films on DVD in the sales. And here she was a few years in her future, an experienced time traveller. Ironically, as soon as she'd stepped into a time machine, the only place she wanted to go was back home.

'This is a precise process? You could take me anywhere?'

Baskerville nodded. 'To the square metre and the second. But I think you've got somewhere in mind.'

'I have,' she admitted.

Anji realised she could go home. Proper home. February 2001. Or perhaps a day or two earlier. Turn back the clock. Go back to Dave. She needn't change the course of history, she realised. When she'd met the Doctor he'd been fighting some monsters called the Kulan – well, she could help him out, tell him how to win.

'The turn of the millennium, Europe,' Baskerville guessed.

'How did you know?'

'Your clothing. Millennium retro. It must have cost you a fortune.'

'Looking at those old TV shows, I'm sure I'd feel right at home there,' Anji told her.

'Malady, are you sure?' the Doctor asked. She could hear the anger in his voice.

'It's what we agreed, remember?' Anji said quickly. 'There's no catch?' she asked Baskerville.

'This is the demo, of course,' Baskerville told her. 'It only works for ten minutes at a time.'

'All right,' she heard the Doctor say. 'Ten minutes. No more. I don't see the harm in that.'

She could still send Dave a warning. She had her mobile. No, wait – don't send Dave anything. Send *herself* a text message. But what? She wouldn't believe it. More than that – wouldn't she remember getting the message, if she'd sent herself one?

'Er… sorry, hang on.' Anji found her phone.

'We have as much time as you need,' Dee chuckled, pleased with her pun. Then she saw the phone. 'Excuse me, what are you doing?'

'Just checking something.'

'That's a phone.'

Yeah, well done, Anji thought – then she realised that by now mobile phones were probably the size of matchsticks.

'You're not to make phone calls from here.'

Anji had a plan.

'I want to make one from *there*. It's a pre-arranged signal, to prove your machine is genuine.'

'Explain.'

'In the past, I will use this, er, antique phone to send a text message to a prearranged number. Then, when I get back to this time, I can check the records to see if the message really was sent.'

On the other side of the glass, she could see Dee and the Doctor mulling it over.

'I don't think that will count as interfering in history or anything,' Anji added quickly. 'It's just a simple code phrase. It's a dead letter number. Otherwise – well, this could all be a fake, couldn't it?'

She'd come up with the ideal message to keep Dave out of harm's way.

DAVE, GO TO HMV, THEY'VE GOT CHEAP STAR WARS DVDS

Dee nodded. 'OK. So what are the exact co-ordinates?'

'Brussels, February 2001.' She gave the precise time and date.

'Brussels? You've got the whole of history to choose from, and you'd go to Brussels in February? According to this, it's raining there.'

Anji shrugged and smiled. 'It's probably raining in Paris, too.'

Chapter Six
Time Trip

So, how do you steer a time machine?' the Doctor asked, looking for pointers.

Dee indicated the control panel. 'It will take a few minutes to align the four dimensional vectors.'

'You can work the machine on your own?'

'Baskerville taught me. The operating principles are very simple.'

'I can hear my ears burning,' Baskerville said, his voice relayed by a tinny speaker. 'I taught Dee everything she knows.'

'You could teach me?' the Doctor asked.

'For the right price.' He turned his attention to Anji. 'Are you ready?'

Anji nodded.

'Lower the screen,' he told Dee.

Dee touched a control and a shutter slid smoothly over the window.

'Hang on,' the Doctor said, 'I thought I was here to watch this demonstration. I can't very well do that with a metal wall in the way.'

'You can still hear us, though?' he heard Anji ask.

'I can.'

'The time energies need to be carefully contained,' Baskerville explained.

'I see,' the Doctor said thoughtfully.

Anji looked around the room. 'I still don't see the time machine.'

'That's because we're in Brussels.'

The whole room was gone.

The sky was grey, it was just as cold as Anji remembered.

'I didn't even… I mean, that was so smooth.'

Baskerville smiled. 'Your phone is beeping,' he told her.

It was finding a network. 'Excuse me,' she told Baskerville.

He nodded, looking a little irritated.

Anji had never enjoyed sending text messages. She'd had an email account since university, SMS was an absurd backward step from that. She tapped away at the phone, trying to get the right letters up – she was out of practice, and hadn't realised what a knack was needed. It took her a full minute to select the right message and send it to Dave.

MESSAGE SENT.

Only then did she look around.

'It's just like I remember it. There's meant to be a statue,' she told Baskerville. 'A little boy… it was over there.'

'It still is,' Baskerville said, pointing it out.

A dark bronze statue, less than two feet tall. Anji frowned. 'Wait, it wasn't there before. It was…' she turned through one hundred and eighty degrees, feeling disorientated. 'There.'

A dark bronze statue, less than two feet tall. Anji frowned. 'How can it…?'

Baskerville hurried to her side. 'Nothing's the matter,' he reassured her. 'The time transfer process has made you a little dizzy. It's déjà vu, that's all. You need to concentrate. The statue is over there, just where it should be.'

'Yes… yes.' Anji nodded. That made sense. 'We can walk around?'

'Of course. Do whatever you need to do to satisfy yourself that the process is genuine.'

Now she was here, now she'd sent the message, Anji wasn't sure what else she could do. She couldn't think of anything to do the first time she'd come here. She wondered whether she should try to track herself down. After all, her earlier self wouldn't be that far away.

'You've been here before?' Baskerville asked.

'Yes…' The dizziness came back.

She saw herself standing in front of the Mannikin Pis, with Dave.

'I'm really not sure Brussels was quite the right choice to be a wild and spontaneous thing,' her earlier self said. It was odd – everyone always said that you didn't look or sound like you thought you did. Anji was a little disappointed to see she was exactly the same as she'd always pictured herself. A little smarter dressed, perhaps.

'Are you all right?' Baskerville asked.

'You tell me,' she said. *That* voice sounded distant and unfamiliar.

'Malady, concentrate.'

'I'm Malady,' she said, reminding herself. She mustn't forget her assignment.

'You are Malady Chang.'

Of course she was. Why was he telling her?

'Take a deep breath,' Baskerville suggested. 'Look at the skyline. What do you see?'

'That Atom thing.'

'The Atomium,' Baskerville said. 'Take a good look. Concentrate on that. Steel spheres, connected with thick metal tubes.'

She saw it. It really was quite striking, she had to admit it. There were escalators and stairs in those tubes. Yes. Anji stared at it. The solidity of it was reassuring. It looked faintly ridiculous, of course – it had been built to represent the future in a generation before she'd been born. It looked like a relic from an abandoned future.

'I half expect Thunderbird Three to launch out of the middle of it,' she laughed.

'Thunderbird Three?' Baskerville asked, puzzled.

Anji felt dizzy. Ever since she'd arrived, she'd felt disorientated.

'I need to sit down,' she told Baskerville.

'Are you ill?' he asked, his voice full of concern.

Was she? Anji didn't know. She'd been fine a few minutes ago, but now felt jet lagged, woozy… her vision was blurred, she'd got a headache.

Deep breaths.

She just wanted things to be like they were before.

Think about real, solid things, things that really existed like men with clocks for faces and giant cyborgs at the end of time and tigers that talked and poodles with hands and aliens, always aliens, with bulbous black eyes and insect-like claws, and fur and sharp teeth.

When she said 'before', she didn't mean 'before she met the Doctor'. She and Dave had been in trouble. There was no doubt about it. At first, yes, it had been wonderful. Not perfect, never say perfect, but as close as she'd got. Someone she could trust, someone she could confide in, talk to, learn from, share a bed with. It had been wonderful, perfect… there's that word again. But it had gone wrong, somewhere along the line. It wasn't something he'd done, and she didn't think it was anything she'd done, but it stopped firing on all cylinders. The reason they'd come to Brussels in the first place was to find that spark again. But her heart wasn't in it – god, the fact she was talking about what they had like it was some knackered old car should have been enough to prove that. She'd thought it was over, that she'd stopped feeling anything for him, but then he'd died and it had been her fault, and she'd cloned him, and come back here; all the time it was Dave that represented everything she'd left behind and so she'd clung to Dave. Clung to him, like that Christmas at her parents' house, when they'd snuck upstairs, only planning a quick cuddle, then they'd ended up with her on top of him, and she had her hand over his mouth because they had to be quiet, and he wasn't being quiet, and then she'd screamed so loud her dad had shouted upstairs to make sure she was all right… and it had all gone wrong, and she didn't know when, and she didn't know why, but she just wanted things to be like they were before. But even that, even there, her memory was cheating on her. Dave and…

'How many spheres are there?' she asked.

'Pardon?' Baskerville asked, a little disconcerted.

She was staring at the Atomium. It was back in place, everything was normal. No space rockets. Just a wet Brussels afternoon.

'How many spheres? I'm trying to count them, but… there're seven. No six, if you count the one in the middle. But that doesn't make sense.'

'There are –'

'Guh,' Anji said. She didn't want to say it, she was thinking… she was thinking *guh*. *Guh*. Her tongue felt stiff, swollen, her eyes didn't seem to be working, either. There was blood in her mouth. 'Eeg, gak, wach, fug, gugh, whuh!'

She felt calm, she was clinging to Dave, everything was going to be all right.

Dee rushed into the room, first-aid kit in hand. Malady was lying flat on the floor, convulsing, jaw clenched.

'What the hell happened?'

'I don't know,' Baskerville admitted. 'Where's the Doctor?'

'Once you set off, he got bored at staring at the shutter. I sent him back to the office with a printout. It'll keep him quiet.'

'Good.' Baskerville leaned over Malady, prised the mobile phone from her fingers and turned it off.

'Malady,' he said softly, into the Asian girl's ear. 'Malady. It's all right. You are back in the sending room. Do you understand? You are in Athens, back in the sending room.'

'Guh.'

'Epilepsy?' Dee suggested,

'There wasn't a trigger,' Baskerville murmured. 'She's an intelligence field agent, she'll have been tested for that. Screened. Or they should have done. Help me restrain her. Be careful.'

He had removed his silk handkerchief. He slid it into the girl's mouth, dabbing away the spittle and the blood. Dee opened her eyelid. The eyes were back to normal, the pupils dilated.

'She's settling down.'

Malady's eyes snapped open. She looked panicked.

'You bit your tongue,' Baskerville whispered in her ear. 'You have a handkerchief in your mouth to stop you doing that again.'

Malady nodded, relaxing a little.

'We don't know what happened,' Dee told her.

'You are safe,' Baskerville assured her. 'You are out of danger.'

Those words relaxed her, as he knew they would. He checked his watch.

'When the ten minutes are up, she should be fine. See to the Doctor.'

Dee Gordon found the Doctor sitting behind Baskerville's desk, the printout unspooled all around him.

'Is everything all right?' he asked.

She smiled reassuringly. 'Of course.'

'It's a lovely place you've got here.'

'Yes, it will be a shame to see it go.'

'You're relocating?'

'Well… yes. This afternoon.'

The Doctor was frowning.

'The Third Prophecy?' Dee prompted.

The Doctor shrugged.

'They didn't tell you? They sent you to Athens today and didn't tell you?'

'Ah. The security service works on a need to know basis. I clearly didn't need to know.' The Doctor's mouth twitched, as though he was trying to stop himself smirking. 'Are you going to tell me?'

Dee checked her watch. 'In two hours, Athens will be devastated by an unexpected tidal wave. We're powerless to prevent it – it's already history. We'll be killed if we're in the area. The loss of life will be immense.'

The Doctor shifted a little uncomfortably. 'It will? And you're happy to –'

'Of course I'm not happy,' Dee snapped. 'But we can't warn people. History would change. We can't change history.'

'I thought that was rather the point of Baskerville's plan.'

Dee paused. 'That's different,' she asserted, unsure why. 'This has to happen, to prove to you that Baskerville's from the future. He knows about the disaster because –'

'– because he read about it in the historical records.'

'Precisely.'

'Which are fragmentary, and history can be changed.'

The Doctor was over at the window, looking down at the city, taking his last chance to.

'Two hours?'

'At midday.'

He looked lost in thought. Finally, he turned back to her. 'So what were the First and Second Prophecies? And, more importantly, what's the Fourth?'

Anji was fully conscious and had been for some time, but it still felt like she was just waking up. That was the first thing she had to deal with.

She felt like she was hung over. Anji was aware that Baskerville was sitting nearby. She was sitting up, which was also a little disorientating.

Should she tell him?

She'd had an adverse reaction to time travel. Something had gone wrong, and it wasn't something Baskerville had been expecting or was prepared for.

Anji had worked it out. It was her. She didn't pretend to know everything about how time travel worked. Hell, she didn't pretend to know anything very much. But when she'd seen herself in the past – met herself, to all intents and purposes – it must have caused some sort of time-travel equivalent of a short circuit.

And she couldn't tell Baskerville, because then she'd have to explain exactly why her 2001 self only looked about three months younger, and was wearing the same jacket. She'd have to tell him she was already a time traveller.

'Malady, my dear, are you all right?' Baskerville seemed genuinely concerned.

'Yes. I feel a lot better.' She did, too.

'That has never happened before,' he told her. 'I'm afraid I'm at a loss to explain what did happen. But before your... attack, you did get a chance to see that the time machine works?'

'Yes,' she said. 'It works, I guess it's me that doesn't.'

Baskerville gave a small chuckle. 'You'll tell your government that it works? That it's worth taking a risk for?'

'I need to consult the Doctor.'

'Of course? Shall we go through now?'

Fitz was quite capable of simultaneously thinking that he was seriously out of condition and in need of a cigarette.

The old bloke probably didn't smoke. He definitely wasn't out of condition. It was a bit embarrassing, actually, to be caught up by a pensioner, when Fitz had a pretty good head start.

At least the old guy was a bit out of breath, Fitz reflected, between wheezes.

He'd chased him all the way up Katherine Street, then down alongside a half-scale train line – there weren't any trains, of course, that would be too easy.

Cosgrove caught up with him by a big circus tent. He had big hands, and a good firm grip. He managed to grab Fitz's shoulder and pull him down to the grass.

The good-looking girl he was with caught up with them by the time Cosgrove had given Fitz a couple of good kicks to the ribs.

'Oh no,' Fitz said, 'I bet you know martial arts, don't you? Go on, then, get on with it.'

'I'm a quantum physicist,' she assured him, in an impossibly posh accent. 'Who is he?' she asked Cosgrove.

'Good question.' Together they dragged Fitz back up to his feet.

'Who are you? Why were you watching us?'

'I'm just a touris–' He didn't get a chance to finish, because Cosgrove punched him in the stomach.

'No you aren't. Now, lad, tell me who you are, and I'll stop hurting you. That's not too complicated for you to grasp, is it?'

'No,' Fitz agreed.

'It's not here, is it?' Cosgrove growled. 'The rendezvous isn't here. So where is it?'

He grabbed hold of Fitz, started shaking him.

'Athens,' Fitz admitted.

'Athens? Athens, Greece?'

'No Athens the fourth stop down from Kings Cross on the Northern Line. Of course Athens Gree–'

Cosgrove punched him in the stomach again.

'Leave him, Jonah,' the blonde said. 'You're really hurting him.'

'Leave him to me, Penny.'

Cosgrove let him drop back down. Fitz stood, glad that his ribs seemed to be roughly where he expected them to be.

'There's no need to worry,' the old man told the young woman, turning to reassure her.

While he was looking the other way, Fitz scarpered.

It wasn't the best plan in the world, in all probability, but it was the best plan he could come up with, and at least it delayed him being punched again.

Cosgrove twisted back round, tried to grab him, but slipped on the grass and fell over.

Fitz would have laughed out loud if he could spare the breath.

The girl was helping him up, rather than coming after him. He hadn't bought much time, but his luck had definitely changed. He could get lost here at the circus – it was full of visitors and performers, and was a maze of tents and caravans.

He rounded the corner of the main tent, and came face to face with the two blokes in trenchcoats.

They looked very familiar. It was then that Fitz remembered

seeing them back in the Mediterranean. They'd been after Malady. They were doing well to get here so quickly.

'Halt. You are the time traveller. You are the one known as the Doctor.'

'Er…'

'Are you sure it is the Doctor, leader?'

The shorter of the two held up a device about the size of a packet of cigarettes, setting off a whole new round of cravings. There was a sickly-sweet smell.

'The control box indicates that the Doctor has one heart,' the alien says.

'Er… he's got two,' Fitz began. 'Oh no, hang on, as you were. Blimey, you keep your records up to date, don't you?'

'If you have one heart, then you must be the Doctor,' the man told him.

'Look, sorry to have bothered you, but I really need to get going. Places to go, people to get punched by, you know how it is.'

The man placed his hand on Fitz's shoulder.

'You don't understand. You are coming with us.'

And Fitz was rather alarmed as the whole universe disintegrated around him.

Roja stood still, watching the window through his spyglass.

All four of them in there – the Doctor, his companion, Baskerville and Dee Gordon – were looking out of the window. That meant the spyglass could read their lips without difficulty. He'd put the speaker on, so Jaxa could hear, too. All the voices sounded the same, of course, but it was easy enough to work out who was speaking.

'– *surely you can see how it would benefit the whole of mankind?*'

'*Perhaps she can see how it's a Pandora's box.*'

'*Doctor? As a man of science, the possibilities of time travel must intrigue you, surely?*'

'It is him,' Roja said.

'We knew that,' Jaxa said irritably.

'We've caught him red-handed. We should get authorisation for a purge and destroy operation.'

'Not until we know all the details.'

'One thing, Baskerville, is that you've not named your price yet.'

'My price? Surely whatever price I asked, it would be –'

'He's turned away from the window. Wait, wait, he's coming back.'

'– simply require half an hour's access to your country's ULTRA computer. The computer used by your intelligence service.'

[Laughter]

'Why on earth would a man from the future need that?'

'I am trapped in this time. Returning home requires a precisely plotted course, and I need more computing power than is available in this time – except for the most powerful computer in the world. And that is the ULTRA.'

'And then you'll hand us the secret of time travel?'

'Indeed.'

'Won't that interfere with established history?'

'You'll appreciate that I can't discuss future events.'

'But you can shape them?'

'Malady, have you considered that this might be the year my history books show that mankind developed time travel?'

'It's too early…'

'What was that, Doctor?'

'Mankind isn't ready. You said it yourself – the Europeans and Americans are on the verge of the Third World War.'

'Fourth, surely?'

'Ah… yes, thank you Ms Gordon. Fourth.'

'Yet here I am, a man from the future. Mankind survives, Doctor, I can tell you that much. The next century will see

marvels, it will see mankind starting to reach its potential.'

Jaxa was looking puzzled. 'It's not the Doctor. He's involved, but it's Baskerville that's instigating this. The Doctor seems reluctant.'

'He's holding out for a better deal, Jaxa, that's all. We know Athens is destroyed in a couple of hours – that's obviously our doing, to sterilise this area. We should call headquarters and get their authorisation for a low grade temp-pulse out at sea.'

'Possibly…' But she didn't seemed convinced. 'They've stopped talking.'

'The Doctor and that Asian girl have gone off somewhere to discuss something in private.'

'Can you find them?'

Roja shook his head. 'They're away from the window.'

The Doctor ushered Anji into the room, got her to close the door while he swept the room for bugs with the sonic screwdriver.

'It can do that?' Anji asked.

'Evidently. At any rate, it didn't find any. Now, quick, what did you find out?'

'I was in Brussels. It was far smoother than the TARDIS. More accurate, too.'

The Doctor looked displeased with the comparison. 'And it's a time machine?'

'I got… well, I got time sick. Really disorientated.'

'You've never had that in the TARDIS,' the Doctor said, some of his pride restored.

'No. But it is a time machine. I was there. Baskerville is on the level.'

The Doctor nodded. 'When I asked how it worked, Dee got a bit snotty. I wonder if she really knows how to operate it. I would have thought Baskerville would want to retain at least some secrets. It doesn't matter, at least not for the moment. What matters is that Athens is going to be destroyed, and we've got a chance to save some lives.'

'Athens is…?'

'Shush. What we need is for one of us to get out of this building and warn the authorities that at midday there's going to be a tidal wave, and that they have to evacuate the city. Meanwhile, I'll investigate this time machine and –'

'Hang on.'

'What?'

'You get to investigate the time machine and go on a yacht, and I just have to go off and call the police?'

'We could hardly do it the other way round. I mean, do you think you're really up to poking around a time machine?'

Anji considered her next response carefully.

'True. And it's not as though you could convince the authorities.'

The Doctor looked confused. 'Why not?'

Anji laughed. 'Well, I mean… *look* at you.'

'I could so.'

'Bollo– Nonsense. Everywhere we land we get accused of murder or something and the authorities don't believe a word of what you say.'

'On Endpoint, I –'

'The exception that proves the rule.'

'Anji Kapoor, I could get this city evacuated like –' he snapped his fingers – 'that.'

'Then we're agreed: you alert the authorities, I investigate Baskerville?'

The Doctor nodded decisively. 'Agreed.'

Anji smiled.

The Doctor tapped his lip. 'Now… we just need a way to get me out of the building.'

The door opened, and Baskerville stepped in, with their chauffeur. 'I'm sorry to press you, but we really need to get away from here. My yacht is moored near here, and it will take about an hour to get it clear.'

Anji stepped forward. 'Baskerville, I have a couple of things to tell you. First of all, I'm not EZ. I'm CIA.'

Baskerville looked shocked. 'CIA?'

'Central Intelligence Agency. I'm an American agent.'

'You are?'

'I… think we can cut a deal. I'm operating on the direct authority of the President himself. Whatever the EZ is offering, whatever you want from them, we can give you more.'

Anji could feel the Doctor was glaring daggers at her, but that didn't stop Anji from feeling smug. Besides, her masterstroke was coming up.

'And this "Doctor" isn't EZ, either. He's an independent operative, the man that stole Jonah Cosgrove's briefcase. He's an impostor.'

Baskerville looked over at the Doctor.

'Is this true?'

Anji leant in to the Doctor and went on tiptoes to whisper in his ear. 'That should get you out of the building.'

It was around then that Baskerville had his man throw the Doctor out of the window.

Chapter Seven
All Fall Down

The Doctor fell about twenty-five feet, about two hundred less than he was expecting to, then resumed his fall, at a reduced speed, a moment later.

Malady – the real Malady Chang, not Anji – had been climbing up the building on some sort of polymer line. He'd grabbed a handful of the back of Malady's sweatshirt. This had broken his fall, but the impact dislodged her, and they found themselves heading straight back down her climbing rope.

'What the hell?' Malady asked, grabbing at the line, feeling the material of her gloves starting to fray.

'Hello again,' the Doctor said cheerfully. He wrapped an arm around her neck and a leg around her, until they were inseparable. That had the result of tipping them over, now they were almost horizontal.

'How did...?'

'Mind the glass,' he warned. Shards of glass were falling along with him, sparkling in the morning light.

'You jumped out of a twenty-third storey window?'

'I don't know which storey it was,' the Doctor admitted candidly, 'and I was thrown out, I didn't jump, but yes, that's the gist of it. Can we discuss this later?'

The line wasn't designed to carry their combined weight. Malady was sure the piton at the end of the line would hold, but wasn't confident they'd slow down enough. She grabbed a little harder, saw the Doctor about to grab the line.

'No! It'll take your hand off.'

The Doctor stuck his free hand, the one that wasn't grabbing the back of her shirt, in his coat pocket, then clutched at the line.

They slowed down, glided to the pavement, landed with quite a jolt.

Malady grabbed for her gun, but it wasn't there.

The Doctor handed it back to her. 'You'll need this,' he said, absent-mindedly examining the damage to the lining of his coat.

After a moment he looked up at her. 'Now, you've probably got a few questions, and I'd be happy to –'

Malady knocked him unconscious with the butt of her gun.

Baskerville was already leading Anji away.

'I had my suspicions about him, of course.'

'Of course you did.' She looked back over her shoulder at the jagged hole in the glass. Warm air was wafting in. She tried to control her breathing a bit, calm down before she had a heart attack. Somehow, although her body was in shock, she couldn't imagine that they'd killed the Doctor. They'd inconvenienced him, obviously, but she was wondering how he'd survived, not picturing him hitting the pavement.

Dee and Baskerville were leading her to the lift. The guy who'd thrown the Doctor out of the window was bringing up the rear, carrying a bulky carry case.

'You've drawn attention to yourself,' she warned Baskerville. 'The police will investigate the body.' She knew she looked worried, this way, they'd think she was worried about that, not the Doctor.

'And in a little under an hour and three quarters, the police will be caught in the tidal wave, and one more body won't make a difference.'

They were in the lift, now, heading upwards.

'You're going to get back in touch with the real EZ?'

He was staring at the roof of the lift, willing it to go faster. 'I'll worry about that when we're clear.'

'You don't have to,' she said flatly.

Baskerville looked at her.

'I'm sure the President would be happy to conduct unilateral negotiations.'

He and Dee glanced at each other. 'We need full access to the ULTRA computer,' Dee told her. 'It's unique. It is the only computer with the processing power we need.'

'America has powerful computers, Ms Gordon.'

'It has to be the ULTRA. And it's secure in an underground bunker below the headquarters of the European Secret Service in Brussels.'

'Hell, whose corporations do you think sold them the computer in the first place?' Anji said, almost swaggering as she said it. 'Do you think we did that without leaving a few back doors? We can get you the ULTRA. We're the richest nation on Earth, Baskerville, you can name your price and we'll match it.'

Baskerville rubbed his chin, lost in thought.

The lift doors slid smoothly open. They were on the roof. A small helicopter sat there, the East European guy in the pilot's seat, the case he'd been carrying stowed behind him. The rotors were already running.

Dee indicated the helicopter. 'We'll negotiate on the yacht.'

Penny Lik was dozing in the main stateroom of the royal airliner. This morning, on the way over to America, she'd been more self-conscious – she told him it was hard to imagine the King and Queen had done what they were planning on doing in this very bed.

Cosgrove told her if she was having problems imagining it, he had covert surveillance videodiscs of them, and she'd laughed and relaxed, so he didn't tell her he wasn't joking. On the way back, she'd simply tried to make him forget about letting the young man escape, and for an hour or so, she'd succeeded. Now they were halfway to Athens, and Cosgrove had preparations to make, so he left Professor Lik to her rest.

They were alone on the plane, except for the three pilots, who were safely locked away in the cockpit.

The hypersonic plane was a variation on the fastest commercial airliner, the Airbus IX. In actuality, there was very little difference between this royal transport and the one in regular service. There were a couple more first-class cabins, the carpets were deeper, the dinner service was fine bone china, the European Airways planes didn't have Da Vinci sketches on the walls. But apart from a few well-furnished rooms, it was almost frugal. Professor Lik's reaction on looking around had been the same as everyone else's - faint disappointment.

The President Minister's plane was quite another matter, but needs must.

He booted up his laptop, and checked the latest reports.

It was eleven o'clock in Athens. There was little doubt Baskerville's prophecies were coming to pass: Cosgrove had made a nice profit betting on the Europe–Brazil match, getting the score, those that scored and the time they scored exactly right simply by following Baskerville's prediction. The actress Bermuda Atkins had died too, suddenly, of some previously unsuspected virus. The Third Prophecy was the tidal wave in Athens - entirely impossible, according to his scientific team. But it was going to happen, and Cosgrove was already utterly convinced that Baskerville had a time machine.

He contacted Station G in Athens, told them to evacuate, with the minimum fuss, and to get their helicopters into the air. There was a military airfield twenty miles inland from Athens - that ought to be a safe base of operations. He found the intercom, and told the pilots to head there.

One of the reports waiting for him on the computer registered the CIA's confusion about why, when it looked for all the world as though the EZ and US were heading towards a shooting war, the royal jet had visited California for less than two hours. The lack of US data security (or their commitment to freedom of information), meant that the details of the flight were already on the datanet, fuelling a dozen conspiracy theories.

None of them mentioned the EZ government attempting to acquire a time machine. A quick search revealed that no one, from the seismology department at Berkeley to a single one of the net psychics, had predicted the tidal wave in Athens.

Baskerville still hadn't shown up anywhere in this mass of data. Cosgrove was worried that his own actions – the exploding Manta, the public search for the case, the use of the royal jet – might start to arouse suspicion. He had to assume the CIA were at least aware that something important was happening. And there was some third party – some organisation that could get on board a military boat in the middle of the sea, and could operate on a world scale, one that had initiative. Both the man who'd stolen his case and blown up the Manta and the man who'd taken his photograph had English accents. Neither had military training. Both had run rings around him. This was worrying.

There was also his feeling that there was something more going on, something beyond the human.

Cosgrove sat back, resolved to take control of the situation.

The Doctor's eyes snapped open.

'A CIA safehouse,' he said.

Malady was standing beside a small video camera, adjusting some of the settings. This was a small room, windowless, like a police interview room.

He was handcuffed to the chair, his arms behind his back.

'What time is it?' the Doctor asked, slipping out of the handcuffs, dropping them in his pocket, then returning his hands behind his back.

'Does it matter?'

The Doctor laughed. 'I know it's before midday. But what time is it?'

'Do you really want me to say that it's me that asks the questions, because I will.'

'If you're going to ask me something, ask me why I'm so confident it's before midday. We're still in Athens, right? So it's before midday. So go on, ask me how I know.'

'We are still in Athens.' Malady turned her attention away from the camera and on to the Doctor.

'Tell me the time, and I'll tell you everything I know about Baskerville's time machine. Does that sound fair?'

'Whose what?'

'Have you been briefed on this mission at all?' the Doctor asked irritably.

'I know there's some hi-tech being offered to the Eurozone Government. I know that the EZ are in contact with someone making that offer, someone who appeared out of nowhere two months ago.'

'His name is Baskerville. What he's offering is a working time machine. I'll tell you all about him – but only after you tell me the time.'

Malady watched him carefully. 'It's five to twelve,' she told him suspiciously.

'We're below ground.' It wasn't a question. 'How far below ground?'

'Doctor, you were going to tell me about Baskerville.'

'Is this floor watertight? Are we in a bunker, or just an ordinary building?'

'Doctor –'

'There's no time to warn anyone,' the Doctor blurted. 'But we can save ourselves.'

'What's going on?'

He broke into a grin. 'I'm glad you asked. At midday, Athens is going to be hit by a tidal wave. There's going to be massive loss of life. Now, you don't know that, but the leaders of the Eurozone do. Baskerville told them. He's from the future, he's read about the tidal wave in his history books, and he's proved he's from the future by making a series of predictions, all of which have come true.'

'Baskerville's from the future?'

'Malady, that really wasn't the bit I wanted you to concentrate on. For the moment, can we stick to the tidal wave? We've got – what, four minutes? – to get out of Athens, or at the very least find somewhere waterproof. Does this safehouse have a safe?'

'Not one that's big enough for two people.'

'One person? You can get in, I'll make my own way to safety.'

Malady laughed out loud. 'God, you're good. I almost fell for it. Can you imagine what would happen when they found me? *If* they found me? "Hey Malady, who locked you in the safe?", "Oh, I locked myself in the damn safe, because my prisoner said I'd drown if I didn't".'

'Did you feel that?'

'Oh come on, Doctor, what next? "There's someone behind you"? OK, I'll bite: what was I supposed to feel, Doctor?'

'An earthquake, I think. Some distance away, but quite concentrated and powerful. Enough to set off a tidal wave.'

The Doctor stood up, handed her the handcuffs and pulled her out of the room. 'It really is time to get going.'

Fitz woke up, which came as something of a relief.

He hadn't moved – the two men in the trenchcoats were still there, so was the big circus tent. He could hear the crowds. He was dimly aware that the old bloke who'd kicked his head in and his good-looking ladyfriend were only a few yards behind him. But they hadn't caught up with him in the time he'd been unconscious. However long that had been.

He felt like he'd just eaten a six-course meal.

His vision was blurred, but – as if to compensate – the smells were overpowering. Grass, the canvas of the tent, the burgers and chestnuts from the food stalls. Fitz wasn't a scientist, but he imagined the blurred vision was something to do with the good kicking he'd been given. He should have been worried it was permanent, but that lobe of his brain must have been whacked, too.

The two blokes were quite ordinary looking. Average height and build. They looked boring, more than anything else. There were two of them, of course, but even so, Fitz felt that he'd have a reasonable chance to get past them.

'Doctor...' one of them said.

They thought he was the Doctor. Fitz had forgotten that bit. What would the Doctor do in these circumstances?

'Oh yes, I am the Doctor,' Fitz assured them, worried he sounded a bit too camp.

'You will give us the secrets of time travel.'

'You know I can't do that,' Fitz said, looking back over his shoulder. The old bloke was right behind him, why hadn't he caught up?

And why did it feel like there were lead weights in his shoes and coat pockets?

The gravity was higher than it was on Earth.

So there was a rather obvious conclusion to be drawn.

'This is an illusion,' Fitz told the trenchcoats. 'A simulation of Earth, not the real thing.'

'Yes, Doctor. Onihr science is capable of such magnificent feats.' The man held up the little box he'd had before.

'But not of sorting out the gravity problem.'

The two men looked at each other.

'If you can't manage simple artificial gravity,' said Fitz airily, 'then you're hardly ready for me to hand you a time machine, are you?'

'You will build us a time machine. You will teach us its secrets.'

'We have fragments of the knowledge,' the other added. 'Our race has spent millennia acquiring them.'

'You find them lying around?' Fitz snorted.

'Precisely. On every planet, there are pieces of the puzzle.'

'Echoes in the rituals or artwork.'

'Artefacts. Components. Relics.'

'The Onihr race collects these, but however brilliant our scientists, we can not fit these pieces together.'

'We want that knowledge. We shall be the masters of time.'

Fitz shook his head. 'I'm not going to stop you trying,' he said – doubting it was what the Doctor would say in the circumstances. 'But I'm not going to help you. So, just take me home.'

'You will serve us, you will –'

Fitz took the opportunity to reach out, and pull the control box from the man's hand.

There were only a few controls. One of them would beam him back down to Earth, he was sure.

A second or two later, he wasn't so sure. No doubt, one of the little square buttons activated the teleport... but what did the other ones do? He pressed one, but it just seemed to spray perfume at him.

The two men, or Onihrs, or whatever, were keeping their distance, circling him.

'Hand that back.'

'There is no escape.'

They were edging closer. Fitz realised he was going to have to press another one of the buttons and worry about the consequences later.

He plumped for one, and tapped it.

A smell like rotting fish burped out of the device.

The two Onihrs paused, just stopping in mid-step, like they were on film which had got trapped in the gate. He'd found the stun setting, Fitz thought for a moment. Then they began to melt, hair blurring into skin, skin blurring into eyes and teeth.

Fitz coughed. 'I'm sorry...' he said softly.

But now they were straightening up. Their bodies were fizzing, fading, and it was clear that there were other shapes in there, superimposing themselves.

Large, dark shapes. Humanoid – stubby legs, slightly longer arms, that bent in the wrong place. Their bodies were top heavy, with wide torsos and hunched backs. Their heads were long, with a blunt snout, tiny eyes. And horns. Horns growing from the end of their snout and between the eyes. Their skin was grey – dark grey.

Their human disguises deactivated, they stepped forward, right at home in the heavy gravity. They were about seven or eight feet tall.

The nearest grabbed the control box from Fitz's hand. The other grabbed Fitz himself, lifting him easily.

'If you won't tell us, we will take the information by force… Doctor,' it spat.

'Take him to the pain inducer,' the other one gleefully agreed.

Fitz gulped.

Anji had slipped out of her suit and shirt, and was down to her bikini. She'd felt embarrassed to do that in front of Baskerville and Dee, even though she was already wearing the bikini underneath her clothes, so she'd gone below to her cabin. When she stepped back up on to the deck of the yacht, she saw her hosts had also changed. Dee was in a three piece swimsuit. She looked skinny, Anji thought, almost unhealthy. She was very pale, too. She still looked poised and confident, though.

Baskerville was in a cotton shirt and bermuda shorts. He looked appreciatively over his sunglasses at Anji. The East European guy was, presumably, driving the boat, or piloting it, or whatever it was you did to boats.

The midday sun was hot, but the sea breeze was very pleasant indeed. The sea was dark, beautiful. Baskerville's yacht was even larger than it had appeared from the air. The six-man helicopter sat on a pad at the stern of the boat.

Dee checked her watch, a rather chunky thing. 'GPS says we're well out of the danger zone.'

Baskerville nodded. 'You're feeling better, Malady?'

Anji knew he was talking to her, but it took her a moment or two to remember she'd been ill. 'Yes. Thank you. I was over the time lag before I'd left the sending room.'

She glanced at her watch. It was midday.

'Athens has been destroyed,' Baskerville said solemnly.

Despite the midday sun, Anji felt cold. 'The death toll?'

Dee was looking downcast. 'Too early to say, of course. The first newscopters have only just arrived on the scene. But it's clearly in the many thousands. Here.' She pressed a control on the small table in front of her, and a screen appeared over it. It showed devastation – a city a storey deep in filthy water, waves washing against and churning over the concrete buildings, fires burning. Cars, trees and rubble washing by.

'Did they evacuate the city?'

Baskerville looked puzzled. 'They had no warning.'

'You warned them.'

'I told Jonah Cosgrove it would happen. He, being a good servant of the superstate, would have told his lords and masters. And then they all sat back and waited.'

Perhaps they did, Anji thought. But the Doctor knew, and he'd gone to warn them, he'd gone to evacuate the city. He'd had two hours to do it. More than enough time for him. Plenty more.

He hadn't prevented it, though. Anji could think of only one circumstance in which he wouldn't have done.

The Doctor was dead.

Chapter Eight
Time and Tide

The Onihrs had led Fitz out of the reconstruction of Earth. It was some sort of solid projection – the Onihrs said it was really advanced technology, but as it hadn't fooled him, Fitz found it difficult to get that impressed by it. They led him along a transparent corridor, and Fitz had finally seen where he was – on board some sort of space rocket, or space station. One star was larger than all the others, and looked like the Earth's sun, only about a quarter of the size. There was no sign of the Earth, but Fitz was sure it was around somewhere.

He also got to look out over the Onihr spacecraft. It was quite elegant, particularly for something built by eight-foot rhinos with hands the size of hams. Fitz had assumed the Onihr ship would be bulky and gunmetal grey, like its owners. Thinking about it, there shouldn't be a correlation between how a race of aliens and their spaceships looked – aeroplanes and ocean liners and bicycles and motor cars didn't look anything like people. Spaceships came in all shapes and sizes, depending on the technology available. This one was crisscrossed with glass corridors, like veins, and the hull was curved, and looked more like blue porcelain than metal. As for the shape… no human object looked much like it. It was the product of an alien race, so it didn't look like a saucer, a rugby ball, a pepperpot or anything. Why would it?

As Fitz reached this new plateau of understanding of alien culture and aesthetics, he and the Onihrs had reached the interrogation chamber. They went out of the corridor into a dark chamber. It was narrow (although nothing in this ship was that narrow), and high-ceilinged, and once they were inside, the

Onihrs had strung Fitz up by the wrists, let him hang about a foot from the ground while they'd gone off somewhere. The higher gravity didn't help one bit.

Twenty minutes later – as far as he could tell, in the dark, unable to reach his watch – Fitz was beginning to wonder if they were ever coming back for him.

Twenty minutes after that, they did.

The two of them had changed clothes. They'd been wearing spiky black armour before. Now they wore billowing heliotrope robes – ones that were far too small for them. They had ceremonial collars – really badly cracked and damaged ones. The matching skullcaps rested, rather ludicrously, on their top horn, the one between their eyes. The whole ensemble seemed thick with dust, and the robes were frayed and crudely patched in places.

'So, Doctor,' one of the Onihrs rumbled, 'have you decide to relent, and to teach us the mysteries of space-time travel?'

'I could tell you,' Fitz suggested. 'But first I have to know what you would do with that knowledge.'

The Onihrs leaned in. He could feel their breath. It was warm, and smelled of meat.

'Conquest,' one of them rasped.

Jaxa's wristband had started to chime.

'We must leave,' Roja insisted.

Jaxa was searching Baskerville's desk. 'We must locate the time machine.'

'Baskerville and his associates will have removed it when they left.'

'Possibly.' Roja was checking his own wrist computer. 'There is no temp trace. Why isn't there a temp trace?'

'It is possible to shield against our time detectors.'

'With great difficulty, Madame Jaxa. They conducted a time test while we watched, yet we didn't register it. And if Baskerville is shielding his machine, that means that he's expecting Agents.'

'You think he is from my era?'

'If he can shield his time machine from us, he may even be from your *future*, Madame. We have to assume that he knows about the impending disaster.'

'How long, now?'

'It is three to twelve.'

'Program a one hour time transference, same spatial location. This building is well constructed, and some way from the shore. It will survive the disaster.'

'We can't be sure of that.'

'No, but we do know that an illegal time machine was operating here a matter of hours ago. The destruction of this city must not be allowed to interfere with our investigation.'

'I have prepared the time transference.'

'Activate.'

An hour had passed. They lurched a little, as the floor had shifted slightly. The windows all had cracks running down them.

'The building survived,' Jaxa said. 'Now, we have to locate the time machine. We can't disintegrate the rogue time travellers without that evidence.'

Roja was looking out of one shattered window.

'Everyone's dead,' he said softly. 'We knew this was going to happen. Baskerville knew. The Doctor knew. So many people could have prevented this.'

Jaxa put her hand on his shoulder. 'So it was written.'

A little over an hour earlier, the Doctor and Malady had emerged from the CIA safehouse, the midday sun making them both blink, after the dingy cellar. The crowds were quite light – it was getting too hot to be outside.

'We're in the Plaka,' Malady told the Doctor, unnecessarily – it was obvious from the surroundings that this was the oldest part of the city. 'We should get to the high ground.'

She pointed over to the Acropolis. Everything felt strange, dreamlike – in just a few minutes, the streets would be… she just couldn't think like that.

'It's nearly a mile away,' the Doctor said. 'We just don't have that long. Ah-ha – in there.'

He started jogging across the street to a branch of Medusa Bank. Malady followed. 'The safe?'

'That's right.'

They pushed their way in, past an old couple.

They got straight to the counter. The Doctor looked around in vain for a teller.

Malady pointed at the speaker. 'Autoteller,' she told him.

'I'd like to see the manager, please.'

'I'm sure I can help, sir.'

'No, I'd like to open an account, but before I do, I'll need to –' the Doctor screwed up his eyes. 'What was that?'

A small plastic card plopped out into the tray on the counter. 'Just taken a retinal scan, sir. Your new account is open, and your access to the IFEC is enabled. You have… no… euros in your account.'

The Doctor pocketed the card.

'I really have to see the manager. It's very urgent.'

'Here at Medusa Bank, we're committed to full customer service, sir, but I can –'

'This is a robbery!' the Doctor declared, jumping up on to the nearest service desk, frightening the autoteller.

Malady ushered the old couple inside, before they could leave. 'In here,' she insisted. 'You'll thank me in the long term.'

The Doctor was playing to the crowd. 'Anybody moves, and my colleague here, Malady Chang, will wave her gun at them.' He bent over. 'You did bring your gun?'

'Never leave home without one,' she assured him, drawing it. 'And, for the record, I'm not sure it's the done thing for bank robbers to shout out their names.'

'I didn't,' the Doctor reminded her, 'I shouted out yours. You'll have to forgive me, I've done most things in my time, but I'm pretty sure this is the first time I've robbed a bank.'

The manager was coming out of his office, behind the counter and its protective glass screen.

'Open the safe!' the Doctor demanded. 'Hurry up!'

'There's no need for anyone to get hurt,' the manager called out in Greek. 'We'll co-operate. Just don't hurt anyone.'

'Wouldn't dream of it,' the Doctor assured him, without the hint of an accent. 'But we've only got about five minutes.'

Malady had just seen the wall clock. 'We've got about three, Doctor.'

'Show me the safe,' the Doctor ordered the manager.

He was already opening up the door to let them in behind the counter. 'It's on a time lock. There's no way I can open it until the morning, and…'

Malady grabbed his collar. 'We don't want the lecture. Show us the safe.'

He led them to the back wall. The safe was a thick metal door, with no visible handle or place to enter the combination.

'How do you get it open?' Malady demanded.

'Don't worry about that,' the Doctor said, patting her head. The door was already swinging open. In his other hand, the Doctor had something that looked for all the world like an electric toothbrush.

The safe was quite a size, lined with brushed steel safe boxes.

'In!' the Doctor ordered the manager. 'Everyone. Come on.'

'In?' the manager asked, not quite sure he'd heard right.

'In!'

There were only two human staff, the manager included, everything else was done by autosecs. There were eight customers. The safe held the twelve of them, just. Malady had to help the old couple in.

The Doctor was pulling the door closed. Malady took a last look through the doorway – and saw a wall of water surging into the square, towards the bank. The pressure had changed, there was a high wind blowing.

Outside the bells of the church of St Nicholas were starting to chime midday. As the Doctor hauled the door shut, and the bolts engaged, the sound was cut off, and the only thing they could hear was the sound of their breathing.

'We'll be trapped,' the manager shouted.

'We'll be saved,' Malady told him. 'Now, quiet, we'll need to preserve oxygen.'

And outside, the bank collapsed as the tidal wave hit.

The pain inducer was rubbish.

Fitz didn't mind that one bit, of course. The Onihrs had spent several minutes gloating about their pain inducer before wheeling it out. It was a box about the size of a television, which sat on a trolley. There was one coiled lead snaking out from it, which ended with a suction pad, which they'd stuck to his forehead.

Then they'd turned it on, and it didn't hurt at all. They seemed to think it would, so Fitz had played along – he wasn't stupid. If he pretended it was agony, they'd keep it at that setting, they wouldn't start going on about how it had ten levels, and this was just level one.

It stimulated the pain centres of his brain. But as such, it was just an intellectual exercise – it was like *remembering* being in pain, or imagining what it would be like if he was. But the weird thing was it also damped down the pain he was feeling from being strung up. So the net effect was that he was better off.

'You are weakening, Doctor,' the nearest Onihr told him. This was the leader, as far as Fitz could make out. He had a spikier horn on his nose, and was slightly shorter than the other one. 'You will help us.'

'What do you know so far?' Fitz asked.

The other one edged forwards. 'We know we need a dematerialisation code. Many of the fragments speak of it.'

'Right. And what are you doing for a power source?'

'We have harnessed mini black holes.'

Fitz nodded. 'And what do you know about… the Vortex?'

The two of them looked at each other, gleams in their eyes. 'We have heard the name.'

Fitz rolled his eyes. 'You'll need to do better than that.'

'You will tell us!' The lead Onihr twisted a dial on the pain inducer, and Fitz's eyes watered as he remembered the time he'd jumped a bit too hard on to the saddle of a scooter.

'Let me down, and I'll tell you everything I know about the Vortex,' Fitz promised.

'Everything?'

Fitz smirked. 'Absolutely every single thing I know. Scout's honour.'

Baskerville had been standing, hands on the railings, staring out to sea, for a while now.

Anji and Dee had been watching the news coverage, trying to take it all in. Knowing it would happen just wasn't the same as seeing it. Dee seemed affected by it, but she'd fobbed off questions about how long she'd stayed in Athens or if she'd known anyone there.

Anji didn't know what to make of Dee. She wasn't quite sure why Baskerville had picked her as a confidante, or quite what she did for a living. She wasn't in much of a position to pry, though – after all, Anji was meant to be a CIA agent posing as a British scientist. She'd be vulnerable if awkward questions were being bandied around.

The television pictures were horrifying. A British rescue team was, by chance, right on the scene. They'd even diverted the royal airliner to just outside Athens to use as a mobile command post. British helicopters were sweeping the area. The pictures concentrated on the airlifts to safety, tried so hard not to focus on the bodies and animal carcasses they could see drifting along in the water.

Baskerville had watched the pictures only once, when the news channel had shown robots picking their way through the ruins. 'RealWar Teletroops,' he'd explained. Not true robots, but remote-controlled machines, operated by soldiers. Cutting edge stuff, but he expressed surprise that 'Malady' hadn't heard of them – the US army was deploying robot legions in North Africa. Anji had changed the subject, and Baskerville had gone back to his contemplation.

Seismologists, oceanographers and just about anyone else a newscaster could loosely describe as 'a scientist' were being pulled into TV studios to be asked why they didn't see it coming. An odd thing that – the TV always talked about 'scientists', lumping them all in together. When they were talking about some financial story, they'd distinguish between merchant bankers, investment bankers, fund managers, futures traders, stockbrokers… they didn't just lump everyone in as 'financiers'. It was a bit like the Eskimos having five hundred words for snow, she supposed, a reflection of the priorities of a civilisation. Although the Doctor had once told her that even someone with only rudimentary knowledge of the Inuit-Inupiaq polysynthetic language groups would know that there were only two words for snow in anything like common use among Eskimo tribes.

Still, there were five hundred English words for people who worked in banks, or who otherwise had a job pushing money around. Most of them repeatable in polite company.

Anji was distracted by an elderly astrologer on television claiming he'd predicted this very disaster on his website this morning. He cited the URL, and a screengrab came up from it, and this was treated by the newsreader as definitive proof he was dealing with a genius.

If there were psychics, they'd do far better playing the markets than writing columns for online magazines. And why dress so ridiculously and act like such berks? If they dressed normally, Anji would at least be able to take them seriously.

She smiled as she reached a new understanding of the way the world worked. Of course they talked and dressed funny. It was the first principle of stage magic – distraction. If you spent your time concentrating on the colourful jumper, you wouldn't be concentrating on challenging the big questions about what they did. More than that, it meant that, at some unconscious level, you started picturing the astrologers in suits, the ones who *were* making a fortune selling stocks and shares. The *real* astrologers. You started thinking that the whole astrology thing really could be plausible.

But what did Anji know? She flew around time and space in a police box, and was currently the guest of a man from the future.

She went over to Baskerville.

'Are you OK?' she asked.

'A little sad,' he admitted. 'I know it had to happen, but even so…'

'If it's any consolation, the disaster served its purpose. You clearly have knowledge of the future. Now, there's no way we can check your story, but you've acted in good faith, you've demonstrated you have a time machine.'

Baskerville nodded. 'I just want to get home,' he said sadly.

'Tell me about it,' said Anji, with feeling.

'I will if you want. It's a time of great scientific advance. There's no disease, no poverty.'

'An end to war.'

'There are wars. There are always wars. Death and taxes aren't inevitable. Wars are.' He almost seemed happy at the thought. 'It's time you made a call, don't you think?'

'A call?' Anji asked.

Baskerville gave a puzzled chuckle. 'Don't you think? It's time for you to call the President and move this to the next stage. You have a phone.'

'In my cabin.'

'Then make the call.'

Chapter Nine
After the Deluge

The air in the vault was starting to get stale, but the Doctor had insisted that they stay put for exactly an hour.

The old couple were worried about their son and his wife – they would have been at work. The Doctor couldn't offer them any words of comfort. The old couple tried to remember if anything like this had ever happened before. They couldn't think that it had.

It hadn't dawned on anyone else that the Doctor and Malady seemed to have foreknowledge of the tidal wave.

All the time, Malady stood, silently, wishing that people wouldn't waste oxygen chatting.

In time, the manager's watch beeped that it was one o'clock. The Doctor opened the safe, using the same tool that he'd used to get them in. Some sort of remote control, Malady assumed. It put her own lockpick to shame. Whoever the Doctor was working for had some nice gadgets.

The water was about an inch deep, and surprisingly dirty. There was already a strong musty smell, the damage was comprehensive – broken windows, mud everywhere, all the leaflets and wallpaper sodden wet.

The old couple were crying, imaging their home like this.

'Come on,' the Doctor said.

'Where?' Malady asked. She was numb – even having seen the tidal wave bearing down, she'd held the faint hope it wasn't real. The safe had been soundproof – for an hour, everything had been so quiet. Outside, all the time, a city had been dying.

'Baskerville's office block. We need to find that time machine.'

'He knew about the tidal wave – he wouldn't have left it behind.'

'It looked like it was part of the fabric of the building – I saw huge power cables. Even if we just find out the power source, it could be important.'

They were outside now, in the Square. The water was deeper, here. It lapped over their ankles. There was near-silence – no traffic noise, no people in the streets, not even birdsong. In the distance, Malady could hear helicopters. There was also a sound like a tarpaulin flapping – the water, she realised.

'Baskerville's building is on the other side of the city,' Malady told the Doctor.

'How did you get me from there to the safehouse?'

'A car. I left it in the underground garage at the safehouse.'

'Every basement and cellar in the city will be full of water,' the Doctor told her.

'The Plaka is mostly pedestrianised, but there's a car park a few streets away. We should be able to find a four by four, or some other car that can use these roads.'

The Doctor nodded. He looked around. 'I could have prevented this,' he told her. 'If you'd believed me, if you hadn't knocked me out.' He hesitated for a moment, clearly sensing what she was thinking. 'I'm sorry – I didn't mean to make you feel guilty. I… this wasn't your fault.'

'It wasn't yours, either.'

The Doctor sighed. 'Perhaps not. Perhaps this was no one's fault.'

Cosgrove passed around the identipics.

He'd warned them about the probable involvement of the CIA, now he was briefing them on the third party.

'There are at least two of them,' he told them. 'This one is a little older, and he seems to be the leader. He neutralised two Service men, immobilised me, stole my property and blew up a Manta. And he did it with a rubber ball. This one – he's some sort of operative, working for the other one. He managed to escape me in California.' He looked up. 'Now, I know what you're sniggering at. You think I'm old. Past it. That they outfoxed an old fool who's spent too long behind a desk. I've been in the Service over sixty years. Think about that. You think I did that by getting soft? If you think that, you just start running, and see if *you* can get away from me.'

He let that thought sink in. 'But this man did get away. Now – I want these people found.'

'If they were in the city when the tidal wave hit…'

'…then they're dead, and I want to see their corpses. Now, I don't think this one's had time to get back from California. I've only just arrived, and I was travelling about as fast as it's possible to travel. *This* one, on the other hand, the leader, he's here. He's here and I want him stopped.'

'Killed, sir?'

'I want to do it. But I want you to beat me to it, if you possibly can. Dismissed.'

The Doctor had insisted on driving.

The Landrover Espial had started first time. The prometheus wasn't working, though – the city traffic computers must be down. The Doctor didn't seem to need it anyway.

The roads were passable, some were even beginning to dry out in the afternoon sun. Some telegraph and power lines were down, some walls and facades of buildings had collapsed. The surface was uneven. Debris. Not bodies. It was macabre, but Malady had thought they were driving over bodies at first. Until she turned a corner, and she'd seen very visible proof that bodies float.

This was horrible.

There were helicopters in the air – a lot of them. A couple were small newscopters, but the others – oddly – seemed to be RAF. Since they'd sorted out Cyprus, there hadn't been much of a British presence in the area. But now there always seemed to be one visible, whichever way she looked.

There might have been a carrier nearby in the Med, out on exercises. But she thought she was au fait with EZ deployments in the whole area. Monitoring them had been her original assignment here, after all. They couldn't have sneaked a carrier, even a submarine one, past her, and the nearest was the *Mandelson*, in the Gulf.

The Doctor seemed preoccupied with something. The fate of the Asian girl she'd seen him with at the airport and getting out the car at Baskerville's office block?

'Navigating,' the Doctor said suddenly. 'Everyone talks about navigating when they drive. Few people get to actually do it. Drive a car in the sea.'

He laughed, but the sound was cold, quite disturbing.

He pulled hard left, the car aquaplaned a little, but turned like he'd hoped it would.

'Who are you working for?' Malady asked. 'You're British, but –'

'I'm not British,' the Doctor told her abruptly.

'English. Whatever you call yourselves these days.'

'I'm not working for anyone.'

'You're in this for yourself? Is that it? You're hoping to get this "time machine" for yourself.'

'No thanks, I've already got one, you see.'

She believed him. Malady realised that at some point she'd accepted there was a time machine. Now she accepted there were at least two. When had that happened? Why would she believe such a stupid thing to believe?

'Doctor, if we're going to work together, then I need –'

He turned to look at her, without slowing the car. 'No. You can follow me around if you want. You can even help me. But anything you "need", you'll have to find on your own.'

He slammed his foot down, the car squished to a halt.

'What's that?'

'You don't know?'

'I wouldn't ask if I didn't know.'

Malady laughed. 'Now, Doctor, you don't expect me to believe that, do you?'

'What is it?'

The robot was about eight feet tall, roughly humanoid – although with its long arms and short legs, it looked more like a gorilla than a human.

'It's a RealWar teletroop. A class three.'

'I see…'

'You must have seen them on the news. RealWar are always boasting about them.'

'They have EZ logos. So they're a European company? Do the Americans have anything similar?'

'RealWar are a Russian corporation, and they're happy to sell to both sides.'

'You say that with a sneer, but isn't that just free enterprise in operation? They've found a gap in the market and exploited it.'

'Now who's talking with a sneer?'

The Doctor smiled. 'It's excellent workmanship.'

Two of the robots were working together – one holding up a building, its back against the wall, the other holding up its arm to act as a bridge to the adjacent building, which was structurally intact. There were half a dozen people hurrying over to safety.

'For the prices they charge…'

'How far away will the operators be?'

'They could be working from the other side of the world. In this case, there will be a base camp close by.'

The Doctor nodded.

Anji held the telephone tentatively.

'Is anything the matter?' Dee asked.

Anji shook her head, unable to think of anything to say.

'What time is it in Washington?' she asked, finally.

'Worried about waking the President up?' Baskerville chuckled.

'Er... what are they? Six hours behind? So it would be...'

'My dear, don't you think the prospect of America getting its hands on a time machine is worth interrupting his breakfast for?'

'Of course.'

'How would you normally contact him?' Dee asked.

'Er...'

Baskerville waved his hand. 'Don't worry about that, Dee. Anji, would you like this conversation to be in private?'

'Yes. That's it.'

'Go to your cabin, if you want.'

'Thank you.' She got up, and walked over to the stairs that led below deck.

She'd been allocated a small cabin, second on the left. There were six cabins in total. As far as she could gather, Baskerville and Dee's relationship was platonic. She'd not seen much of the East European guy, but he didn't share with Dee – or Baskerville, for that matter. And, somewhere on this yacht, was – she presumed – the time machine itself, removed from the office block before disaster hit.

Anji took out her mobile, rang directory enquiries – she'd asked for the operator, but it turned out to be a fully automated service, and asked for a number for the President of the United States, saying she was CIA. The service automatically connected her, and the phone started to ring.

She assumed the cabin was bugged, at the very least. Tonight, she'd be undressing under the bedsheets, and probably showering in her bikini. It was like she was a contestant on Big Brother. She'd have to be careful how she played this phone call, too.

Anji didn't expect to get straight through to the President, but she was a bit annoyed to hear some old dear tell her she was through to the White House general enquiries line. It was obviously the one the little kids and nutters were directed to.

'Hi, I'm a CIA agent,' Anji began.

'Of course you are,' the woman said in that way that you'd describe as 'sweetly', but which was oozing with patronising scorn. 'How can I help?'

'Tell the President it's Malady Chang, and then put me through to him.'

The phone clicked, then started ringing.

'Yes,' a deep, firm voice answered.

'Mr President, this is Malady Chang.'

He hesitated for what seemed like three years.

'Hello there, Malady. I guess in the circumstances you're using any phone you can?' He was playing along.

'That's right, Mr President' – was that what CIA agents called the President? – 'I have to tell you that this line might not be secure. But Baskerville has a time machine, and I've seen it work for myself.'

'Understood, Malady. So…'

The door to the cabin opened, and Baskerville walked in, and took Anji's phone from her.

'We can end this charade. Mr President, this is Baskerville. Mr President, your agent here has seen that I have a working time machine. She says that your government has access to the European ULTRA computer… Are you saying that she's lying, sir?… I require half an hour's access to ULTRA. In return, I will give you the blueprints that will allow you to build a time machine, and I will supply certain components, special minerals and software that will allow you to build a working version… I will only hand over the blueprints to you, personally. And we will do that in Istanbul… Istanbul, Mr President, or no deal… Be at the Green Hotel, Istanbul, in exactly twenty four hours. That's one twenty, European Standard Time.'

Baskerville pressed the button that ended the call, and turned to Anji.

'Thank you, Ms Chang.'

* * *

Cosgrove slumped back in his seat, amazed.

'A trick?' Penny Lik asked him. The young Service lieutenant who'd called him into the communications room was nodding. There were four other techies there, sat at their consoles, connected to ear and eyephones. None of them thought it was genuine – not on an open line, without even basic encryption.

Cosgrove wasn't so sure.

'I've met Baskerville, and that was his voice.'

'Voice patterns of the other man match the President.'

'But they wouldn't use an open line,' one of the techies complained, and Cosgrove knew the man was right.

'Do you know who the girl is?' Cosgrove asked. 'She didn't sound American.'

'All we know is that she isn't Malady Chang.'

The picture of an attractive Chinese girl in USAF dress uniform appeared on all the video screens. It was a formal portrait – although she looked too old for it to be a graduation photograph. Perhaps it had been taken to celebrate a promotion.

'*That* is Lieutenant Commander Malady Chang. And *this* is what she sounded like last year when she attended a meeting in New Kabul.'

'*Not very much. I'm interested to see you. But there's something I'd like to get finished. It will only take three or four minutes –*'

A Californian accent, unmistakable, and almost entirely unlike the woman on the phone.

'*She* sounded English,' one of the techies agreed. That was Stevens, a linguistics expert. The first time Cosgrove had worked with him, he'd been impressed when he'd just said hello, and Stevens had deduced Cosgrove had a Swiss mother and hadn't lived in Scotland since the late fifties.

'You can do better than that.'

'I can. Like you, Professor Lik, that woman is a university-educated third-generation immigrant brought up in London. Her family were originally from Pakistan, though, not Korea. She's… there's something else in there.'

'Something else?' Cosgrove asked.

'Yes. Everything about the way we speak is influenced by our surroundings. If you work abroad, your voice starts picking up new inflections. That woman… she sounded like she was in her twenties, but spoke like a woman twice that old. There are other things in there I don't even recognise.'

'Something else,' Cosgrove told them. 'She asked for "the operator". Do any of you youngsters even know what that means?'

They shook their heads.

'No, you wouldn't. So, we have an anomaly. Another one.' He rubbed his chin. 'Stevens, Inform London –'

'London, sir, not Brussels?'

'I said London, lieutenant.'

'Sir.'

'Inform them that the President of the United States is going to be in Istanbul this time tomorrow.'

He nodded and set about his work.

Brooks turned to Cosgrove. 'We need to increase security to the ULTRA computer.'

Cosgrove smiled. 'No. Let's give them access, see how they get in, and what they really want to use it for.'

'Sir.'

To the next man along: 'We also need to locate the man from Neverland and get an ID on this Anglo-Indian woman.'

Finally, to Brooks. 'And we've still not found "the Doctor". I want him located. See if you can hack the CIA database to see where Malady Chang is posted at the moment.'

Cosgrove turned away.

'Sir,' Brooks said.

'Don't you understand your orders, Brooks?'

'Sir… I've found them. The Doctor and Malady Chang. They're in a Land Rover, heading towards the business district. Here in Athens.'

Cosgrove turned to the screen. There were three cameras on them – one long shot, showing almost a quarter of the city, one following the Land Rover ploughing through the water, the third aimed square through the windscreen. The Doctor was driving, Chang was in the passenger seat.

'So they are.'

Like the rhinoceroses of Earth, the Onihrs had poor eyesight, but more than made up for that with a highly developed sense of smell.

The Onihr leader could hardly bear to look at the Doctor at the moment. The alien was burning leaves, blowing the smoke through his mouth.

'That is your fifth burning leaf tube in almost as many minutes,' the deputy leader growled.

'Sorry,' the Doctor said. 'I'm trying to get off nicotine pills.'

'You were going to tell us about the Time Vortex.'

'I will, I will. Can I just get the circulation back to my wrists?'

The deputy leader grunted his impatience. The leader concurred.

'You will tell us... *now.*'

'Er... right. Time travel. Well, there's my TARDIS, of course –'

'We know of Chronodev from the fifty-first century. We know the identities of the four surviving elementals.'

'Right-oh. Good for you. Then who else is there? Time travel is pretty common these days. The fabric of space-time just seems a bit more malleable, don't you find? Oh yes – in the thirties we met Kala. She was a Time Agent, a human from the forty-ninth century. Noel Coward had some big shears that cut through the Very Fabric of... don't look at me like that, it's true. There was that experiment at Station Forty. Then in the eighteenth century we met Sabbath –'

'What do you know about Sabbath?' they both growled. 'We must know more about Sabbath,' the deputy leader added.

Fitz pointed at his own chest. 'Hey, hang on – you've got the Doctor here, right in front of you. Concentrate on what's important.'

The Onihrs looked at each other.

'This room has a lovely view,' the Doctor added.

The Onihr leader turned to follow the sound and smell of the Doctor – it wasn't difficult keeping up with him.

'Wow. Is that the Earth?'

The blue-green disc was obvious against the blackness of space.

'We do not know the local name for the planet. We were on routine patrol in this galaxy and detected disturbances in the fabric of space-time.'

'But you were down there, chasing that Chinese bird and hanging around that theme park.'

'We were monitoring you, Doctor. The human female was also monitoring you. Our disguises were necessary for covert operations on the planet.'

'So you're not interested in the Earth?'

'It's a primitive planet.'

'It's one of the Doct– of *my* favourite places in the universe.'

'It is?' the deputy leader asked. 'Why?'

'Well, to be honest with you, I'm not sure. Let's have a think. It's beautiful to look at. As you can see. It's big –'

'Onihros, our home planet, is four times the size.'

'– but not too big. Er… the shopping's good. There are some nice people there.'

The Doctor paused to light his sixth leaf stick. The deputy leader was studying his snouttop computer. The rich smell of data pervaded the air.

'You are hiding something from us, Doctor. Something about the Earth.'

'Nah.'

'You have a special affinity with the planet. You have visited it on many occasions. It has acted as a magnet to time travellers and other fourth-dimensional beings. Why?'

The Doctor shrugged. 'I honestly can't say.'

'He is hiding something from us, leader.'

'I agree, deputy leader. There is only one thing for it.'

The Doctor's shoulders slumped. 'Don't tell me… the pain inducer, only this time you'll start on level five.'

The Onihr leader paused. That hadn't occurred to him. 'No,' he grunted finally. 'The only course of action is to conquer the Earth. Deputy leader, prepare the invasion fleet.'

Chapter Ten
The Secrets of Time

The Doctor parked the Land Rover right outside Baskerville's office block. Here, closer to the sea, the city was in ruins. Across the road, another office block had collapsed completely, its top floors concertinaed into the ground level. The water was knee high, filthy, full of concrete rubble and sodden paper debris.

Malady followed the Doctor out of the car, wading through all this.

'We'll need shots after this,' she called over to him.

'And a towel,' the Doctor agreed.

It took both of them to push open the revolving door of the office block, against the water.

There was a creaking sound, like a ship's timbers.

'The building's unstable,' Malady told the Doctor.

He didn't acknowledge her.

'Which storey did you say I was on?' he said instead.

'Pardon?'

'When I fell out of the window, you told me which storey it was.'

'I didn't actually count them.'

The Doctor moved behind the reception desk.

'Hello, sir. Visitors aren't allowed behind this desk, I'm afraid.' It was the autosec.

'The power's still on,' the Doctor mumbled to himself. 'Using the lift would be too risky, though.'

'If you could move to the other side of the desk, sir, I'll be able to help you with your enquiry,' the autosec said calmly.

Malady was already heading for the stairwell. 'It's going to be quite a climb,' she warned.

Outside, there was a terrible splash, as some concrete crashed into the ground.

'I don't think this building's going to last much longer,' she said, although the Doctor wasn't listening.

He came back over. 'We'll use the lift.'

'You said it wasn't safe.' What she meant to say was that it obviously wasn't safe – the building was creaking, she could almost feel it twisting off its foundations.

'No, but it's fast. If the building's really going to fall down, I'd much rather I was in a steel box with all sorts of safety features than just some stairwell.'

If the building was really going to fall down, Malady thought, then she'd much rather be somewhere else entirely.

The Doctor pressed the button for the lift. When it didn't immediately arrive, he started jabbing repeatedly, as if that would make the lift come down any faster.

'Who's Cosgrove?' he asked, while they waited.

'Pardon?' She knew the answer, but the question had come out of the blue, and Malady didn't want to play all her cards if she could help it.

'I borrowed his briefcase,' the Doctor told her.

'You did?'

'Yes. Shortly before I blew up his boat.'

'That was you?'

'You know about it?' the Doctor countered.

'I saw it.'

'So you know Cosgrove?' He smiled, knowing he'd caught her out.

'Jonah Cosgrove is –'

'Jonah?'

'Yes. It's an odd name, but… well, my first name's Malady, and yours is "The".'

'It's not that, it's… it doesn't matter. Carry on.'

'Cosgrove is the head of the British Secret Service.'

'Eurozone Secret Service, surely?'

The lift arrived, and they stepped into it. The Doctor pressed the button for the twenty-somethingth floor.

'The British military was meant to merge with the rest of Europe's as part of the Act of Federation, yes. But not quite everything got put into the mix. The British government liked to maintain a little… independent capability. Cosgrove is the deputy head of the EZ Security Service, but his *real* job is to fight for King and country.'

'And the other EZ countries don't know about it?'

'Less than a hundred people in the world know about it, and most of them work for the Service. They're the cream of the crop.'

'Cosgrove being the crème de la crème.'

'Exactly. He's been at the heart of the British Secret Service since before the moon landings. He survived the Martians, the Euro Wars, the fall of Learman. He's normally utterly invisible. He stays in London. The fact that he's involved at all was enough to have the President authorise me to look into it.'

The lift doors opened.

'This is the floor,' the Doctor said. 'Come on – we don't have long.'

'What are we looking for?'

'It doesn't matter what I'm looking for. You're looking for anyone who's trying to kill us.'

Malady drew her gun. 'Bring them on.'

The Doctor followed the Onihr leader on to the command gallery, wittering all the way. All around them, Onihr officers moved into place, with practised ease. The leader admired their discipline, their sense of purpose.

'You can't invade the Earth,' the Doctor was saying, through clouds of leaf smoke. 'They'll resist. They're tenacious creatures, humans.'

'We have analysed their defensive capabilities.'

'Five minutes ago, you said you knew nothing about them.'

'Five minutes ago, we didn't. Now we know everything.'

Olfactograms of various human weapon systems appeared in the air.

'What's that smell?'

'That, Doctor, is the state of the art of human weaponry. And here is what our war computers calculate will happen when we launch our attack.'

The drift of the waft was unmistakable.

'You see, Doctor! Our technology is thousands of years in advance of that of the humans. We will prevail! The prediction is that the war will last seven minutes, Doctor.'

The Doctor had stopped in his tracks.

'The human race have nuclear weapons.'

'We will not allow them to blow themselves up,' he assured the Doctor.

'That isn't what I meant – they could launch them at you.'

The Onihr leader spent several minutes laughing at that.

Anji lay on her bed, staring at the ceiling, wondering what she'd got herself into.

Where were Fitz and the Doctor? Fitz could still be in California, but wouldn't have a clue how to find her, or even get in contact. Anji wasn't even sure the Doctor had told him they'd be leaving the TARDIS at Heathrow. *She* didn't have any way of getting in touch with the Doctor, so why would Fitz? They really ought to carry mobiles, or communicators like they had on *Star Trek*. Then again, they should carry all sorts of stuff – a first-aid kit, matches, a torch. Just basic stuff. The Doctor had all sorts of junk in his pockets, but never anything useful. She didn't want them to get a uniform, or even fully kitted out, or anything – it would just be nice to have some proper training.

She decided to check what she had in her pockets and bag.

Tissues. That wasn't exactly an inspiring start. The keys to her and Dave's flat. Loose change, mostly from the late eighteenth century, but some twentieth-century American coins, too. Suncream. A theatre ticket. Her mobile. Her Psion organiser. A page from the *Financial Times*.

A featureless black box the size of an audio cassette that she had difficulty placing at first.

It was the Doctor's time detector – he'd handed it to her back at the beach. She ran her finger along the edge, and it came to life, faint lights flickering across its surface.

She could use it to find the time machine. It was somewhere on the yacht, after all.

First, she made sure she knew what she was doing – the Doctor had just run it along – there. It bleeped a little at her, because she was a time traveller. It didn't bleep at the fold-down bedside table or the lamp because they weren't. It couldn't be simpler.

She held it out at arm's length, so it wasn't just registering her all the time, and set off towards the door. After a moment, she returned for her bag – somewhere to hide the detector if asked.

Baskerville and Dee were up on deck – she could hear them moving around. She'd finally spotted the East European guy up at the wheelhouse, or whatever it was called. Which meant the coast was clear.

She edged out of her room. Somehow, it didn't seem to be right doing this in swimwear. On the other hand, she thought, glancing down, if anyone but Dee found her, they wouldn't be looking at the time detector.

The device was steadfastly refusing to bleep. Anji shook it, wondering if it was on the blink, but it didn't make any difference.

There were three levels – decks, she corrected herself – one formed the control tower… hell, she didn't even know what that was called. The bit that was above the main hull bit.

Anyway, she'd got the basics of the layout of the yacht – the lowermost deck had a small hold, but was mostly turbines and engines. The deck above that was the one she was on now – cabins, the galley, a small workshop and laundry. Then there was the main deck, with its control tower, helipad, and area for sunbathing. There was a dining area/lounge there, too.

So there wasn't too much to search. Her money was on one of the cabins.

She tried the door to one, and was surprised it was open.

Dee's room, unless Baskerville or the East European guy were keeping something very quiet. Anji inched around the room. If she could hear them up on the deck, there was a very good chance they would hear her if she made enough noise.

The dressing table had a few expensive bottles of perfume on it, a few small items of jewellery. The wardrobe had a variety of changes of clothes, including a very snazzy-looking velvet catsuit/ballgown thing. There was a small zip-up bag, which turned out to be a VSCD case with three VSCDs in. There was a very expensive and powerful-looking laptop propped up against the bedside table.

No sign of any time machines, and nothing registering on the time detector. The way these things worked, it was bound to be in the very last place she looked.

Anji moved on to the next cabin.

'The time machine was through here.'

The Doctor held the door open for Malady, who stepped through. 'Is that it?'

The Doctor followed her in. The time machine was sitting in the middle of the room, the power cables still leading up to it, the lights still blinking on and off.

'I don't understand...'

Malady was looking around the room. She pointed through the thick glass window with her gun. 'What's through there?'

'That's the sending chamber.'

Malady was opening the door.

'Be careful – there may be time spillage.'

'I'll take the risk,' she told him, witheringly.

'Why didn't he take the time machine?'

The Doctor flicked a couple of switches, then remembered Malady was in the sending chamber, and decided things might start to get complicated if he accidentally sent her into the past.

'It's a bare room,' Malady told him.

The Doctor poked his head through. 'There was a coffee machine in here before.'

'Well, there isn't now.'

The Doctor returned to the time machine. 'I didn't get much of a chance to examine this before.' He looked up as Malady came back in. 'No... I'm sorry, this doesn't make sense.'

'The whole time travel thing, or just a bit of it? Come on, Doctor, that's a metal box with some lights on it, not a time machine. Do you think it looks like a time machine?'

The Doctor moved around it, unsure what Malady expected a time machine to look like.

'Why take the coffee machine, and not the *time* machine?' the Doctor asked again. 'He knew the tidal wave was coming. He knew to the *minute.*'

The Doctor looked over to Malady, who was looking up at the door. He turned to see what she'd seen.

Two graceful figures stood in the doorway. There was a middle-aged woman with long grey hair, and a small boy, probably no older than ten or twelve. They both wore neat purple one-piece outfits, and had gold circlets on their heads. Both were aiming stubby pistols.

Anji was in Baskerville's cabin.

The room was Spartan, virtually empty. Two identical pinstripe suits hung in the wardrobe, there was what looked like a CB radio on the dressing table, but there was almost nothing else of interest.

Anji stubbed her toe on something under the bed. She bent down to take a look. Under the bed was the silver carry case, the only thing Baskerville had salvaged from his office.

She pulled it out and opened it up.

It was the coffee machine, the one from the sending room. The jug was still half-full of coffee.

She waved the time detector over it, but from the lack of a signal, it still looked remarkably like a coffee machine, and not like a particularly bijou TARDIS.

Someone was coming.

Anji was squeezing herself under the bed before she knew what she was doing. There was someone coming down the steps to this deck. A moment later, the cabin door opened. She saw Baskerville's sandalled feet step in, then the door closing.

She hoped he hadn't come downstairs for some coffee.

He sat on the bed, his ankles inches from her face. What if he found her? Some people would pay good money to find a semi-naked Asian girl under their bed.

He was moving around on the bed. She seriously hoped he wasn't going to sleep. She checked her watch – it was a minute to two. But he could be having a siesta.

He was talking into the radio.

'Oblimova? Good.' His voice sounded different. There was an accent there – the same vaguely East European accent as his chauffeur.

Baskerville's feet appeared again, and Anji began to ease herself backwards. If they should touch her...

'The bomb worked. Look, there's been a change of plan. We're doing a deal with the Americans, now. Yes, well, dollars are as good as euros. Better in many ways. Now, we need to –'

Back a bit further...

Beep!

The time detector in her bag cheerfully registered the time traveller who had just brushed across it.

Two seconds later, Baskerville had grabbed bag and owner, and pulled Anji out from under the bed.

She stood awkwardly. He let her readjust her bikini.

'Er… hi,' she said, wondering how he'd kill her.

'Doctor,' the woman said. Her voice was calm, authoritative. She looked and sounded more like a university English lecturer than a… whatever she was.

The Doctor stepped forward. 'You know me?'

The boy was watching him with thinly veiled contempt. 'We're going to take you to our master to face trial. The whole universe will hear of your crimes.'

To their surprise, the Doctor grinned at that. 'Excellent,' he declared. 'That really is excellent news.'

'He's pleased, Jaxa,' the boy said, scandalised.

'You relish the idea?' the woman asked.

'Of course,' the Doctor said, leaning in. 'Perhaps there, I might find out what you're accusing me of.'

He glared at her, waiting for the answer.

'You're Time Agents, are you? I've met your sort before.'

'You have?' Malady asked.

'Yes, England in the nineteen-thirties, a place called Little Marpling. They were so keen to maintain established history, they were prepared to explode a nuclear weapon to stop a group of renegade time travellers.' A thought struck him. 'It was you, wasn't it? The tidal wave was you, covering your tracks.'

'No!' the boy shouted. 'That was all part of the web of time. But if it hadn't been –'

Jaxa placed her hand on his shoulder, silencing him. 'Roja…' She turned to the Doctor. 'I was a Time Agent once, but not a military officer. Now I work for a more noble cause. One that doesn't take kindly to your interference here.'

'Moi?' The Doctor looked offended.

Malady was watching them both carefully, getting their measure.

'What do you think the Doctor has done?'

'He is supplying time travel technology to a primitive era.'

The boy was studying a readout on a wristband. 'He isn't from this time zone.'

'You aren't?' Malady asked.

'Guilty as charged,' the Doctor admitted. 'But I'm here for the same reason as you.' He thumbed back over his shoulder. 'That time machine isn't mine, it belongs to an explorer from the future, a man who calls himself Baskerville.'

Jaxa moved over to the time machine, ran her hand along it. 'This isn't a time machine.'

'I've seen it operate,' the Doctor said. 'I was there.'

Jaxa pressed her gun against the side of the cabinet and fired. The cabinet gently fell apart, the four sides unpeeling like a banana skin.

'Light bulbs,' she told him.

The Doctor went over, checked the machine. She was right – there was nothing here but lightbulbs and LEDs, the only electronics were there to make the lights flash.

'The time machine has been removed,' the Doctor said. 'Look, there's room there for something the size of a suitcase. Baskerville took the working parts with him.'

Roja was still studying his wristband. 'There is no sign of a temp trace.'

Jaxa was reaching for a silver tube at her belt. 'Doctor, you must be removed from this continuum and taken –'

'Wait a moment,' the Doctor interrupted. 'Make up your mind. If you're right and this isn't a time machine, then what, exactly, am I guilty of? Supplying light bulbs?'

Roja was looking confused. 'He's right, Jaxa. If this isn't a time machine, then no crime has been committed.'

'But the Doctor himself claims that it *is* a time machine.'

The Doctor smiled smugly. 'If you're going to put me on trial, you'll need better evidence than that. It'll be my word against mine.'

Jaxa was having none of it. 'You'll be taken to a place where your actions can be assessed and punished.'

As she unclipped the tube, Malady made her move – she swept down with her hand, chopping Jaxa's gun out of her hand. She then swung round, kicking Roja hard in the face. He fell down, grabbing at his nose.

Malady grabbed the Doctor's sleeve. 'Time to go,' she told him.

The Doctor looked back over his shoulder. 'Who *are* they?'

Jaxa's Story

Let me tell you how they did it (how they did it back in history, I mean).

Before it was done to me, I was an historian, so I ought to have known. I did know. On the threat of war, the Admiralty issued press warrants to their officers. Gangs of marines were sent out, led by some old, worn-out lieutenant, and all the merchant ships were prevented from leaving port.

Everyone's heard of the press gangs. The common image is that they roamed the streets, grabbed drunks from the benches of the taverns and dragged them back to their ship. That happened, but not as often as you've been led to believe from old films. It didn't have to.

The press gangs did most of their work in the harbours, going on board the ships. The crew of an English ship in an English port didn't get shore leave – if they did, the captain would never see half of them again. Trusted men were granted it, in small groups, but you could spend ten years on your ship and never set foot on dry land. The mountain came to Mohammed – every ship arriving in port was boarded by travelling salesmen, tobacconists, minstrels, barrels of beer, and women, of course. Plenty of women. More often than not, there were more 'Blue Sallys' on board a ship in port than there were crewmen.

And that's where the press gangs went first – the lower decks of the big merchant ships. They gave you a choice about it, too, contrary to what you might have heard. They told you if you volunteered, you got paid a bounty. If you didn't volunteer, of course, you were pressed into service anyway.

It's no coincidence that the phrase Catch-22 was coined about a war. Every time there's a war, people make claims about the first casualty, and it's always an abstract - truth, freedom, reason. No one ever talks about the first recruit, but that's an abstract, too - logic. The Admiralty became a bastion of inescapable logic, the sort that confused Alice and kept Kafka up at night.

But there was something attractive about it, too. Suddenly, everything became maths, a straightforward proposition, the world became much easier to understand. You're either with us or against us. Everyone's in uniform, everyone knows their place. There are regulations, rules of engagement, there are orders. What was happening might not make much sense - fighting for peace was always, at best, a problematic concept - but why it was happening is perfectly straightforward. Everyone knew how they would be spending their days, what they had to do, what the reward would be. If it was a choice between death or glory... well, not many people volunteered for option (a).

But that didn't stop some people from running. I would have, when he came for me, if I'd had the choice.

The gangs caused chaos, of course - the press gangs had regulations, but they weren't regulated. They were ruffians - half the gang would only just have been captured themselves, and didn't see why anyone else should get away. Anyone they found got beaten to the ground, checked to see if they wore sailor's clothes underneath their coat, or had tar on their hands. Dead giveaways.

There were ways to avoid the press gang, ways more imaginative than just hiding or running. Get your friends to accuse you of some crime, get locked up for the night by the magistrate, then have them drop charges in the morning, when the gang had gone. That was a good one.

The best way, traditionally, was not to be physically present in the eighteenth century, to exist on a world with no sea, to live in the forty-ninth century, a far distant era of unparalleled peace and prosperity.

That was my way of avoiding the gangs. Extreme, I know, and imagine my surprise when it didn't work.

He was from the eighteenth century, you see. He was at war, looking for recruits. He also had a ship, which he rather fancifully sailed in the Mare Tranquillitatis. In his day, he would explain later, the astronomer-astrologers knew beyond any doubt that the dark patches on the Moon's surface really were seas, hence the names. That they weren't actually bodies of water wasn't important, it was the idea that was, it was their absolute faith that made his voyage possible. When I suggested to him that such a sentiment made no sense, he merely smiled.

He looked… well, I'm a film scholar and archivist. My job is to return to the primitive times, and to go back and recover all the films and television programmes that were withdrawn, deaccessioned and junked. And to me, he looked like the middle-period Orson Welles, that is, after he started putting on weight but before he grew the beard. He might not have literally looked like that, you understand, and might not have appreciated the description, but I really didn't care.

I was dying.

A time jump had gone wrong – placed me in the wrong century, before the Moon had an atmosphere, before the terraforming. I was barely three decades away from safety, I could reach out with my hand, almost touch it.

The radiation was intense, and more than enough to destroy the fragile ubertronics of my time machine. The heat burned at my skin, toyed with me. In the circumstances, the total vacuum was a mild inconvenience.

Sabbath stood there, his coat-tails flapping in a non-existent sea breeze. His moon had an atmosphere, as well as men with umbrellas for noses, kittens the size of elephants, and rocks that sang shanties in fluent French.

He offered me a choice. If I didn't come with him, he'd… take me anyway. He needed timefarers for a great enterprise he was undertaking, and he was having difficulty finding a workforce. He said something about paying peanuts and only getting monkeys, which I took to be a private joke.

So I took his hand, and as I did, I felt the sea breeze on my face, and knew I'd never be able to go back.

Chapter Eleven
Bankruptcy

The Doctor and Malady were running out of the lift before the doors were even fully open.

They were out of reception, splashing towards the Land Rover in seconds. The Doctor had the keys in his hand. He pointed them at the car, pressed the control to activate the central locking.

The Land Rover exploded.

While the Doctor examined the keychain, puzzled, Malady looked up. Jaxa was at a window, far above them, pointing a gun.

A second shot scored the air, but exploded harmlessly twenty feet from them.

'They've got us pinned down,' the Doctor said.

'She has – we don't know where the boy is,' Malady corrected him.

'Come on!' the Doctor started running close along the side of the building.

Malady followed, one eye looking back, trying to spot the boy.

She almost missed the helicopter in front of them.

It was a Raven, a stealth gunship, a stalwart of the European air force. Malady had never seen one up close. It was larger, more solid, than she had imagined. The rotor blades were angled down a little, and were kicking up waves of spray.

The helicopter turned, almost lazily. The door at the side was open, an old man was crouched there, a rifle in his lap.

'Do you recognise him?' the Doctor asked.

She did. 'Jonah Cosgrove.'

'Give me your gun.'

'It doesn't have the range.'

'The *gun*,' the Doctor hissed.

Malady handed it over. The Doctor passed it from hand to hand, as if deciding whether to fire left- or right-handed.

Cosgrove had his rifle on his shoulder, and was carefully aiming it. They were sixty feet apart – possibly less. His gun did have the range. It also had computer-assisted scopes, but Malady suspected Cosgrove wouldn't need them.

The rifle muzzle flashed, just as the Doctor fired the pistol.

Two seconds later, Cosgrove, the Doctor and Malady were all still alive, which surprised her.

The Doctor fired again. The first time, Malady had thought she'd imagined it, but she saw it again: a smear of a spark in the air between them and the helicopter.

Cosgrove fired, so did the Doctor. The third time, the third spark, and Malady realised what the Doctor was doing.

He was shooting Cosgrove's bullets out of the air.

Cosgrove hadn't worked it out. The helicopter was coming ever nearer – he was shouting something to the pilot – he thought there was something wrong with his gun.

An energy bolt sizzled between Malady and the Doctor, then on underneath the helicopter, before exploding into the half-collapsed office block opposite.

Malady turned to see the boy, only a few feet behind them, looking annoyed with himself for missing.

He aimed his gun again.

Malady did exactly what her training told her to – she ran straight for him. The second energy bolt detonated where she had just been. She caught up with the boy as his face was just registering that she was heading his way.

She brought her forearm down to the child's wrist, deflecting his gun hand, brought her knee up between his legs, slammed his chin with the heel of her palm, then grabbed his wrist, planning to either get him to drop the gun or break his wrist. In the event, she did both.

He squealed. Malady recovered his gun, then gave him a swift chop to the back of the neck, and he fell face first into the floodwater.

She watched him struggle on to his hands and knees, spitting out dirty water, tears in his eyes, his hand hanging limply.

Chalk one up to the good guys.

She turned on her heel, raised the ray gun and fired at the helicopter. The energy bolt hit the tail fin, blowing a great chunk out of it. The helicopter pulled up and away, and she could hear Cosgrove turning the air blue as he ordered the pilot to get them back down there.

The Doctor was watching them go. Malady joined him.

'We need to get inside,' the Doctor told her, looking around for a building that didn't look like it was about to collapse. 'There,' he said finally.

Cosgrove was angry with the pilot for retreating, but now they were out of the area, he accepted it had been the right decision. The helicopter was labouring, the engine didn't sound healthy. Besides, he'd just had a call from the communications centre on the royal plane.

The helicopter pilot had wanted to get down to assess the damage, and had found a raised bit of wasteland where that was possible. With the engines powering down, it was possible to have a more meaningful conversation with the comms room.

Penny Lik had found something she thought Cosgrove might find useful. When she told him what it was, Cosgrove could only agree.

Jaxa found Roja propped against the wall of the office block, trying to stop himself crying.

'She hurt me. She stole my gun.'

'You let advanced technology fall into the hands of a primitive?'

'I didn't *let* her. She hurt me.'

122

For the first time in the two years she'd known him, Roja looked his age, and it struck Jaxa just how inhuman it was to expose a twelve-year-old child to danger.

Eighteenth-century ethics for you. Her employer prided himself on being ahead of his time, of being a man of the future. But his future was children down mines and up chimneys, it was only a third of women dying in childbirth, it was hunting animals to extinction to make billiard balls and exotic rugs, only to discover that man himself was just a jumped-up monkey.

Sabbath's cabin boy was one of the lucky ones. Found in the street, he'd been given clothes and a bed, he'd been taught to read and write. When it had come to Sabbath's attention that he'd proved adept at that, he'd become a Boy First Class, his training had become intense, if specialised – mathematics, chronology, astrology-astronomy, high-energy physick.

Operational training with Jaxa was just part of his studies. This boy would be one of the Admirals of the Fleet, when he was a man. And when there was a Fleet.

'Stand up,' she ordered. He struggled to.

'There are locals after the Doctor and his companion,' Roja said. 'They have aircraft.'

'Then we will kill them.'

Baskerville smiled at Anji.

'Will you start, or should I?' he asked reasonably, using the cultured English accent, not the East European one he'd used when he didn't know she was listening in.

'You're not from the future?' He couldn't be, or the detector would be bleeping.

'No.'

'So where did you get your time machine?'

Baskerville shook his head. 'I have to keep some of my secrets. Now, my turn: How much do the CIA know?'

'Nothing.'

Baskerville looked her up and down, as if appreciating her for the first time. Anji kept her arms by her sides – if he wanted a good look, he might as well have it.

'Nothing?' he asked.

'I'm not CIA.'

That clearly surprised him. 'You *are* working for the EZSS, after all?'

'I'm not even sure what that is.'

'The Eurozone Secret Service,' he said, sounding a little pained.

'Oh right. No. I'm Anji Kapoor. I'm a trader at MWF, a London bank.'

Baskerville wasn't sure what to make of that. 'Ethical fund management?'

Anji sighed. 'Not always.'

'Why not?' he was testing her.

'Because, ultimately, we're there to make money for our customers and shareholders. And there are very few stocks as reliable as tobacco and defence contractors.'

'*Defence* contractors?'

'Arms manufacturers, then.'

'The people that make cluster bombs, strike aircraft and guided missiles. Defensive systems like those?'

'Yes. I don't create the demand by trading shares.'

'But you are a vital part of the process. Without the shareholders, how would they expand? Without people like you, how would they ever develop new... defensive... systems?'

'Is this third form debate going anywhere?' she asked, irritated. 'Without a military, the West would have been invaded by Russian tanks, or bombed to oblivion. Offensive weapons act as a deterrent.'

'Indeed.' Baskerville was smiling at her. 'Before we go any further... have you heard of Chechnya?'

'Yes. Part of the former Soviet Union. The Russians invaded.'

'The Russian tanks invaded, and eventually it was bombed to

oblivion. I was there when the first nuclear device was detonated. Half a million children and old women turned to ash in an instant.'

Anji put a hand on his shoulder. 'I'm sorry. I didn't know.'

'Don't be sorry, my dear. I was a General in the Russian Army at the time. It was me that pressed the button. And for the last ten years, since I left military service, I've been what you might call a freelance defence contractor.'

'An arms dealer?'

'Do you know what this planet's main industries are? Forget agriculture, forget the automobile. The four biggest industries on this planet are arms dealing, illegal narcotics, illegal arms dealing, and the oil trade. Narcotics and the oil trade have been in steady decline for decades. Arms manufacturing is, as you say, as blue chip a stock as you could hope for.'

'The market for time machines is even better?'

Baskerville shrugged. 'Not exactly. It's more a way of drumming up business. Increasing my cashflow.'

'By getting the Eurozone – or the Americans, whoever will cough up – to give you money.'

'Giving me money… yes. I hadn't thought of it in quite those terms, but yes. They will give me money. Now… I think I've told you plenty about myself. How about you, Miss Kapoor. It is "Miss"?'

She nodded. 'What would you like to know?'

'You're young.'

'I'm twenty-seven.'

'But you're good at your job?'

'Yes.' It might have sounded arrogant, but as far as Anji was concerned she was just stating the facts.

'And you clearly have initiative. The CIA and the EZSS have been after me for years. They don't know my real name, only one of them knows what I look like. Yet here you are, standing in my cabin, looking very fetching I might add, and you've managed to get to the truth of it in a matter of hours.'

Anji shifted a little uncomfortably. 'Well, yes.'

'I don't have an electronic presence,' Baskerville said. 'There were army records, of course, ID numbers. But I faked my death. Most people who fake their death adopt a new identity – usually someone about their age who died. I… didn't. The whole world is data, now. Every square centimetre is just a set of GPS co-ordinates, every human being is just a serial number. The intelligence services have their listening posts, they have the keys to datanet encryption, they have their CCTV and image recognition software. This is a world where every syllable uttered is stored and logged. But I don't exist. They don't know my name, I don't have an email address, I don't even have a phone number or a IFEC account in my name. So they can crank up their search engines until they cannae take the strain, but they'll never find me. And as long as they can't find me, I'm invincible.'

Anji's phone started to ring.

Baskerville looked down at her bag.

Anji looked embarrassed. 'I'm not expecting a call.' She fished it out of her bag and pressed it to her ear.

A moment later, she handed it over to him.

'It's for you.'

Baskerville's face fell.

'Baskerville, it's Cosgrove. I hope I'm not interrupting anything?'

'Er… no.'

'I hear you're dealing with the Americans, now.'

'I…'

'There's no use denying it, old chap, we've got you monitored, now. You're on a yacht in the Med, about fifty miles out from Athens. I'm in Athens myself, right at the moment.'

'Yes…'

'Now… you're meeting the President of the United States in Istanbul tomorrow. I will be there, bidding on behalf of His Majesty's Government. I can give you access to the ULTRA.'

'Is there anything you don't know about me?'

'I know where to aim the smart missile. In my experience, that's all you ever need to know about a person. Now – you've met the Doctor, I believe?'

'Yes. I killed him.'

'No you didn't.'

'I threw him off the top of an office block, that usually does the trick.'

'It didn't in this case. Now, don't worry, I'll sort out the Doctor problem. Think of it as a goodwill gesture. I'll see you tomorrow in Istanbul. Good bye!'

Baskerville handed Anji back her phone.

'Where were we?' Anji asked sweetly.

Every alarm in the museum was ringing.

The huge entrance hall was knee deep in water – you took half a dozen steps down from the street to get in, and so the whole ground floor had acted as a reservoir for the floodwater.

The Doctor and Malady waded through.

'Where are we headed?' Malady asked.

'In here, Cosgrove's lot can't use surveillance satellites or helicopters to locate us. And Jaxa and Roja won't be able to hit us with sniper fire, they'll have to get closer. They're trained, but – well, the boy didn't last long fighting hand-to-hand, did he?'

Malady still felt guilty about beating up a child. She had his raygun in her hand, and he had been firing at her – she had no doubt she'd be dead now if she hadn't. But there was a basic belief hardwired into her brain that you don't hurt children.

She hadn't hesitated last time. She hoped she wouldn't hesitate next.

They were wading towards a large staircase at the end of the entrance hall, one that curved up to the upper galleries. It was mid-afternoon, and sunlight poured through the small windows lining the ceiling, like golden spotlights, casting deep shadows.

This hall was full of enormous sculpture. Malady was no expert, and all the signs describing the exhibits had been washed away, but she recognised Greek gods when she saw them.

'I guess these must have stood in the temples,' she said.

The Doctor looked back at her. 'Yes. Don't worry, they'll survive a bit of water. They've survived worse than that over the centuries.'

Most were sitting. They'd have been twenty feet tall standing up, Malady guessed. What was knee-high water to her barely lapped their ankles. They were perfectly white, perfectly proportioned – idealised forms of beauty. It wouldn't be difficult to worship them, she thought, particularly before they'd been dwarfed by the office blocks outside, and had stood taller than a house.

'They aren't going to stop coming after us,' Malady said.

'No.'

They could already hear more helicopters overhead.

'Normally we could make an escape through the sewers,' the Doctor said. 'Out of the question for the moment, of course.'

'We're cornered.'

'We're alive, and as soon as we step outside we won't be.'

They'd reached the stairs. Seven steps up, and they were on dry land again. It felt odd not to feel the water dragging against her shins.

The Doctor paused for breath. 'Sorry,' he said, 'it's been quite a busy day. Let's get up to the galleries upstairs, we'll come up with a plan there.'

'So who are you?' Anji asked Baskerville.

'I was surprised you hadn't heard of RealWar. That is my little empire. I'm sixty years old, Anji. Too young to have lived through the Second World War. My parents could remember it. And we were the first two generations in human history where the young men didn't expect to be called up to fight. Yes, there were wars –

Afghanistan, the Gulf, Mexico – but they were fought by specialists. Professional soldiers, not conscripts.'

'You joined up.'

'I did. And I did because I wanted to fight. Somewhere, deep inside all of us we all want to fight – all men anyway, perhaps it's different for girls. But you know what American and European kids did? They didn't join the army, they still wanted to fight, but they didn't want to *die*. So you know what they did?'

'Er… became football hooligans?'

Baskerville nodded. 'Some of them. Many became footballers – or took part in other competitive sports. Some took up shooting, or martial arts.'

'God, all the teenage boys I knew spent all their time watching television.'

Baskerville grinned. 'Precisely. *Most* of them just did that – sat in front of the television, watching wars, or kung fu movies, or contact sports. And playing computer games – shooting people, beating them up, infiltrating enemy bases and stealing secret plans. They played at being precisely the sort of soldiers they would never dream of becoming in real life. You know why?'

Anji laughed. 'Because when you're killed in *Half-Life* you don't actually die.'

Baskerville nodded. 'Exactly. A very simple, yet also very intelligent reason. The best reason in the world, in fact… but it did make fighting wars increasingly difficult, because governments were expected to run wars like computer games, with no one really dying. At first, they just pretended no one was dying – just didn't show those bits in their briefings. But that didn't fool anyone.'

'So you came up with the solution?'

'Oh yes. RealWar. Teletroops – robot soldiers, controlled from a distance. Cheap, completely expendable – but the bullets they fire are just as real as if there was a real squaddie firing them.'

Anji gave her best 'everyone knows that' look. 'You invented them?'

'Yes. Invented them, marketed them. But I assumed... I'm a Russian, Ms Kapoor. We still haven't got the hang of capitalism. We have... well, capitalism in Russia is exactly what the Soviets used to tell us it was – gangsters and faceless international financiers screwing us out of all our money. I assumed the robots would be driven by professional soldiers, but –'

'But the real whizzkids are the computer gamers. And the computer gamers love to play a game that isn't a game, they love to fight a real war where there's no risk of dying.'

Baskerville nodded. 'It took my ten years to realise that, but you've got it straight away. You really are good at your job.'

'I'd buy shares in your company,' Anji admitted. 'Robots fighting robots... that's almost ethical, isn't it?'

'Ah.' Baskerville hesitated. 'Well, my robots are cheap, but not that cheap. In the event, only the EZ and the Americans can afford them in anything like the numbers where they're an effective substitute for a human soldier. So... more often than not, it's robots versus humans. Another thing I didn't anticipate... the teletroopers don't like their opponents to be robots. They relish the idea of going after humans. They have to be drafted in to fight other robots, but to go up against *people*... they'd pay for that privilege. Once the powers that be realised that... well, market forces. So the robots started paying for themselves.'

Anji felt ill. 'People paid to kill other people?'

'Only to kill *bad* people,' Baskerville said sarcastically. 'It was how the war against terrorism was won. The computer told you who was a terrorist and who wasn't, with eighty percent accuracy, anyway, and the teletroopers went in and blasted them away, paying good money, all from the comfort of their living rooms. And if you weren't fighting, you were watching – the ultimate reality TV show, for the highest stakes imaginable.'

Baskerville sat back. 'And, with my patents on the software and hardware, with my licensing agreements, with the tie-in books and games and toys and videodiscs... well, I became the richest man on Earth. Well… I think so. As I don't have an electronic presence, it's all black accountancy, but…'

'So… who do they fight now?'

Baskerville smiled thinly. 'You see my problem? How to maintain my position as market leader?'

'You're engineering the war between Europe and America?'

Baskerville nodded.

'Millions will die.'

'Yes. Millions will die, and for everyone that does there will be two angry parents and two angry children and a dozen angry friends baying for revenge. And, for only a few dollars subscription, they can take that revenge. It'll be the ultimate grudge match, and the TV rights alone will be worth trillions. But what then? It's the problem for all fight promoters, all the makers of action films… what do you do after the ultimate battle, the fight to end all fights? How do you do that without killing the golden goose?'

'You stop?'

'Only if you're one of the weak.'

Anji looked at him. He was smiling.

'You have an answer to that question? Something involving this time machine of yours?'

Baskerville nodded. 'Oh yes.'

Chapter Twelve
The Spy Who Shot Me

They had men, covering all the exits, with orders to shoot anything that came through.

They couldn't land helicopters on the roof. There were three doors at ground level. The Doctor and Malady had gone in through the main entrance, one of the others was blocked by debris, the other hadn't been opened since the tidal wave had hit. The Doctor and Malady were still in the building.

Cosgrove had a limited number of men available, but he had enough. He ordered all the doors covered by teletroops, got a squad of men to set up by the main entrance, and kept two helicopters in the air, circling the museum.

The Doctor and Malady were working together, now. Cosgrove still didn't think the Doctor was CIA, though. But they must have common interests – and that common interest could only be to prevent his acquiring time travel.

Anyway, there was now a fourth party involved. A middle-aged woman and a young boy, in purple uniforms which no one could identify, carrying laser handguns.

Time travellers from the future. They had to be. Penny Lik suggested they could be policemen from Baskerville's time. She read a lot of science fiction, but Cosgrove thought she was probably right – the authorities of the future would be at least as concerned about the spread of time-travel technology as the twenty-first century was about ABC weapons. So they'd send people back to stop proliferation. Once you accepted the possibility of time travel, the main objection became that there just weren't *enough* time travellers. Surely they'd be all around –

tourists, researchers, spies, military men, businessmen, all travelling back to do their jobs? Cosgrove was glad his instincts had been proved right, that there was an *unearthly* component to all this.

Cosgrove gave orders for the two newcomers to be captured, if at all possible. They had last been seen retreating back into the office block where they'd found the Doctor, but Cosgrove fully expected them to resurface.

Jaxa pressed a medi-stim to Roja's neck.

'We should sterilise the area,' Roja was saying, still wincing from the pain.

'There may not have been a crime,' Jaxa reminded him.

'The woman stole my gun. They should all be eradicated.'

'Then you have let future tech fall into primitive hands. The crime is yours. Would you like me to eradicate *you*?'

Roja was sitting up, now. 'That's not fair,' he said, sounding like a spoilt brat.

Jaxa considered her options. The handgun would have to be retrieved, of course. The Doctor was a known rogue time element, and one her master was particularly interested in, but merely being present in a time zone that was not your native one wasn't a crime. Particularly in the case of *elementals*, who didn't have a native time.

They needed to find Baskerville. He was the key to this – if he was a rogue, he wasn't known to them. His death would tie up loose ends here, and would represent something that could be presented as a positive result, without causing any awkward political ramifications. But killing Baskerville and letting the Doctor go, whatever the legalities of the situation, would not please Sabbath. She could hear him talking in that slightly sarcastic tone of his, telling her that she'd caught the small fish, but let the big one go, and that she had no sense of the larger picture.

'Our priorities are clear,' she said finally. 'We must recover or destroy your handgun. We eliminate Baskerville. Then we capture the Doctor and return home with him. We deal with him there.'

'But we're not the only people after the Doctor.'

'No we aren't. But nothing else need concern us – if anyone tries to prevent us achieving our objectives, then we eradicate them.'

Jaxa handed Roja her gun.

'But what will you use, Madame Jaxa?'

'I will find something,' she assured him.

She unclipped her timeporter from her belt and opened it up.

'We will teleport over to that museum. The Doctor and his companion will be on one of the upper levels.'

Roja was looking out of the window. 'There is a lot of human military activity.'

She replaced the timeporter. 'They have simple projectile weapons, they needn't concern us. She tapped her neck, and the cowl extruded over her head, covering it. Roja did the same.

She activated the timeporter.

The Doctor sat at the base of a large vase which, according to the sign, dated back to the time of Alexander the Great.

In the galleries, there was no evidence of the tidal wave. Malady had wondered if there would be any survivors huddled up here, but if anyone had been here when the wave struck, they'd since evacuated.

The Doctor was lost in thought, his eyes closed. 'Have you ever had a bar of music in your head, one that you can't place, and however hard you try you can't hum the next bit?' He asked. 'It's frustrating, isn't it? Just imagine what it's like to have nothing but that. Living a life like that.'

He didn't elaborate. Malady wasn't entirely sure he was talking to her.

'Cosgrove's men will be here in a minute,' she told him gently.

'Plenty of time to come up with something,' he assured her.

Malady returned her attention to her new raygun. There were a variety of dials and switches on the top of the weapon. She decided not to play with them – the setting it was on was effective, and she didn't want to accidentally put the safety catch on. She wondered how many shots she'd get before it ran out of power.

Cosgrove moved in, two men in front of him, three behind.

They fanned out as they entered the main entrance hall. It didn't look like the Doctor and Malady were here. It was waterlogged – in their position, Cosgrove would get across the hall and up that staircase to the first floor.

They moved forwards in a line, executing a search pattern – if the Doctor was here, they'd know about it.

There were huge statues here – Apollo, Zeus, an achingly beautiful Aphrodite. These things had endured for centuries. Millennia. They were older than his own civilisation.

Hard to think there had been a time when there wasn't a Service. Some of the secret societies, of course, claimed to date back into antiquity. But how would you ever prove that?

What would that mean, anyway?

Cosgrove believed in tradition. He was a patriot, he fought for the United Kingdom. Great Britain. But not because it was *old*. Because he genuinely believed it was a way of life worth preserving and fighting for. There were fragments of a British way of life that were still worth clinging to.

He looked up at Aphrodite again. Today she really was rising from the seawater. She was perfect. Every curve, every line, every detail.

'Sir!' one of the men called out.

Something was happening on the staircase in front of them.

That was the best description Cosgrove could come up with for the moment: something.

The light was changing. Shapes were forming.

The time police, he realised. They were materialising – using some future technology to beam straight into the museum.

He brought his machine pistol up and fired three rounds into the nearest shape to him.

The first volley passed straight through, ricocheted off the back wall. The next did the same. The third killed the target.

It was the woman, and she was thrown back by the force of the bullets hitting her before she'd fully materialised.

Madame Jaxa looked surprised.

'I'm dead,' she told Roja, who was kneeling down. She could hear the human soldiers splashing across the entrance hall towards them.

'No.'

'The bullets… they arrived before me. They're inside me, I can feel them. I'm dead. Don't let them kill you, too.'

Roja stood, fired at one of the soldiers, who vanished in a burst of light. The others dived for cover behind the statues.

A moment later, one edged round the corner of his plinth. Roja could hear him doing it, see the water sloshing around as he made his move.

He disintegrated the man, and the corner of the statue, with a single shot.

Three more soldiers opened fire. Roja felt some of the bullets ricochet from his clothing.

He bent down, activated Jaxa's timeporter.

His tutor vanished, returned to their home time.

Perhaps there the medics could save her.

Roja knew they couldn't. But perhaps they could. Perhaps.

He was crying, the cowl he was wearing suddenly felt very hot, restrictive.

He fired at the base of another of the statues, watched it fall like a tree that had been chopped down, saw some of the soldiers dive out of the way, and some of them that didn't.

He hurried up the stairs.

The statue of Aphrodite came crashing down, the head breaking off as the torso hit the floor, a great wave surging out.

The head was the size of a small car. Cosgrove barely avoided it, but was bowled over by the surge of water.

Two of his men had been killed before that. Another two died under the falling masonry.

Cosgrove pulled himself upright, water pouring off him. The insides of his boots were wet, he could feel cold water trickling down his back. Aphrodite stared up at him, her perfect face half submerged in the water. He felt angry at seeing her like that, violated.

'Stevens, are you there?'

Stevens was, and came splashing over. 'The boy went upstairs,' he said. 'That gun of his…'

Cosgrove nodded.

'Where's the one I shot?' Cosgrove asked.

'I didn't see.'

'I killed her. She's not there.'

They did a quick visual search of the room. The waves from all the splashing about were already beginning to subside, but the light was good, there was no sign of the woman.

'You got her, sir. Perhaps the boy used that gun on her, to stop us getting hold of the body.'

Cosgrove nodded. 'Good thinking.'

'Sir, the kit the boy was wearing was bullet proof. He took four rounds, didn't even knock him off his feet.'

The technology was impressive, Cosgrove thought. He'd once been hit while wearing a Kevlar vest. The bullet didn't kill you, but you knew you'd been hit. You got pushed over, you had a bad bruise for a month.

'I killed the woman, I can kill the boy.'

* * *

137

Malady and the Doctor looked to the top of the staircase at the sound of the first shot.

A moment later, it was clear there was a firefight going on downstairs, between Jaxa and Roja and the British special forces.

It wasn't so clear who was winning.

The Doctor was getting to his feet. Malady pulled him down.

'No. Stay put.'

They were half hidden here, able to get a good look at anyone coming up the stairs without being immediately obvious to them. A moment later, her instincts were proved right. Roja came running up the stairs. His face was covered in a balaclava-like hood. He was carrying another raygun. He was clearly in retreat.

Malady waited a moment, until she was sure that Jaxa wasn't right behind him. As she moved to stand, this time, the Doctor pulled her down.

She thought he was trying to stop her shooting, but he was just waiting until the boy was nearer. Roja wasn't looking for them – he'd obviously forgotten his mission. Something had distracted him. Given the gunfire a moment before, and the absence of Jaxa, it wasn't too hard to guess what.

The boy stumbled straight past them.

Malady and the Doctor leaped out, as if they'd practised the move together. Malady grabbed the boy, the Doctor twisted the gun out of his hand.

The Doctor yanked the hood off.

The boy's eyes were red with crying, his nose was running.

'Get off me!' he shouted, but he just wasn't strong enough to put up much of a struggle.

They could hear clattering footsteps coming up the stairs.

'Cosgrove's men,' the Doctor said, lifting something from the boy's belt, a silver tube.

He examined it, then twisted the end. A control panel unfolded, Malady wasn't quite sure how.

'Simple enough controls.' The Doctor grabbed his lapels. 'Now,

Roja, what was your mission?'

'I'm to take you back to Sabbath.'

'Ah… Sabbath. You're one of his, are you? What's your story, then?'

'I'm his Cabin Boy.'

'Yes, of course you are. Just his style. You do realise you don't exist, don't you? It was *Tom* the cabin boy. There was no one on the Black Pig called Staines or Bates. There was a Barnabas, and a first mate who didn't have a name, but –'

'Doctor, what are you talking about?' Malady asked.

'If you don't exist,' the Doctor said, 'you make the perfect agent, don't you? Not so easy to catch. Impossible to kill.'

'I exist. Let me go and I'll show you I exist.'

'And how would you do that?'

'I'd hit you. Then I'd show you.'

'Is that how we're to justify our existence in the new order? By how hard we can hit people?'

'You can see me,' Roja said. 'So I exist.'

'People see all sorts of things, don't they?'

'I exist. I exist. People remember me.'

'They think so therefore you are?' The Doctor shook his head. 'I'm sorry, but it doesn't work like that.'

Malady was shaking her head. 'I don't understand a word of this.'

The Doctor smiled. 'English pop culture, Malady, don't worry about it. Just another bit of misplaced self-aware seventies nostalgia with no place in the twenty-first century.' He twisted the top of the silver tube and the controls furled up and slotted themselves back in place.

'Time to go.' He squeezed the end of the time machine, just remembering to grab Malady's hand at the last moment.

Cosgrove and Stevens arrived a moment later to find Roja yelling into thin air.

'I exist! I do! Come back! I exist!'

Cosgrove blew the back of his head off with a single shot.

'No need to shout about it,' Cosgrove told him quietly.

Chapter Thirteen
Tomorrow Never Lies

Malady watched the boy, Cosgrove and the other British special forces soldier fade away.

She wasn't sure what the Doctor had done.

'You killed them?' she asked. But the helicopters had gone, too.

'I moved us in time, but not in space.'

'How far?' The sunlight was in the same place it had just been.

'Exactly a day.'

'We're in the future?'

The Doctor grinned. 'Yeah. But here they call it "the present".'

He handed her the gun he'd taken from the boy.

'Cosgrove didn't work it out,' the Doctor said, relieved. 'He must have thought we'd travelled in *space*. By the lack of helicopters, it sounds like he scaled down the search. If he'd just waited here, he'd have got us.'

The Doctor opened up the time machine again, started checking the settings.

Malady looked around. 'OK… we made it. I really didn't think we were going to. But we got away.'

'I don't think this has much charge left,' he said, waving the time machine. 'Two journeys at most. We should conserve energy, find some other way to get about. I need to find my companions, too. Anji's probably with Baskerville, Fitz could be anywhere on Earth by now.'

Malady nodded. 'And whatever it is Baskerville has planned, he's a day closer to it, now.'

The Onihr leader studied the latest status reports.

Fitz watched him, wondering what the Doctor would do in his place. He suspected it wouldn't be to hang around for a day and a half, hoping something would come up, but that was the best Fitz had managed so far.

'So… what are you planning?' he asked. There was always a chance the Onihr leader would tell him.

'First we fire our EMP cannon, disabling all electronic devices on Earth, then we introduce the metal- and plastic-eating megaviruses, that will reduce all metal alloys and plastics to biodegradable sludge. Then we will invade, dragging all their world leaders from their places of safety and decapitating them. The fifth minute of the invasion will begin with –'

'It's OK, I get the idea.'

The control gallery was facing the Earth, now.

Sending a message to Earth seemed entirely futile. What would Fitz say? 'Don't make any plans for this evening'? Locating the Doctor and getting a message to *him* was a possibility, but the only way Fitz could think of doing it was to ask the Onihrs – and they still thought he *was* the Doctor.

'Time travel detected, leader,' one of the Onihrs growled.

'Where?'

'On the surface of the Earth.'

The air filled with the smell of fresh hay. It had been a while before Fitz had realised that the Onihrs were almost blind, but had a highly developed sense of smell. He'd been quite proud when he'd worked it out. It explained the flowers growing from the walls of some of the rooms – decoration.

He was sure there was probably a way to turn their blindness to his advantage, or to cunningly contrive a disguise using different scents.

Buggered if he could think of how, though.

'It is located here, leader.'

The leader picked up Fitz and lowered him in front of the console.

'Explain.'

'Er... can you show me a picture?' he asked.

A picture of Greece from space appeared.

'Greece,' he explained. 'Er... Athens?' That was a guess, but he thought Athens was around there somewhere.

'Human communications have used that word many times during the last day, leader. There has been a tidal wave there, and significant loss of life.'

The Onihr considered this information, clearly not sure how to proceed.

'Rather than invade the Earth,' Fitz suggested, 'you should perhaps concentrate on that.'

The Onihr leader and his technician sniffed the air, curiously.

'Explain.'

'Well, instead of using all this technology to just conquer the Earth, why not use it to track that time machine?'

The Onihrs hesitated.

'I mean, you can do that, can't you?' Fitz asked. 'You keep going on about how advanced you are.'

The Onihr leader grabbed Fitz's collar. 'We can do that, Doctor. It will take time, but we can do it.'

He lowered Fitz back to the floor, checking his anger.

The technician was looking a little concerned. 'It may take some time, leader.'

'Proceed.'

The Doctor and Malady found themselves a quiet spot.

The helicopters had gone, most of the floodwater had subsided, although everywhere was still damp, there were great puddles in the street.

The bodies had been removed.

Malady put her eyephones on. 'I'm going to call the President.'

The Doctor seemed more interested in the eyephones than what she'd just said.

She made the call.

'Malady,' the President said warmly. 'I was speaking to a Malady Chang yesterday, but it wasn't you.'

Malady had no idea what he was talking about.

'A young Englishwoman?' the Doctor asked.

'Who's that, Malady? You didn't say you were with someone.'

No she hadn't, and she chided herself for that.

'It's the Doctor,' she explained.

'Is it?' the President said. 'I knew I'd heard that voice somewhere.'

'You've met the President?' Malady asked.

The Doctor shrugged. 'Possibly.'

'I'm Felix Mather, Doctor.'

The Doctor racked his brains. 'Ah yes. 1989. I stole your space shuttle.'

'That's right.'

Malady looked at the Doctor. He must have been about ten at the time.

The Doctor smiled. 'Remember afterwards, when we landed at Edwards? The look on the face of the –'

'Sir, Doctor, I'm sorry to interrupt, but if we could save this for another time?'

A hesitation at the other end, then. 'OK, Malady, what have you got?'

'If we could deal with the impostor first. You know who it is?' she asked the Doctor.

'I strongly suspect that it's Anji Kapoor, a young companion of mine. What did she tell you, Felix?'

Malady winced. Even the First Lady referred to him as 'Mr President' in public.

The President outlined what they already knew – that Baskerville had a time machine, he was willing to hand over blueprints in return for access to the ULTRA computer.

The President was to deal face-to-face with Baskerville in

143

Istanbul, and he was in Air Force One, heading that way for a meeting in just a few hours.

Malady waited for her new instructions.

'I think we can handle it from here, Malady. Stand down, and get back to Station E for a debrief. But take your time – you've earned a rest.'

'Felix,' the Doctor interrupted. 'To prove he has time travel, Baskerville made four prophecies to Cosgrove. Three of them have come true, the third was the Athens tidal wave. We need to know what the fourth was.'

'I'm not sure how I could –'

'You've got the whole CIA and FBI at your disposal, you're the leader of the free world and you're meeting Baskerville in a couple of hours. I'm sure a man of your resourcefulness can find a way.'

Malady could almost hear the President glaring at the Doctor.

'I'll do it,' he said finally.

'How did you know?' Anji asked, tucking her hair back behind her ear.

They could see Istanbul on the horizon, now. The pilot (Anji had finally learnt that his name was Leo), had anchored the yacht, and started to prepare the helicopter. Dee had gone to her cabin to pack.

'How did I know what?' Baskerville asked her.

'You made those prophecies. But your time machine can only go into the past. So how can you see the future?'

'Ah yes. Well, being the richest man in the world has its advantages. Fixing a soccer match is really not as difficult as you'd think.'

'The young actress who died…'

'Really should have paid more attention to biosecurity.'

'And Athens?'

Baskerville took a deep breath. 'Yes, Athens.'

'Four thousand dead or missing. A million people homeless.'

'Yes. I've killed more people in my time, directly and indirectly. But I have to admit I'm not proud of myself.'

Anji found it difficult to look at him. 'How?' she heard herself saying.

'A large bomb, placed in exactly the right place on the seabed. It dislodged just the right amount of material to create a localised tidal wave... and just enough to bury all the evidence. Quite a feat of engineering. The people who arranged it were worth every penny.'

She couldn't think of anything to say. Nothing that would express how she was feeling.

He was an old man, sixty if he was a day. He was quite slight. She could break his neck, throw him overboard. She was sure she could do it physically. She was damn sure she could justify it morally.

But a minute passed, and she still hadn't done it. It wasn't fear that Dee and Leo would kill her when they discovered what she'd done. They probably would, but she didn't care about that.

The reason she hadn't killed him, she realised, was that she still wanted some questions answered, and if she killed him, she'd never know.

'You think it's a crime,' Baskerville said softly.

'Don't you?' she asked, angry.

'I suppose it is. But what's wrong with crime? I've always thought the world should be run along Mafia lines. When the Soviet Union fell, the Mafia took over. As a soldier, I hated to see gangsters and pimps running the country. But they paid good money, at a time when the government couldn't even pay its own workers, let alone provide for anyone else.'

He suddenly seemed quite tired.

'Areas controlled by criminals have far lower crime rates, that's the irony.'

'They rule by terror. They charge protection money.'

'And governments rule by default, and charge taxes. I tell you what, my dear, if a gang tried demanding forty or fifty percent of people's income, they wouldn't last very long.'

'There would be anarchy. Who would be in charge?'

'Whoever made the streets the safest, whoever could supply the most of what people demanded. It's the free market, you should appreciate that.'

'It's not what the majority want.'

'Yes it is. You don't vote for someone who looks good on the datanet and who isn't quite as awful as the other chap. But you do get someone who knows the local area, someone who wants to look after it, someone who's got an interest in keeping the local businesses running. Not like the Eurozone, where someone who's never even been to your country decides to close the factory that's your town's only employer because he needs to tidy up a balance sheet or reduce a subsidy budget.'

'Those people are accountable.'

Baskerville shook his head. 'No. They're elected, but that's hardly the same thing. Do you think they have the *real* power? Do you know who controls the world, Anji? Do you know who it is who guides the markets, regulates supply and demand? Follow the money, follow the flow of capital.'

Anji readied herself for some racist bile. If Baskerville – or whatever his real name was – really had grown up in post-Soviet Russia, she could excuse him it, she supposed. Their civilisation had literally collapsed, a superpower that put the first man into space had been reduced to lawlessness in a very few years. She didn't know how long it had taken to rebuild. It would have been many years after her native 2001, and they weren't that many years after 2001.

So, he'd blame the 'international financiers', or the 'Western Bankers', or maybe he'd come right out and just say 'Jews'. Or he'd blame some other immigrants, or dole scroungers, or single mothers. He'd blame someone who was manifestly doing even worse, getting even less, out of the system.

'No one,' Baskerville said quietly. 'That's the most frightening thing. There are all those conspiracy theories about secret cabals running the world. My conspiracy theory is that they're a myth, put about by people who desperately don't want their citizens to realise that there's no one in charge. There's no one flying the plane, and no one knows where it's heading.'

'The market –'

'The "market" is a myth. No… it's just a cosy way of saying "the situation we're in". It's a way of talking about the flow of capital, the trading of shares and commodities, the IFEC computers and traders pressing a button or running a program that sells a trillion euros worth of shares because the President Minister of the UK is looking a bit peaky.'

Anji shuffled a little on her feet. There was a bit more to it than that. Admittedly not much more than that, though.

'It's not a perfect system. You have an alternative, I suppose?'

Baskerville nodded.

'Actually, yes I do.'

The Turkish government was a little surprised to receive word that the President of the United States wanted to meet the Turkish President to discuss the North African situation, and wanted to meet him at barely a day's notice.

They apologised profusely – the Turkish President would need to fly back from the Far East, where he was heading a trade delegation, and the earliest they could arrange a secure venue would be that evening.

And the White House told them not to worry about it, and asked them to clear a floor of the Green Hotel for them to wait at.

Just as they'd planned.

Air Force One landed just before midday. The limousine and motorcycle outriders were waiting. President Mather made a short speech, expressed his desire to see the 'international situation' resolved, pledged support to the victims of the Athens disaster, and then stepped from the podium to the limousine.

There was a small anti-American demonstration, but nothing that would make the news back home that evening. Just the usual sort of people blaming him personally for all the troubles of the world.

It was about fifteen miles from the airport to the hotel, but the roads were cleared for the Presidential party.

At the hotel, the President was ushered upstairs, then into the suite that had been cleared for him. An aide told him that an American teletroop had hacked the system, managed to disable the safety overrides and had attacked a school bus in Tripoli. It required an urgent response, so before that he needed briefing.

A matter of greater urgency was that he needed to use the men's room.

Mather was surprised just how opulent the bathroom was – there was an ornate carving on the ceiling, the floor was marble, inlaid with gold.

And Jonah Cosgrove was standing there.

'Felix,' he beamed, his Scots burr unchanged from the last time they'd met. 'How very good to see you.'

The President knew better than to call for his security. 'I know back in your day America and Britain had a special relationship, but I can unzip my own fly.'

Cosgrove grinned. 'Just get some intern to do it. You've got traditions to uphold, old chap.'

Mather sighed. 'How can I help an old friend?'

'Baskerville,' Cosgrove said simply.

'Uh-huh?'

'He's playing us off each other.'

'Is that right?'

'He'll raise his price.'

'As I understand it, it's a price worth paying.'

'As I understand it, the whole of eternity is big enough to share between us.'

'You think the Eurozone and the United States should both get time travel?'

'That wasn't the "us" I had in mind. Look, Mr President, we both know that whoever *doesn't* get time travel will just steal it from the other side. They'd get the blueprints the same day. You've got access to ULTRA, we've got access to every computer at the Octagon. So let's just split the costs down the middle, eh?'

Mather considered the offer for a moment. Cosgrove glanced up at the ceiling, tapped his foot against the marble floor.

'We don't tell Baskerville,' Mather said finally.

'Why not?'

'Because there are things he doesn't need to know. We go in separately, we play along with whatever he's got in mind. Make him waste a lot of effort trying to play us off against each other.'

Cosgrove nodded. 'Yes.'

'Now, can I please go to the bathroom?'

'I was just leaving. Be seeing you.'

'Wait. Do you know what the Fourth Prophecy is?'

Cosgrove hesitated.

Mather smiled. 'Let me rephrase that. You know what the Fourth Prophecy is. Please tell me.'

Cosgrove thought about it for a moment. 'OK, you have done me a good turn today so I shall do you one back. Do not go into Toronto town centre today.'

'You have to give me more than that.'

'An atomic device is going to detonate in –' he checked his watch – 'four hours. Not a bomb. Apparently it's a civil nuclear device, one that was going to be used for some engineering project.'

'If a nuclear bomb went off… in this political climate, we'd assume it was the Eurozone, and launch a counterattack.'

'In the circumstances, best if you don't,' Cosgrove said. 'You tell your people to expect it.'

Mather looked aghast. 'Tell people I knew it was going to

happen, but did nothing about it?'

'I knew about Athens,' Cosgrove said. 'The future has happened. There's nothing we can do to change that – not yet. We have to stick to our guns. I'll see you at the airport.'

Chapter Fourteen
When Rhinos Attack

Malady and the Doctor were watching the arrival of the presidential entourage at the Green Hotel from a bar at Athens airport. Malady was drinking a Scotch, the Doctor was nursing a small orange juice.

The airport was too far from the tidal wave to be affected, but had become a focal point for the relief efforts. The concourses had become a makeshift dormitory for some of the tens of thousands who were now homeless. Relief flights were pouring into the city – and people were also leaving in droves.

Surprisingly, then, the bar they'd found was almost empty. The sounds of the people chatting, babies crying and children playing filtered up here, but the people themselves stayed down in the concourses. The back wall of the bar was taken up with a big digital datascreen. The disaster in Athens was already struggling to keep its position at the top of the news. There had been a shooting in Tripoli, one vociferously condemned in the Eurozone Parliament, but which the Americans were keeping almost supernaturally quiet about.

The commentators saw it as just another step towards war between Europe and America. That was inevitable now, they were saying.

A report from London – there were anti-European demonstrations there. A near-riot in Trafalgar Square, people throwing Euro notes on to a bonfire. The voiceover claimed that a new opinion poll had suggested that if Europe and America went to war, then 84 percent of the British public would side with the Americans, and against the semi-elected government.

Cut to the House of Commons, where the President Minister –

looking even older and more weary than he had of late – was almost drowned out as he recited Britain's obligations under the Articles of European Zoning.

Then cut to scenes in Tripoli – another riot, this time burning President Mather in effigy and stamping on the Stars and Stripes.

Malady's eyephones rang.

'Toronto,' the President told her. 'A civil nuclear device goes off in four hours. That's the Fourth Prophecy.'

'We're at Athens airport, and there's still time to get –'

'It's a eight hour flight, Malady, you won't have enough time. I'm going to alert the Canadian authorities that we've had a tip-off. They've got enough time to evacuate at least most of the city.'

The Doctor was reaching into his pocket. He took out Roja's time machine, and placed it on the table.

'Tell the President there's no need.' His eyes were full of fire. A chance to save people, Malady realised. A chance to atone for the deaths and suffering here.

'We're on our way,' she said, hanging up.

Her eyephones started ringing again. She switched them off.

The Doctor activated the time machine.

The Onihrs' screens flared, the room filled with scent.

'We have detected an anomalous electronic device.'

Fitz had been dozing off. The Onihrs had taken up his challenge, and, as far as he could tell, the full resources of the Onihr ship were now dedicated to detecting time travel. From what he could gather, though, they had about as much of a clue how to go about it as Fitz would have. They could detect time machines, apparently, but not time travellers themselves.

But they were doing their best. Fitz shook himself awake, and looked at the screen.

There was a map, overlaid with a regular pulsing.

'Our analysis suggests it shows a time displacement of several decades.'

'Location?' the leader asked, lumbering over to one of the consoles.

It was zooming in. First the screen showed the Earth, then the Northern hemisphere, then Europe, then the eastern Mediterranean, then Istanbul, then a small silver helicopter powering over the Bosphorus.

'The device is in that human aircraft. It is heading for a landing area.'

'Leader!' one of the others shouted out, unable to contain his excitement. 'There is a lifeform in that ship showing signs of time displacement.'

They'd run some instruments over Fitz a few hours before, and from that, somehow, they could tell he was a time traveller. The jargon was as impenetrable as ever, but apparently 'crossing the time field' left a 'unique energy signature'. And Fitz had that unique signature.

So did the person in the helicopter. Which meant, if he was feeling pedantic, that it wasn't 'unique' at all.

It also meant it was probably the Doctor or Anji. His instinct said it was Anji – he suspected the Doctor's signature really would be unique.

'We shall launch an attack. Ready the landing party.'

The leader turned its vast head to Fitz. 'Onihr technology has triumphed, Doctor.'

'Congratulations,' Fitz said warmly, wondering what he should do next.

Dee called the President's hotel suite on Baskerville's behalf. They were two floors below the presidential suite – she gave them the room number – and invited the President and no more than one bodyguard down.

When Dee opened the door, she was surprised to see Cosgrove standing there, in front of an oriental woman in jeans, a T-shirt and designer glasses.

'Hello Mr Cosgrove,' she said, without missing a beat. 'Miss, are you by any chance Malady Chang?'

'Penelope Lik,' she said. 'And it's not "Miss", it's "Professor". "Emeritus Professor", if we're standing on ceremony.'

Dee gave a stiff bow. 'Why don't you both come inside?'

Baskerville was waiting inside, with Anji. Dee watched the Asian woman carefully. Baskerville trusted her, but Dee didn't. In the last twenty-four hours, the young woman had claimed to be working for three completely different sides, and had used two names. She couldn't be trusted. It takes one to know one, Dee thought wryly.

Cosgrove looked relaxed. Dee glanced at her watch – which contained a portable weapons detector – he was carrying a pistol, in a shoulder holster. He had a throwing knife, tucked behind him, and four small explosive charges concealed in his belt. The woman was unarmed.

'So glad you could make it,' Baskerville said. He seemed calm enough.

Cosgrove's head leant slightly towards Anji, and he raised an eyebrow.

'Anji Kapoor,' she said, standing up and offering her hand.

Cosgrove took it and gave it a chivalrous kiss.

'You surround yourself with beautiful women, Baskerville. I approve.'

Dee smirked – neither Professor Lik or Ms Kapoor appreciated the flattery.

'If we could get to business?' Lik asked.

Baskerville held up a hand. 'Not everyone is here.'

There was a knock on the door.

Baskerville looked up at Dee. He didn't want to be left alone with Cosgrove and his armoury.

Anji seemed to pick up on this. 'I'll go,' she suggested.

As she did, Baskerville turned to Cosgrove. 'You spoke about solving our little Doctor problem. I take it the problem's solved?'

Cosgrove's smug expression flickered a little. 'The Doctor is working with a CIA agent, Malady Chang. I almost had them in Athens yesterday, but they escaped.'

'And you don't know where they are now?'

Cosgrove shook his head.

Baskerville moved aside to let the President, his bodyguard and Anji into the room. 'Well: let's ask. Welcome Mr President. Mr Cosgrove here was just asking after Malady Chang. One of your agents, I believe.'

The President wasn't pleased to see Cosgrove there. Well, he wouldn't be.

'Lieutenant Commander Chang was in Athens yesterday, helping with relief efforts. She's since left the city. I ordered her to take some rest and recuperation.'

'And the Doctor?' Cosgrove asked.

Mather blinked. 'I believe the Doctor was with her.'

Cosgrove smiled, but there was no joy in the expression. 'Lucky Doctor.'

Dee happened to look over Anji, and as she did, she saw the woman was looking relieved.

But she was the one who denounced the Doctor, she'd got him killed, when Leo had thrown him out of the window.

Except the Doctor hadn't died.

Dee looked away from Anji, not wanting to give away anything herself. If Anji was working with the Doctor, then she was working against Baskerville.

'So,' the President was saying, 'where do we go from here?'

Baskerville sat on the edge of the desk. 'To the airport. We'll negotiate in secret.'

'At the airport?' The President was looking over at his bodyguard.

'We can't allow the President to go there without a full complement of –'

Baskerville held up his hand. 'He can take you. Or he can stay here, and I'll just negotiate with the Eurozone. It's entirely up to him.'

'The President's security would be at risk,' the bodyguard objected.

'That's why you have a Vice President,' Cosgrove murmured. 'I'm sure Ben Russ is champing at the bit.'

Mather gave him a withering look.

Baskerville checked his watch. 'If we could reach a decision.'

'I'm going,' the President said.

'Sir, I –'

'I'm going,' he repeated, and that was that.

Baskerville stood, straightened his tie. 'Good. My helicopter is waiting. If we could –'

But he didn't finish the sentence, because the aliens arrived.

Anji had been watching the proceedings carefully.

The President was a distinguished-looking African-American in a telegenic blue suit. He was in his sixties, she guessed, but healthy. His bodyguard was straight from the CIA brochure – blond, and no doubt blue-eyed behind the sunglasses.

Cosgrove was ancient, decades older than Mather or Baskerville, but in absurdly good physical condition. His assistant, despite all that protesting about her credentials, clearly had a crush on him, at the very least.

Baskerville was in one of his sharp suits, Dee was in smart businesswear.

Anji didn't feel as out of place or out of her depth as she had assumed she was going to. She was a bit vague on who Cosgrove was, but he was the head of MI5, or the SAS, or something. He was a soldier, not a politician. But he was senior, and clearly powerful.

And the Doctor was alive, and had teamed up with the Chinese girl Fitz had met. No one had mentioned Fitz. He was probably sunning himself on a Californian beach.

Now what? Events were clearly moving on, and Anji was clearly in the thick of it. She'd have to play it by ear.

But she didn't get a chance, because the aliens arrived.

It wasn't the same as when the two time travellers had appeared out of thin air in the museum, but it was close enough for Cosgrove to recognise it, and give himself a couple of seconds to prepare for it.

The air by the back wall rippled, and three shapes stepped from it.

They were enormous, as wide as they were tall, and only roughly the shape of men.

They were hunchbacked, with small legs, long arms. Their heads were elongated, and ended with a vicious-looking horn. They looked like rhinoceroses. Half-men, half-rhinos. They wore spiky armour that looked like wrought iron. Each carried a metal object that could only be a gun of some kind.

Cosgrove moved out of the way.

Dimly, he registered that Anji had done the same. Interesting. He'd had her down as a civilian, but not even the White House bodyguard had her reactions.

The bodyguard had drawn his pistol.

Cosgrove did the same, but kept it down, out of sight.

The bodyguard fired, at virtually point blank range, but it didn't do any good.

The creature nearest to the bodyguard raised his weapon, fired, and a white line of light bisected the bodyguard.

Penny Lik screamed, and was the next to die. Cosgrove was surprised how angry he felt.

One of the creatures was grabbing for the Asian girl, Kapoor, but she was managing to duck and weave out of its way. They were almost too large for the room, they were having to bend down to avoid scraping against the ceiling, and Kapoor was taking advantage of that.

One snatched her handbag, parted the leather with its claw, as if it was Clingfilm.

It rummaged through the contents, found what looked like an old-fashioned mobile phone, and growled something.

Cosgrove had hunted rhinos.

It wasn't something he could admit anywhere these days, of course, even at his club. It had been sixty years ago, in Africa, and he'd bagged one, gaining a lot of admiration from the hunter who'd been leading the party.

Rhinos were extinct in the wild and in zoos, now, he'd seen that reported on the news a few years ago. They only existed in clonetivity.

He stood, raised his gun, and one of the creatures was at him within seconds. Cosgrove shot its gun, blew a hole in it that exposed a glowing mechanism. The creature tried firing it, but he'd disabled it. That only served to anger its owner, who swung its arm at him. It was too powerful to block. Cosgrove ducked, came up, tried to punch it in the side.

The creature didn't even register the blow. Instead it reached down, picked Cosgrove up. It was like being lifted by a crane. Cosgrove brought his hands together, slammed them down hard on the creature's arm. It was like hitting a statue.

Cosgrove wriggled, tried to grab at the thing's eye with one hand. Everything had a vulnerable spot, and it wouldn't like the ball of his thumb, or his thumbnail, in its eye.

He poked it, but just seem to enrage the beast more.

It threw Cosgrove down to the floor, leaned in.

It snarled something in its alien language.

It opened its mouth, roared in Cosgrove's face, half-deafening him.

Cosgrove shoved his gun in the open maw, angled it up slightly so it was aiming up at the brain pan, and fired.

The skull was thick, so he didn't blow its brain out. Its eyes glazed over, though.

It had also lost control of its legs. Cosgrove barely rolled out of the way in time as it crashed down.

The reaction from the other two creatures was instantaneous and startling: they panicked.

One of them, the one holding the mobile phone, shrieked an order.

A second later, the air had rippled, and the two surviving creatures had gone.

Cosgrove sagged, exhausted.

Dee was trying to catch her breath.

She'd not felt like this since she was a girl. She'd had asthma, the sort you grow out of, she'd only had a couple of attacks, nothing too serious, although it had felt like it at the time.

It felt serious now.

Her lungs ached, her mind just wasn't doing anything at all.

'What the hell were they?' a woman's voice was saying. It was probably her own.

Anji and Cosgrove were on their feet again. The President hadn't had time to move.

Professor Lik and the bodyguard were smeared over the ground.

Dee felt sick.

Baskerville stood, tried to compose himself. He and Anji were the first to get to the alien corpse.

'What is it?' Baskerville asked.

'An alien,' Anji said quietly.

The body looked untouched, pristine. Dee tried to piece it all together.

'Cosgrove shot it,' she said feebly.

Cosgrove was getting back on his feet, but he needed to prop himself against the wall to do it.

Baskerville was agitated. 'We get out of here, now.'

Mather was looking down at the remains of his bodyguard. 'I need my security team –'

'They wouldn't last long,' Dee said, and it came out sounding far more callous than she'd hoped. She was more worried about

Baskerville, who looked scared for almost the first time Dee could remember.

'I can get us to safety,' Baskerville insisted.

'I'll look after you,' Cosgrove pledged.

Mather laughed.

'I know how to kill them, now,' Cosgrove insisted.

'We get moving,' Dee ordered.

'And we bring the body,' Cosgrove said, looking down at the alien.

Baskerville nodded, then turned to Anji. 'Miss Kapoor, do you have any idea why they were so interested in your telephone?'

The Onihr ship was in uproar.

Fitz had watched the three-Onihr landing party depart. All they needed was one of those little control boxes. So that meant all *he* needed to get out of here was one of those little boxes.

Well, he also needed to know where they stored them. And how to work it. But it was something to aim for.

The Onihr leader gloated to 'the Doctor' about how they were going to teleport down and take the time traveller and their time machine (which they assumed was the device they'd detected).

They'd also said their attack would be fast – a snatch and grab raid, one where any resistance would be met with maximum retaliation.

But even the Onihrs who stayed behind on the ship seemed surprised how quickly the landing party returned.

When only two of the Onihrs returned, surprise turned to shock.

Shortly afterwards, when it became clear that the leader hadn't returned, that the humans had managed to kill him, that turned into an uncomprehending silence.

The deputy leader shuffled forwards to hear the report.

One of the human weapons had killed the leader with one shot. They had massively underestimated human ingenuity, for the second time. They had recovered the time machine, though.

It looked remarkably like Anji's mobile phone.

'This device is the human time machine,' the deputy leader told him. 'You will make it operate.'

Fitz took it from the Onihr, turned it on and selected something from the menu.

It started to bleep out the *X-Files* theme tune.

'This is a telephone,' he told him. 'A communications device. It's nothing like a time machine.'

'Our instruments prove that it has travelled through time.'

Fitz brandished it. 'It has, I'm sure. But that doesn't make it a time machine. Did you kill the owner of this?' he asked, beginning to feel a little numb himself.

'A man and a woman died,' one of the landing party confirmed.

'The woman holding this device?' Fitz asked, not wanting to hear the answer.

'No.'

Fitz took a deep breath, felt a bit more calm. What he was going to do next was horrible, insensitive and exploitative, but it was the break he'd needed and he wasn't going to let it slip away.

He whirled to face the Deputy Leader.

'I warned you,' he snarled. 'I warned you the humans were not to be underestimated. Your leader's arrogance killed him, not the humans.'

The Deputy Leader looked taken aback – at least that's what Fitz assumed. He'd no idea what an offended rhinoceros looked like.

'You sully the honour of our leader.'

'No. I'm merely telling you the truth. You're playing with fire. If you can't deal with the humans, then how do you ever hope to deal with the implications of time travel?' He fished for a suitably portentous phrase. 'You're meddling in the fundamental elemental forces of the universe. They'll destroy you. My concern is that you will accidentally destroy this whole tangent of the galaxy!'

He wasn't sure he meant 'tangent', but it had the desired effect.

The Deputy Leader looked cowed.

'Hand me that!' Fitz demanded, and was passed Anji's phone. He slipped it into his jeans pocket.

'And hand me one of those control boxes.'

The Deputy Leader, used to taking orders, not yet giving them, handed it over.

Fitz, not quite believing his luck, tucked that into a jacket pocket.

'Now, you must prepare to leave this solar system. You have done enough harm here.'

The other Onihrs murmured what sounded like consent, all eyes (or noses, Fitz supposed) on their new leader.

The Deputy stood his ground for the moment, then straightened up.

'No!' it roared. 'No! We will destroy the humans. We will purge them from the universe for this action! Prepare the invasion!'

Fitz sighed. It had all been going so well.

Chapter Fifteen
Time-Flight

Anji sat in the helicopter as it swept over Istanbul, but she hardly registered the historic city beneath her.

The helicopter was full up – Dee was flying, Cosgrove in the co-pilot's seat. Baskerville was sitting next to the President... and she, being the smallest, was squeezed in the back with the dead alien.

It stared at her, through one glassy, dead eye. Its skin was smooth – up close, it looked more like a seal's or a dolphin's than the hide of a rhinoceros. But the head was almost an exact replica of the Earth animal. The boxlike snout, the fearsome horn, those funny little round ears right at the back of their heads.

The armour was a substance that looked and felt like some hitherto unsuspected alloy of wrought iron and rubber.

There was a nobility in the creature's face. It was an undignified way to treat the corpse, she thought.

They were heading for the airport. That's all Baskerville would tell them.

The President twisted round to talk to Anji – it was pretty difficult to hear him over the noise of the rotors.

'I assume you're the woman who I talked to yesterday?'

Anji nodded. 'Sorry about this –'

He was shaking his head. 'Wouldn't have missed this for the world.' He leant in a little closer. Anji could barely hear the next thing he said, so there was no chance Baskerville could.

'You're with the Doctor, right?'

She nodded. 'You know him?'

'I knew him, yeah. More than twenty years ago. He must be

getting on a bit now?'

Anji smiled. 'He doesn't act his age.'

'Did he see his daughter again, do you know?'

Anji blinked. 'He's never mentioned a daughter.'

'I bet he never mentioned hijacking the space shuttle, either?'

Anji laughed. 'He's mentioned it once or twice. I think he's proud of that.' She paused. 'You'd think he'd be proud of his daughter, too.'

'He is, miss, don't worry about that.'

The helicopter was coming in to land by a small hangar, covered in logos and signs in Russian. Or Cyrillic script, at any rate.

Baskerville had radioed ahead. There were three men on the tarmac, with a large medical-style gurney. Anji got down from the helicopter, and the three of them set to work covering the alien in a tarpaulin and lifting it out.

Baskerville and Dee ushered Cosgrove, Mather and Anji herself towards the hangar. The main doors were inching open.

'Where are we going?' the President asked.

'Somewhere we won't be disturbed,' Baskerville said. He was carrying the silver case containing the coffee machine. Dee had a bag that looked like it had that laptop of hers in it.

'Baskerville, I'm the President of the United States, you can't just –'

'Mr President, if all goes to plan, then by this evening you'll be the President of Time. It's worth the risk.'

Cosgrove watched the exchange, looking amused. 'Don't worry, Felix, I've told you: I'll look after you.'

Anji looked ahead. The hangar doors were open enough to see inside now.

A black Concorde sat there, a set of steps set up alongside it.

'What the hell?' Cosgrove asked.

'Isn't she a beauty?' Baskerville said.

'I flew on Concorde plenty of times, but –'

'But you thought the last one went out of service when BA went

164

bust? Well, it did. But I bought one, and made certain modifications.'

Cosgrove watched him carefully. 'How long is it since you arrived from the future?'

'My time machine landed several years ago. Making money is not that difficult with the knowledge and science of the future at your disposal.'

Anji couldn't help but admire Baskerville's ability as a liar. Or his taste in aircraft. She'd never ridden on Concorde before. She'd seen it sitting on the runway at Heathrow a couple of times. The matt-black colour scheme he'd picked made it look even more like some designer item – like the Porsches and hi-fis Anji had grown up wanting in the eighties.

They headed up, inside the plane.

It wasn't the tallest building in the world any more.

If you cast your net a little wider, it was practically a stump – the Lunar Tower, built in lower gravity, was four times taller. But the tourists still flocked to the CN tower.

The Doctor and Malady joined them. It was as good a place as any to start searching Toronto for a nuclear bomb.

The CN Tower might have been designed as aversion therapy for those suffering from vertigo. You got to the lookout level via glass-sided elevators... and the floor of the observation deck was also made of glass.

Malady didn't have a hint of vertigo. She'd climbed mountains, abseiled, flown in hang-gliders. But the glass floor was enough to make anyone a bit nervous.

Except the Doctor, who apparently hadn't noticed the floor was transparent. They'd gone outside on to the observation gallery.

'Ah... Toronto in the summer,' the Doctor sighed.

It was a beautiful city. From up here it looked like a giant Lego set. They were looking out over the new lakeside development. The lake itself was dark, flat.

'Where would you hide the atom bomb?' the Doctor asked.

'It's a civil nuclear device,' Malady explained. 'A clean nuke.'

The Doctor snorted.

'Relatively clean,' Malady conceded. 'Safer than traffic fumes or industrial waste.'

The Doctor was shaking his head, clearly not impressed by that line of logic. 'So… what are they used for?'

'Well, their use is still relatively rare. Big engineering projects, mainly. If there's a mountain in the way of a new road, that sort of thing.'

The Doctor looked around.

'No mountains,' he noted quietly. 'Perhaps they've all been levelled. Haven't the CIA told the Canadian authorities about the Prophecy?'

'They have, and they've had a security clampdown and run a whole set of safety checks on the device, to make sure it's functioning normally.'

'But they won't tell us where it is.'

'Nope. Because there's a security clampdown, they aren't telling anyone.'

The Doctor sighed. 'I suppose there's a logic to that.'

'They've told us, not in so many words, that there's only one nuke in the city. We also know they're using this one to clear the harbour.'

'That they know of,' the Doctor said. 'Still… the odds are it's the one mentioned in the Prophecy. The only one we're likely to find, anyway.'

'The Prophecy specifically said it was a civilian device.'

The Doctor nodded. 'Not a terrorist attack or a military blunder. Well, that settles it, it's got to be the one. So, how do we find it?'

Malady handed over her binoculars. 'Large warehouse, about four miles to the north.'

The Doctor peered out over the city. 'What am I looking for… ah yes.'

'We know the name of the building contractors working on the harbour project. That's a local warehouse of theirs. The only one being guarded by RealWar robots.'

They were keeping out of sight of the road, but from up here, it was easy to spot them marching around the builders' yard.

'We've got enough charge for one more time jump,' the Doctor said. 'From here, it's easy to pick precise co-ordinates.' He was already starting to fiddle with the controls on the time machine.

Malady took the binoculars back. 'We don't know what the security there is like.'

'No,' the Doctor replied patiently, 'but we do know what the consequences will be if we don't stop that nuclear device from going off.'

Malady thought about that. 'Perhaps, by warning the authorities, we've done all we needed to do?'

'I wish it was that easy. Put it this way: if the bomb… if the *nuclear device*… goes off, will you be happy you did all you could?'

Malady shook her head. 'Baskerville's seen the future, can we change that?'

'We have to try. I'll put us just inside that warehouse.'

Baskerville passed down the cabin, a bottle of champagne in hand.

Dee Gordon, Baskerville's assistant, dozed on one of the leather seats. Anji Kapoor… the enigma… was sat opposite him, sipping at her champagne.

Of those awake, only Mather abstained. It wasn't Cosgrove's idea of a stiff drink, but it was a drink and that was near enough.

'Louis Roederer Cristal,' Cosgrove told her, after his first sip. 'Not the best year, but most years are like each other, nowadays.'

'Is that because you're getting on?' Mather joked.

Cosgrove failed to see the funny side, and if Anji was amused it was only faintly. 'It's because vineyards are micro-irrigated, climate controlled and the picking is done by robots.'

Mather laughed.

The Concorde was levelling out. From the position of the sun, it looked like they were heading north-east. Over the Black Sea, then. Into Russian territory.

Cosgrove didn't like this at all. He grabbed Baskerville's arm as their host made another pass with the champagne. 'Where are we heading?'

Baskerville looked him in the eye. 'Somewhere safe. Would you rather be in Toronto?'

Anji looked up. 'Toronto's all right,' she said. 'It's a bit like New York built by the Swiss, but –'

'The guide books will need updating shortly,' Baskerville told her coldly.

She was looking at him accusingly. Cosgrove frowned. What was going on there?

Who was this girl?

'Anji, why don't you and Mr Cosgrove here examine the alien?'

Fitz edged out of the control gallery.

The Onihr deputy leader had warmed to his theme of revenge and organising the destruction of the Earth.

Which was a bit annoying, because Fitz now had the teleportation device to get back down there. If it was going to be atomised a few minutes later, it hardly seemed worth it.

The couple of Onihrs he passed barely seemed to notice him as he made his way down the transparent corridor. He wasn't entirely sure where he was heading, and it was hard work in the alien gravity.

He'd have to stop the Onihrs. That was obvious. Rather less obvious was how.

As soon as he found a quiet spot, he took the Onihr control box out. It was simple enough – there were only four controls, as far as he could make out. One of them controlled the holographic disguises they wore on Earth. Another one controlled the teleportation. What the other two did was a complete mystery.

Baskerville entered the code that allowed him access to the cockpit. Leo was there, managing the autopilot software.

'Can they catch us?' Baskerville asked.

'Impossible. Baskerville, they can't even see us.'

'Stealth technology… it's not all it's cracked up to be, you know. I've sold enough of it in my time. Any country with a mobile phone network can detect a stealth plane.'

'We're well into unmonitored territory here. Neither the Americans or the Eurozone have hypersonic jets in intercept range, and they won't launch them in the current climate, because the other side will think they've just launched a world war.'

Baskerville took his place in the co-pilot's chair. This was exactly as they'd planned. He checked the news feeds on the datanet. Tension over the Tripoli shootings. There was pressure on the Americans for the President to make a statement. But he was 'holed up in his hotel room in Istanbul'. They weren't telling anyone he'd been kidnapped. Maybe they didn't even know – the Americans might think he was still at his mysterious meeting. Still, the news agenda was about to change.

'Time to deal with Toronto,' Baskerville decided. He reconfigured the co-pilot's controls for RealWar interface.

He entered the 'back door' codes that, unbeknownst to even a single one of his customers, enabled him to take any RealWar robot in the world and see through its eyes, control its every action.

He entered the unique registration code for one of the robots in Toronto.

And, on the screen in front of him, he saw the nuclear device.

The Doctor and Malady swirled into existence in a small office in a mezzanine level in the warehouse.

It was some sort of foreman's place – full of paperwork, requisition orders, maps and invoices. The light was off, so was the computer. The room smelt of pickle, clearly a favourite of the man who worked here.

There was a small safe.

'How big is the bomb?' the Doctor asked.

'The size of a small car,' Malady told him.

'It's not in the safe, then.' He checked under a pile of paperwork, before realising it wasn't likely to be under there, either.

Malady peered out of the office window, out over the warehouse. 'It's down there.'

From here, they got a good vantage point. Behind a screen, there was a large articulated lorry, corrugated silver sides, but with no markings. Three human guards and four humanoid RealWar robots stood guard.

'Ready to move out,' the Doctor said softly.

'There's no way of confirming it's in there,' Malady told him.

'We could go and look,' the Doctor suggested.

'It looks well-guarded.'

'Yes, it does, but –'

One of the RealWar robots raised an arm and fired its machine gun. None of the three human guards had time even to register the attack. They fell where they stood.

The sound of the shots echoed around the warehouse. The other RealWar robots stood motionless, apparently oblivious. The robot that had fired raised its arm and advanced towards the truck.

'That's our cue, I think,' the Doctor said, heading for the door.

Malady drew one of the energy pistols, and followed him out.

The robot was opening the door at the back of the lorry. Its hands were a little too large for the delicate operation.

Malady and the Doctor hurried along the gantry. RealWar robots had their place, but Malady knew they weren't perfect – their cameras and microphones were notoriously poor. Operators had a narrow field of vision and were almost deaf, particularly when the heavy hydraulic limbs were moving. It meant that they could only concentrate on one task at a time.

The robot had manage to grab the door handle.

'It's remote-controlled, isn't it?' the Doctor asked. 'Is there any way of telling who's operating it, where they are?'

Malady shook her head. 'Absolutely impossible. It could be from anywhere in the world.'

'Judging by what they're planning to do, it's someone a long way away.'

They'd made their way down narrow metal steps to the warehouse floor. In that time, the robot had got the door of the lorry open.

They could see into the trailer. The atomic device sat in the middle of the container, looking fairly innocuous.

Malady raised her arm, pointed the energy pistol at the robot, and fired.

The shot hit it square in the back, and the robot went down, its limbs sprawling.

'No!' the Doctor shouted.

Malady shrugged. He must have been worried she'd hit the nuke. 'I didn't miss,' she told him.

The other three RealWar robots stood to attention.

'Ah.'

The robots raised their arms in unison, the sound of the machine guns loading up filled the air.

The Doctor started running for the lorry.

'Keep them busy!' he called back, over his shoulder.

Malady dived for cover, as the robots started firing at her.

Out of the corner of her eye, she could see the Doctor clambering up over the fallen robot to get into the truck.

One of the machines was heading that way, the other two were heading for her.

She ducked behind the metal screen that hid the truck from

view, deciding it was the best cover. It was half-inch steel plate. As the robots started firing, she was relieved that it could stop the bullets.

They were marching towards her position – another drawback of the robots was that they weren't built for covert ops: they hissed and clanked. No more than a tank or armoured car, according to the manufacturers, who had a point.

And the fact robots couldn't do everything kept her in a job, so who was she to complain?

She straightened up, raised her gun, spun round the corner to face the robots.

Then dived back for cover as they opened fire.

The bullets streaked past her, scorching the air.

The Doctor climbed into the trailer of the articulated lorry, and hurried over to the bomb. The gunfire outside echoed and echoed off the corrugated metal walls of the container, and it was almost enough to deafen someone.

The bomb, though, looked refreshingly simple to defuse.

He took the sonic screwdriver from his pocket, and removed a piece of the casing.

The Doctor was always faintly disappointed that real nuclear bombs didn't have digital countdown clocks on them. It would add to the sense of urgency if numbers were ticking down.

This bomb wasn't even armed. That must have been what the robot – or rather its operator – was trying to do. At the moment, this was just a metal box with a quantity of plutonium in it. His job was to make sure it stayed that way.

'Ten... nine...' the Doctor began, trying to inject some tension. 'Eight... seven...' The casing was off, now, revealing the arming mechanism surrounded by the usual scribble of wiring.

'Six... five...' Now, what would be the best way of doing this?

'Four... three...'

He squeezed the sonic screwdriver, releasing the arming

mechanism. He caught it, drew it out, gently.

'Two...' All he had to do was snip the wire, now. No chance of setting it off accidentally – not unless it had been armed first.

He reached into his pocket for his wirecutters.

'One...' He slid the wirecutters around the cable. Oh Doctor, he told himself, you've done it, and with less than a second to –

A robot arm grabbed his leg, pulled him off his feet and dragged him halfway to the back of the truck.

The Doctor grabbed the bomb's casing. It was securely attached to the floor of the trailer, and holding on would keep him inside, close to the bomb.

The robot kept pulling, unconcerned by the prospect of tearing the Doctor in half.

The Doctor glanced back over his shoulder. The robot was hunching in the doorway, almost too big to get in.

It was quite crude as robots went – a simplified skeletal frame, with primitive hydraulics passing for muscles. It had two camera eyes, and a heavily armoured chest section, which was presumably where it kept its radio relay and on-board processors.

The hands were little more than clamps.

Clamps were enough, of course.

It was hurting his leg, now, increasing the pressure.

There was heavy gunfire from outside the truck – all bullets, no energy blasts. So, Malady wasn't getting a chance to shoot... but she was still alive, and avoiding the robots.

The Doctor's robot was planning to arm the device. You could do that with an arming key, but you could also do it with a direct interface. Looking for it, the Doctor could see just the right sort of port on the machine's wrist. Normally used to connect it to diagnostic computers, he supposed.

The Doctor released one hand, reached down with the sonic screwdriver, unscrewed the robot's wrist, and prised the clamp off his leg.

The robot withdrew the stump, looked at it, mirroring the

operator's surprise.

The Doctor returned to the nuclear device, found the wire and the wirecutter.

The robot raised its other arm, the machinegun slid from its housing.

The Doctor scooped up the detached hand, and bowled it at the robot.

Instinctively, the operator tried to catch it, or bat it away, or *something*, but misjudged the ability of the robot to balance. It toppled over, like a toddler who'd just forgotten how to walk.

The Doctor was about to snip the wire, when he had a better idea.

Outside, there was a single laser blast, a small explosion, and the sound of a robot crashing to the ground. Followed immediately by a burst of gunfire from the other one.

The Doctor got to the back of the truck, kept low, out of his robot's field of vision. It was getting back to its feet – a task made more difficult by the loss of its hand.

Malady had got lucky with that first shot – blasted the robot right in the transmitter, cut the signal to whoever was controlling it. The Doctor bent over the dead robot, reached into the cavity formed by the blast.

He unclipped a couple of circuit boards, slipped them inside his jacket.

'Malady!' he shouted. 'Get over here!'

Malady broke cover. She now had an energy pistol in each hand. She ran towards the truck, pointing the guns behind her, firing at the robot. She sprang into the container, just as the nearest robot got itself upright.

Together, they got the doors of the truck closed.

'Now what?' she asked, clearly irritated. 'They'll just open the doors, and –'

'We'll be gone,' the Doctor said, pulling Roja's time machine from his pocket. 'What's more, I can couple it up to these circuits

I got from the robot. We'll be able to teleport straight along the carrier wave to whoever's operating those robots.'

'Er…'

The Doctor was puzzled – why wasn't it activating, like it had before?

'It ran out of juice, remember?' Malady asked.

The robots opened fire. The bullets clattered against the truck, punching little dents.

'So… we're trapped, aren't we?'

A bullet whizzed past the Doctor's ear. The walls of the container weren't going to last much longer.

The Doctor looked around. There was Malady, the nuclear device and him.

'I need a power source. Hand me one of those guns.'

He took it, but quickly ascertained that he had no idea how to get to the power cell.

'You disarmed the bomb?'

'Uh-huh.'

'Well, at least we won't be dying in vain.'

The Doctor leaned in to the nuclear device. 'Of course.' He opened up the time machine, then handed it to Malady. 'Hold that,' he ordered. Then grabbed into the heart of the nuclear device and pulled out a metal hemisphere.

'Doctor, that's the plutonium core.'

'It's half of it. Not enough to trigger an explosion. Plenty for our purposes.'

He took the time machine from Malady, plunged it into the heart of the core. The time machine was a sophisticated piece of nanotech, its ubertronics were quite capable of automatically adjusting to the new source of energy. The display unfurled, as before.

Malady still looked nervous. 'We're going to the lion's den? Right to where the operator of those robots is?'

'No. I didn't have time to track the radio signal.'

'But we only get one trip.'

'Yes, don't worry. I've got the perfect place in mind.'

He pressed the button.

In one of the rear compartments of the Concorde, Anji and Cosgrove were examining the corpse of the alien.

Cosgrove had started by checking the weapon the creature had been carrying. But he'd damaged it beyond repair when he'd shot it. He looked disappointed.

'Help me with this armour,' Anji suggested. She was trying to remove the breastplate, but it wasn't budging.

' "What man dare, I dare / Approach thou like the rugged Russian bear / The armed rhinoceros or th' Hyrcan tiger, take any shape but that, and my firm nerves shall never tremble." '

'*Macbeth*,' Anji said.

Cosgrove looked down at her admiringly. 'Yes. Well done. I always liked the Scottish play. I suppose one good thing about the Learman years was that the schools got their priorities right when it came to English Lit. Your generation was very lucky.'

Anji didn't have the faintest idea what he was talking about. 'After my time,' she told him. 'I did it for GCSE.'

Cosgrove looked puzzled. 'How old are you? I'm sorry – if you don't mind me asking.'

Anji raised an eyebrow. 'There are some things a gentleman never asks.'

'I'm no gentleman.'

'I can tell, or you'd be helping me with this armour.'

Cosgrove stopped looking at her and started helping. 'It's like it's welded on,' he concluded after a few moments' struggle.

'Perhaps it is.'

He was examining the muzzle. 'There's a nose guard. That might come off.'

It came away very easily. Anji examined it. The front was the same spiky metal rubber stuff. The inside, though, was packed with what looked like glowing circuitry.

'What do you make of that?' she asked Cosgrove, passing it over.

'It's electronic.' He poked his fingers in two large sockets, then leaned in to examine the corpse.

'I think these things fitted over its nose.'

He laid it back over the creature's snout. He was right, they were a perfect fit.

'Breathing apparatus?' he suggested.

Anji wasn't convinced. 'Where's the air supply? The tubes?'

'You can get rebreathing devices that are compact.'

'Yes, but there's still a small air cylinder. Look, you can see there just isn't room for one.'

She took it again and turned it over in her hand. The circuits were glowing softly.

'It's active,' she said, then, 'can you smell that?' She held the device to her nose. 'That's really weird. It's like one of those scratch and sniff cards. She could smell flowers, a citrus sort of smell, and also something like woodsmoke.

Cosgrove was looking puzzled. 'I've just got no idea what that is. Look. We should wait for an expert. We could end up damaging it.'

With that, he left, going back to the passenger cabin, and the free champagne Baskerville had laid on.

Anji sat looking at the body of the alien. She wouldn't put it past it to get up and start charging around. Do that inside a plane in mid-flight, and everyone would die.

Cheery thoughts.

The door to the compartment opened, and Baskerville stepped in.

'What have you discovered?' he asked. He was looking nervous. Then again, Anji was sure she did, too.

Anji handed over the nose guard and admitted she didn't know what it was.

'This is an alien,' Anji told him.

Baskerville nodded. 'Yes.'

'You weren't expecting them.'

'Ms Kapoor, I thought I'd taken every possible eventuality into account when drawing up my plans. Well, I was wrong.'

He poked the alien's head. 'Ugly thing, isn't it?'

'No. Baskerville, I don't think you realise how serious this is. They want time travel.'

Baskerville looked at her.

Anji thought about it a bit more. 'That's got to be it, hasn't it? It's the reason you've got Cosgrove and the President here. They're clearly very advanced aliens, but that doesn't mean they have time travel. So they've come here looking for you, as someone who can give it to them.'

'Do you know what fascinates me, Ms Kapoor?' He gave the corpse a good slap. 'This thing came ninety billion light years, or whatever, and it beamed into a hotel room containing – amongst others – the President of the United States, a very senior member of the European Intelligence Services, and myself, someone who, to the best of everyone's knowledge, is a time traveller from the distant future. With all those people to choose from, they came after *you*. Why do you think that is?'

Anji had been wondering that herself, of course. 'I don't know.'

'You don't?'

'Possibly because I've been in your time machine? I stood out as someone who'd travelled in time.'

'No,' Baskerville said, too quickly.

'Why not?'

Baskerville hesitated. 'Well, for a start, I went to Brussels with you, remember? And Cosgrove had his trip the day before.'

'Then I don't know.' It had to be the Doctor, she thought. They knew she was associated with the Doctor. Or perhaps she stood out because she'd done so much time travelling, or because she was out of her native time, or because she'd crossed her own timeline in Brussels.

Baskerville was examining the corpse. 'There's something in its ear.'

He tugged it out. It looked a lot like an earpiece.

'Some sort of communications device?' Anji asked. She held it up to her ear. 'Yes – listen, it's a test signal, it just keeps repeating operating instructions.'

Baskerville took it from her and listened. 'In what language?'

'English,' Anji said, puzzled by the question.

'It's just growling and gargling. You speak alien. There's more to you than meets the eye, isn't there, Ms Kapoor?'

She hadn't killed him back on the yacht, because she hadn't had all the answers. For the first time, it dawned on Anji that she was still alive for exactly the same reason.

Baskerville was looking a little starry-eyed. 'I wonder if Dee could get it to transmit.'

'And if she did?'

'Well… a number of new business opportunities would be open to me, wouldn't they?'

'You'd deal with aliens?'

'Wouldn't you? I'm not going to let some politically incorrect nonsense about putting the human race first get in the way of a good deal.'

'They were trying to kill you.'

Baskerville smiled. 'My dear, they were trying to kill *you*. Hardly the same thing, is it? Don't worry – I need you alive for the moment. After all, you're the only one who understands the language. My organisation is always on the lookout for people with special talents. You can be my chief negotiator.'

Chapter Sixteen
Dealbreaker

The Onihr deputy leader drew in a deep breath, and examined the control gallery.

A room full of highly trained, professional warrior-scientists, preparing for their task. There was no greater testament to their fallen leader than the dedication of those men he had left behind.

The deputy leader wasn't sure he could match up.

Onihrs are immortal, barring attacks such as the one that befell the leader. Immensely long-lived, at any rate. The leader had commanded this ship for thirty thousand years. The deputy leader had served under him for twenty-five thousand of those years. He had not expected to ever become leader himself. He had trained for it, he had the knowledge, but he wasn't *prepared*.

The humans were vicious things, more vicious even than the databanks had suggested. The tactical analysis hadn't foreseen the death of the leader, so they could be wrong about victory in an invasion.

Somewhere in the deep recesses of the deputy leader's mind, there was doubt. Some instinct that made him question what purpose the invasion would serve.

An act of revenge? Against a primitive species that barely comprehended its actions, that had the merest flicker of space travel. They were no threat to the Onihrs, and if they ever were to be, it wouldn't be for millennia.

'Deputy leader!' one of the communications technicians barked.

'Yes?'

'The leader's communicator is active!'

The monitor screen parped and the scent of a human wafted over.

Gibbering human language started up, a deeply unpleasant sound.

A moment later, another human voice, but one speaking in the Onihr tongue.

'I am Baskerville. I speak through an interpreter.'

The deputy leader swung his snout to the screen. 'I am the deputy leader of the Onihr race.'

Gibber, shriek, chatter.

'I wish to speak to the leader.'

'The leader is dead, killed by one of you monkey-creatures.'

Pause.

Mumble, quack, eep.

'I speak to you through his radio. I did not know it was your leader. I was present at his death. I did not kill him myself, the man that did was acting in self-defence, following the death of two humans.'

'The death of eight billion humans would not justify the death of our glorious leader.'

Pause.

Squeak, squawk, gibber.

'You targeted us deliberately. We have something you want. Please tell us what. We may be able to arrange a trade. There is no need for bloodshed.'

'You sound like the Doctor,' the deputy leader spat.

'The Doctor?' This was the interpreter speaking, not waiting for its master. 'He's up there?'

'Yes.' The deputy leader sniffed the air. 'Somewhere.'

He swung his head around. 'Where is he?'

Tucked away in his little room, Fitz had got the control box to work.

He wasn't sure how – he'd just kept pressing buttons, hoping none of them was the self-destruct switch. Not a perfect method, but the best he could come up with.

Now it was talking to him, showing him pictures, instead of spraying perfume at him. The voice was pleasant, male, vaguely Celtic.

He'd called it Pad.

'Pad, when the leader went through his invasion plans, he said he could disable all the electrical equipment with an Ee and Pee something or other.'

'The EMP cannon.'

'In English?'

'The EMP cannon,' it repeated.

'Er… in shorter English words that, say, a small child would understand.'

'A…' it hesitated, whirred, '…gun that… uses electricity to create a… big magnet… that breaks electrical equipment.'

'A powerful weapon.'

'Yes.'

'A big weapon?'

'Yes.' There was an edge of impatience in Pad's voice.

'Where is it?'

'The EMP cannon runs the full length of the ship, from the engines at the rear to the parabolic projector at the front.'

'What defence is there against it?'

'None. It is crude, but totally effective. It is possible to shield against small electromagnetic pulses, but this weapon can burn through all known shielding.'

'If the Ee and Pee cannon was disabled, then would the Onihrs be able to invade Earth?'

'They would encounter heavy resistance, and face twenty percent casualties. The probability of total victory is over ninety-nine percent, with a ninety-five percent chance of that victory within one day, a ninety-two percent chance of that victory within six hours. There is a fifteen percent chance of humans destroying their own civilisation with nuclear weapons rather than surrendering, or as an accidental or collateral consequence of the Onihr attack.'

'Would they go ahead with the invasion in those circumstances?'

Pad whirred. 'The EMP cannon is active, so no statistical data or precedent exists.'

Fitz mused on that for a while. Was a nuclear holocaust after a day of hopeless resistance any better than five minutes of no resistance at all? He was tempted to ask Pad.

It bought more time, that was certain.

Anji was definitely alive, the Doctor almost certainly was. Anji knew about the Onihrs, now, so perhaps the Doctor did. The two of them might only need a day to sort things out.

'How would I sabotage the Ee and Pee cannon?' he asked.

And Pad told him.

Baskerville was in the rear compartment with Anji, and he'd just called Dee in with them. Leo was safe in the cockpit.

So Cosgrove and Mather were alone for the first time.

'Where's he taking us?' Cosgrove asked.

'No idea.'

'You don't have a GPS tracker?'

'If it was working, I'd know where we were, wouldn't I?'

They were both peering out of the window. They'd crossed the Black Sea. The terrain below looked like it could be the Ukraine. Equally, it could be Russia, or Georgia. Maybe even Eastern Turkey or Kurdistan. Five countries that just about covered the spectrum of political affiliations, none of which were entirely safe, three of which were in the middle of civil wars.

'We've a chance to agree strategy, while Baskerville's busy with that alien.'

President Mather's instinct was to keep his mouth shut, but then he remembered who he was talking to. Cosgrove had been entrusted with secrets that were kept from Prime Ministers and Presidents. Mather knew more than most – he'd been CIA, he'd been an astronaut working on all three SDI projects, he'd been Secretary of State during the Canisian invasion. But he suspected Cosgrove knew more than he did.

'Those aliens,' Mather said. 'Do you recognise them?'

'No,' Cosgrove said. 'You?'

'No.'

'It adds another dimension to all this.'

'Makes a squabble between the United States and the Eurozone look insignificant? I suppose they'd be above all this.'

Cosgrove laughed. 'I was wondering if they'd take sides, actually. The Eurozone might be able to offer them something they want.'

'You, a loyal servant of Europe? We both know you'd fill in the Channel Tunnels given a chance.'

Cosgrove looked offended. 'I'm no Little Englander. There's not a drop of English blood in my veins. But, then, there's no such thing as Eurozone blood, is there? You've dealt with them, Felix. They're bloodless, faceless. There's no history, no values, just political expediency. All they want is someone else to pay their farmers and fight their wars for them. When I speak up, they offer to increase my salary. They've turned me into a *mercenary*. The only reason they have power is that there's not been a major war on their watch. And that record is going to come to an end, in a matter of weeks.'

'It might not.'

'You don't sound convinced.'

Mather took a deep breath. 'Well, perhaps that's because I know you're right.'

'It's madness, it's suicide, and it's inevitable.'

'Nothing is inevitable. Jonah... we've known each other for a long time.'

'Yes.'

'I trust you. More than pretty well any of my advisors.'

'Good.'

'We work together? We can stop the war?'

184

Cosgrove nodded. 'Mr President, if we have a time machine, we can do anything we want. We can *un*do anything we want.'

'Undo?'

'It must have occurred to you.'

'I saw time technology as a...'

'A what? Something to open up a new market for American goods? Somewhere else for your tourists to go? A major employer, like the Apollo programme?'

'All of those things. It'll revolutionise the world, Jonah. It'll change the world, like the Industrial Revolution, or the creation of the atomic bomb.'

'And we'll be the masters. Are you familiar with the works of Agathon?'

Mather looked witheringly at him. 'Can we assume I'm not.'

'He was a Greek philosopher. He said that not even God could change the past. We'll be able to. We'll be above the gods themselves.'

'You and me?'

'*Just* you and me. We'll rule over Time itself. As partners.'

The Onihr deputy leader filled the small TV screen in the rear compartment. Anji and Baskerville were hunched in one corner – she'd pointed out that having their dead comrade in the background of the picture might send out the wrong message, but it was difficult to work round.

'You want time travel,' Baskerville said. 'I have time travel. You have advanced technology – I suggest a trade.'

Anji translated, not knowing how. It sounded like she was just repeating everything that was being said.

'Onihrs don't trade with primitive lifeforms.'

Baskerville looked uncertain.

Anji didn't wait for him. 'Then you won't get time travel, and this discussion is at an –'

'Wait! We will negotiate.'

Baskerville smiled. 'Good. We should meet face to face. I will prepare a meeting place, and contact you with the co-ordinates. We will speak soon.'

He cut the link. The screen went dead, the Onihr deputy leader faded from view.

And the Doctor was up there. How had he managed that?

Anji turned to Baskerville. 'Happy?'

He didn't look it.

'I think I might be in too deep.'

'You've kidnapped the President of the United States and some senile psycho with a licence to kill, you want to trade time travel with a bunch of giant alien rhinos, and you think you're in too deep? What could possibly make you think that?'

He looked troubled.

'Are you all right?' she asked. 'The last thing we need now is for you to go off the rails.'

'We're nearly there,' he told her.

'Where?'

'A facility I own.'

'A base?'

Baskerville seemed amused by the idea. 'A secret hideout? No, it's a factory. I've never been there in person, before.'

'In Russia?'

'On the Steppes, yes. A secure place to negotiate with Mr Mather and Mr Cosgrove. The personnel at the factory have got orders to fire on everyone except me, and the capability to bring down anything that's launched against them. No one else, not even those creatures, will be able to track me there.'

'What do you want?' she asked.

'I beg your pardon?'

'You have a time machine. So, leaving aside the aliens for a moment, what else could you possibly want?'

'I told you – access to ULTRA.'

'You told me at first that you needed it to calculate a course back home to the future. But if you're not from the future…'

Baskerville looked at her. 'I think it would be instructive to hear you finish that sentence,' he said carefully.

If Anji could finish the sentence, she wouldn't have asked him. She considered it logically, tried to go for the simplest solution.

'…then you need the ULTRA for something else,' she concluded, after a moment.

'That something else being?'

'I'm not sure what the ULTRA is. So I don't know what you'd do with it. You said it was an intelligence database… so it's got some information on it that you want. Or want erased. But it isn't about you, because you don't have an electronic presence, or whatever you called it. There's nothing on there for you to erase. So what else does the ULTRA do? Surveillance? Access to another system?'

Baskerville looked up, worried.

Warm.

'Access to another system,' Anji concluded. 'To do what? Start a war between the US and Europe? You don't need a computer to do that.'

She dried up, tried to think back to what he'd been talking about before, on the yacht. He was wearing his best poker face, now.

Golden geese. Stealing money.

'Money?' she asked.

Baskerville's face fell. 'Great heavens, you really are good, aren't you?'

'Money?' she repeated, this time disappointed. 'You have a Concorde, you have a helicopter, you have a yacht. There comes a point where you don't really need any more money, doesn't there? You're already drinking the most expensive champagne. If it's not good enough, well, I'm sure you could afford your own vineyard.'

'IFEC,' Baskerville said. 'ULTRA will give me complete access to IFEC.'

The intercom buzzed. 'We're coming in to land, Baskerville.

Everyone should get to their seats.'

Anji followed him through, puzzled.

Mather and Cosgrove were sitting opposite each other, and had clearly been in conversation. They straightened up, looking like guilty schoolboys.

'Seatbelts, gentlemen,' Baskerville reminded them. They both belted up.

Baskerville took a seat, Anji sat next to him. Dee was hurrying through to the cockpit, perhaps to help out with the landing.

The plane was banking down, gently. It had slowed down considerably, even in the time it had taken Anji to come through and take a seat. They were heading through the clouds, now, so there was no visibility.

Anji checked her watch. They'd been flying for about two and a half hours. It took Concorde about three and a half to cross the Atlantic, so they must be well inside Russia.

Baskerville smiled over at her. He trusted her – she could have told Mather or Cosgrove that he wasn't a time traveller, she hadn't. Anji was unsure why she hadn't, but knew it was the right thing to do.

She wondered where he'd got his time machine. There were time machines everywhere, of course, she'd learned that from her travels with the Doctor. It was a bit like L-plates. Before you started driving lessons, you didn't notice any learners. Once you started, every third car seemed to be from a driving school. And everywhere the TARDIS landed, there seemed to be a time traveller there or thereabouts. The only thing the time machines had in common was that they were all completely different.

He'd killed the original owner, she could presume that much. Perhaps that was why he was so keen to sell it – it was hot property. And maybe that was why the TARDIS had diverted them here – a time traveller had died, a wrong needed righting.

The Concorde banked hard to the right, splashing Anji's champagne over her.

'Just routine,' Baskerville called out, 'nothing to worry –'

The plane banked hard left. Anji saw a streak of fire through the window.

'What the hell?'

'That was a ground-to-air missile.' Cosgrove shouted. 'We're being fired on!'

Chapter Seventeen
Stand Off (ish)

'It's a Concorde, Baskerville,' Relker told him. 'Ground to air defences are active. We'll down it.'

The Doctor leant back in his chair, his hands behind his back. 'Dee, what do you make of it?'

Malady moved over to the radar. 'It's not registering on radar. It could be modified for stealth. You're sure the radar is working?'

'Of course, Miss Gordon. We think it is a stealth craft. That makes it hard to hit with heat-seekers,' Relker admitted. 'We were right to fire on it?'

The Doctor smiled beatifically. 'Of course. Those were my orders, after all – fire on anyone approaching who isn't me. Let it land, then have your men surround it, stop it from taking off again. Keep everyone on the plane for the moment. Oh and Relker, if they resist –'

'– kill them?' Relker asked, with relish.

The Doctor was horrified. 'No. If they resist, get under cover. Non-lethal force only.'

Relker looked disappointed, but saluted and left the office.

Malady waited until he'd gone and rounded on the Doctor. 'When he finds out...'

'Let's keep that from happening for as long as possible, eh?'

Malady had given up asking him how they'd ended up here. They'd had one time jump. The Doctor had materialised them in... well, at first Malady had thought it was his house. Somehow, the cathedral-like space of wood panelling and bookcases looked just the sort of place the Doctor would call home. The Doctor had seemed relaxed there, too. He'd handed her the time machine, then gone over to an odd five-sided writing desk, which had some sort of computer built into it. The Doctor had used it to track the radio signals that had been controlling the RealWar robot, followed them back to the teletroop at the source, then announced that the signal had been bounced off all sorts of satellites.

Then he'd opened the door, and it turned out they'd been right in Baskerville's base all along.

In a blue shed.

A shed that had the word 'police box' along the top, and which was laid out so that the inside was bigger than… well, it was an optical illusion of some kind. Quite a clever one, but Malady had seen better.

All very confusing.

Outside the shed, the Doctor had been more cautious. They were in a research lab. Spotless white corridors, no windows. They'd sneaked past a couple of open plan laboratories full of computers and test rigs and into this office.

Then Relker had found them.

Malady had just been about to try to blast her way out of the problem, but Relker had welcomed the Doctor as Baskerville, and herself as 'Dee', who the Doctor explained later was Baskerville's assistant. They were expected, and it was good to finally meet Baskerville, but how could he possibly have arrived here without his men knowing? The Doctor had told them he liked to keep some secrets, then asked the men to increase security. Apparently, the standing orders were already to shoot anything that came close to the complex.

Which meant wherever they were must be pretty isolated.

All the notices and safety posters were in Russian. Other than that, they hadn't a clue where they were.

They'd been led to Baskerville's office, which was almost bare.

'I wonder how many mercenaries there are in total?'

The Doctor moved on to the second drawer, not finding

anything in the first. 'Why do you say they're mercenaries?'

'I recognise a couple of them. Russian Mafia. One of them, Laikov, is a suspect in the killing of the North Chinese ambassador last year.'

'For a man from the future, Baskerville keeps strange company.'

'What is this place?'

'Can you hear that noise?'

She could, faintly.

'It's a production line,' the Doctor explained. 'I think this is a factory of some kind.'

'Making time machines?'

The Doctor shrugged. 'I doubt it – Baskerville's selling blueprints to his time machine, not mass marketing it. Perhaps this place makes coffee machines.'

'Coffee machines?'

'He took the coffee machine from his office in Athens, remember?'

'If this is a coffee machine factory, then the last thing he'd do in an emergency is rescue the coffee machine.'

The Doctor looked thoughtful. 'True.'

They could hear the Concorde coming in to land. The sound was muffled, but Malady now thought they were above ground – at least two storeys from the top of the building.

After a moment, the engines died down.

'Baskerville's probably on that plane.'

'Certainly, I'd say.'

'So we haven't got long before he convinces them of who he is.'

'No.'

'So shall we stop messing around in filing cabinets and stop him?'

The Doctor slammed the door shut. 'Malady, you took the words out of my mouth.'

'We need to radio for backup.'

'How long would it take for them to arrive?'

'Hours, so the sooner we get it done, the better.'

Baskerville sat in the co-pilot's seat, incandescent.

'I am Baskerville, you idiot!' he screamed into the microphone, not for the first time.

'Baskerville is here already,' a Russian voice replied.

Dee sighed. This was going around in circles. She checked the CCTV – back in the cabin, the President, Cosgrove and Anji Kapoor were still in their seats, chatting. She switched circuits – there were sixteen or seventeen Russian Mafia mercenaries at various points around the plane. They'd put a small van in front of the plane, a forklift behind, to stop it from moving.

The Concorde had some defensive systems, but only to tackle air-to-air attacks, not against a ground assault.

They were penned in.

'Ask him to describe Baskerville,' she suggested.

Baskerville turned to her, his face red, eyes glaring. 'I am Baskerville.'

'I know that,' she said wearily. 'Haven't you worked it out, yet?'

Baskerville looked at her for a moment. 'The Doctor?'

'He beat Cosgrove, he survived being thrown out of a twentieth-storey window, then a tidal wave in Athens, he got past a RealWar squad in Toronto.'

'So how did he get here? He was in Toronto… what? Twenty minutes ago?'

Dee stopped. He was right. It was impossible.

'Ask him to describe Baskerville,' she repeated.

Baskerville did so.

'He's in his forties. Long dark coat. Brown hair. Blue eyes.'

'Not a brilliant description,' Baskerville told Dee. 'It could be anyone.'

'It could certainly be the Doctor.'

'Are they restless yet?'

Dee glanced down at the CCTV. 'The President is watching

television with Anji. Cosgrove is looking out the window. The mad old fool's probably planning to make a break for it.'

'If he does, I don't fancy the mercenaries' chances. Perhaps I should let him out.'

She leant up to the microphone. 'Relker, this is Dee. That man is an impostor.'

'We've got a Dee here too, ma'am.'

'A Chinese-looking girl?'

'Yes.'

'Does Dee Gordon sound like a Chinese name to you?'

'Dee does. I mean – I don't know Chinese. But the only name I've ever been given is Dee. And that could be a Chinese name.'

Dee buried her head in her hands. 'It's possible to have too low a profile,' she told Baskerville.

Baskerville reached out and adjusted a control. 'I've had enough of this.'

Anji sat in her chair, watched the news on the small television screen set in the table.

Footage of Mather entering the Green Hotel, three hours before (it felt a lot longer). There was still no sign of the President, who the network felt should have made a statement about the Tripoli shootings.

The network had concluded that the President was in his hotel room, unwilling to face the anti-American and anti-war demonstrators who'd congregated outside.

It was a little surreal to have him sitting alongside her, watching the news reports.

'Never believe what you download off the datanet,' he told her in that rich voice of his.

'Do your people know where you are?'

'Yes.'

'Some sort of homing device?' Cosgrove asked.

'Nanotech. One of my eyebrows, apparently. I don't know which

194

one. I've often tried to spot it.'

Anji tried not to stare at them.

'Advanced stuff,' Cosgrove said, admiringly. 'Does it help us at all?'

'It means they know where I am.'

'We're on the Russian Steppes. I don't think the USAF make house calls here.'

'They will to protect their President.'

'Where are they?' Anji asked.

'On their way,' the President insisted. 'Concorde's fast, and the jets will be coming from the Gulf.'

'We could take Baskerville's time machine by force.'

Mather nodded.

'Would you be able to operate it?' Anji asked them.

'You seem very chummy with him,' Cosgrove suggested.

'No,' she said simply. 'Just keen to stay alive.'

Cosgrove raised an eyebrow. 'Who are you? If you don't mind me asking.'

'She's a friend of the Doctor,' Mather replied.

'And that's an explanation?' Cosgrove asked.

'It's a pretty good indication we won't get an explanation. Cosgrove, what time is it?'

'You're wearing a watch.'

'I know. Look at the news.'

'And there's a clock on the screen... and both this and the watch are showing the right time.'

Anji took a deep breath. 'If you two just said what you meant, instead of talking in secret code all the time...'

'Toronto,' Mather said.

Cosgrove raised an eyebrow. 'Yes. Toronto.'

Anji peered at the screen. It looked more like Tripoli to her. The same pictures of the school bus they'd had on before.

'You're still doing it,' she told them.

'A news blackout?' Cosgrove suggested.

'In the land of the free?'

'In a Commonwealth nation, old chap.'

'Trust me, if there was a nuclear explosion in the same *hemisphere* as the US, there wouldn't be anything else on the news.'

'Nuclear explosion?' Anji asked, trying to piece all this together. 'The Fourth Prophecy?' she guessed, suddenly.

'Yes.'

'And it's not happened?'

'No.'

Cosgrove stroked his chin. 'Which rather makes me wonder why Baskerville got it wrong.'

Fitz sauntered towards the EMP cannon maintenance duct, trying to act like he owned the place. Every so often, when he was sure no one was looking, he'd sneak a glance at the plan of the ship Pad was displaying.

He had passed a couple of Onihrs along the way, and they'd looked him up and down, but not tried to stop him.

The ship was huge. He guessed it was about a dozen miles long, about as wide, about as tall. The size of a vast city, even bearing in mind its inhabitants were twice as big as people.

His legs were getting a bit stiff now he'd walked halfway down the ship. He shouldn't have asked Pad where to go – he should have just guessed it was as far as physically possible from where he'd been. The gravity seemed to be getting bigger. Or stronger. Heavier. Whatever the word was.

Up in space, there was no way of telling what time it was. His watch was broken – probably during the good kicking that old bloke had given him in America, just before he'd been brought here.

The walk was a good chance to have a good think. It wasn't helping though – his best plan was still to sabotage the EMP cannon and slow down the Onihrs' invasion of Earth.

'Doctor,' a growling voice barked from behind him.

'Er, yes?' said Fitz, stopping in his tracks.

'The deputy leader requires you on the control gallery.'

Fitz groaned and turned round.

He could see almost all the way back to the gallery from here. It wasn't quite a straight line – the transparent corridors wove in and out of the superstructure of the ship. But he could see the route he'd taken.

Five miles. Six, probably. Maybe seven. With all that weaving, it was quite possibly eight miles.

'Doctor,' the Onihr asked. 'Where were you heading?'

'Er… just taking a walk.'

'A walk? An odd alien custom.'

'You're the one with all the corridors, mate.' Fitz scolded himself for using the word 'mate'. It wasn't very Doctorish, was it?

'These are mainly used by the maintenance robots,' the Onihr told him. 'We teleport all but the shortest of distances.'

Fitz looked down at Pad, sighed.

'Er… I have a control box, but I think it's broken.'

'May I?'

The Onihr took it in one huge paw. 'No – look, it's just a question of…' he tapped the third button, then the second, then the fourth, and they were on the control gallery.

The Onihr passed the control box back to Fitz.

'Cheers,' Fitz said.

The deputy leader was wearing an ornate black and gold suit of armour. It looked practical – bloody practical, actually – but Fitz got the idea it was at least partly ceremonial. It was dripping with fragrant oils. It was overpowering, visually and nasally.

'Dressed to impress,' Fitz said cheerfully.

'I shall lead the delegation to Earth,' the Onihr announced.

'Doing a deal?'

'Yes.'

'Need any help?' It was a cheap way to get back home, Fitz thought.

'No, Doctor, you shall remain here.'

'I know the, er, humans. I could help you get what you want.'

'If the human does not give me time travel, I shall tear its head off and take time travel for myself. Then I shall raze all the cities of the Earth.'

Fitz smiled affably. 'OK. Er… good luck.'

Relker was getting cold, waiting. Night would be falling soon. The shadows were long, the air was getting a tang of cold. Even on a summer's night, it would be bitter. Oleson was standing next to him, already shifting from one foot to the other and rubbing his hands together.

The Concorde had been sitting on the runway for an hour, now. The stand off was absurd. Whatever the plane was coated with was thick enough to block IR scans of the interior, but there were a few windows, and the spotters around the plane had been watching, doing a headcount. There were hardly any people on board – the pilot, the man who claimed to be Baskerville, his assistant (who claimed to be Dee) and no more than four or five people in the main cabin.

Even just using the men out here on the runway, they could storm the plane and take it in moments.

Relker was unsure what Baskerville was waiting for. Or, for that matter, who the people on the Concorde were, or why they were here. They knew all about the operation here. But if it was one of the Russian governments cracking down, they'd have sent tanks. The Americans or Eurozone would send helicopters.

The Trojan Horse. That's the image that kept coming back to Relker. They – whoever *they* were – had sent the Concorde simply to baffle him. They'd landed it here, made him and his men waste valuable time and energy wondering what on earth it was here for.

A Eurozone plane (a retired Eurozone plane, but don't dwell on that), adapted using state of the art American stealth technology.

Containing a man claiming to be their boss, who claimed – bizarrely – that he had the President of the United States on board, when anyone with a newsfeed knew the President was in a hotel in Istanbul.

Shoot them all and let God sort them out. That was Relker's preferred option.

A RealWar class two slid easily from the main building. The hover tank. Hovercraft technology had suddenly come back into vogue, with the development of new materials. This didn't look like a weapon at all, it looked like a sculpture – it was smooth chrome, all sleek curves. He saw the Concorde, the evening sky, even himself and his men reflected against its metal surface.

The gun ports opened, all three cannons emerged.

Baskerville was making a move. Relker wished he'd been consulted first.

He reached for his radio. 'Baskerville, what's the HT for?'

Nothing.

Relker was reaching down for his gun when the Hovertank started firing at his men. Some of the idiots were standing up, to see what the noise was. Others had their heads down, and those were the ones who weren't killed instantly.

The tank moved methodically forwards. His men should know better than to take it on – even if their bullets got past the armour, the chances of hitting a vital component were ridiculously small.

Hopefully someone had got a jammer on them, or something that could cut the command signal.

'Baskerville?'

Oleson was looking over at him, also puzzled. 'What the hell is it doing?' he asked.

'Baskerville's not in his office.'

'If he's controlling that, he must be. Or someone must be. It's the only teletroop hub in the complex.'

'Handy to know,' another voice chimed in.

An old man in an expensive, fashionable business suit. He looked about eighty, the lines and wrinkles in his face were an inch deep, his hair was neat, but thin. But his eyes were sharp and he seemed unaffected by the cold.

'Who?' Relker asked.

'Cosgrove. Jonah Cosgrove,' the old man replied, as he broke Oleson's neck.

Relker brought his gun up, aimed it and fired.

But Cosgrove had gone.

Chapter Eighteen
Boom and Bust

Mather and Anji had a grandstand seat.

The complex consisted of three areas. The nearest was the runway their Concorde sat on, hangars and what were other support buildings for the airstrip. Beyond that, larger, more industrial-looking buildings. A factory, or warehouses at the very least. Beyond that, smaller buildings – office space, accommodation blocks. It was a compact site, no more than a dozen buildings in total.

Anji tried to figure the place out. She couldn't see a road – now she was looking, she couldn't see any car parks. So, you got here by air. Which fitted in with the isolation of the place. This really was the middle of nowhere. Almost all around was nondescript moorland. Flat, with a couple of lonely-looking trees in the middle distance. No sign of any other habitation, or even agriculture. Not even planes in the sky. Through the windows on the right side of the plane, they could see the runway had been built a short distance from a cliff edge, although it was difficult to see how high the cliffs were.

Although that side would be easy enough to defend, the complex looked more like a light industrial site than a military one. Now, somewhere there was clearly an anti-aircraft battery – they had been shot at. But this wasn't a fortress. The buildings were made from corrugated metal and flimsy-looking concrete slabs. There wasn't even a perimeter fence. The men surrounding the plane weren't in uniform, they looked like mercenaries, or paramilitaries. Its best defence was its isolation.

Anji had watched as the tank – the same type of shiny, egg-shaped vehicle she'd seen on the news back in that Ibiza restaurant – came out of the hangar building. At first, both she and Mather had assumed it was simply reinforcing the men guarding their plane.

They'd been a little surprised to spot Cosgrove outside. Neither of them had seen him leave, or had any idea how he'd got down from the plane. He'd managed to find cover, and edge towards what looked like the command post, near the hangar door.

Then the tank had started firing at the soldiers on the runway.

It had three guns, which all operated independently, and found their targets. Anji was fascinated by the efficiency of the thing – until she remembered she was watching men die.

Mather didn't understand what was going on. It was too soon for his air force to arrive, let alone for robots to be deployed.

Anji quickly worked out it must be Baskerville in control, working from a computer on board the Concorde.

Within a minute, Dee and Leo came into the cabin, carrying pistols. 'We're moving out once the runway is secured,' Dee announced.

Mather leant over to Anji. 'If we get a chance, we have to disable the AAA system here.'

She worked out he meant anti-aircraft artillery before she opened her mouth to ask. 'How would we go about that?'

'There will be a radar post somewhere close by. We should aim to disable that.'

Dee was opening up the front door on the left side of the plane. She had already cocked her pistol. Now she was using the door as cover, waiting for her moment.

'What is this place?' Anji asked.

'It's a robot factory,' the Doctor whispered.

He and Malady were right on the edge of the factory floor. Mechanised production lines were assembling RealWar robots, conveyor belts stretching hundreds of feet. The line nearest to them was assembling the class threes, the humanoid type. There was something compelling about the process – it was perfect choreography, almost like a dance routine. Arm moves into place, welder emerges, welder welds, welder withdraws, robot moves on to next stage.

Malady was watching this with more practical things on her mind. 'It's the RealWar factory.'

'Does this mean you know where we are?'

'No. We knew RealWar was a Russian company, but the location of its offices and research centres are a closely guarded secret. Most of Russia is unmonitored. It's either too isolated or too poor for satellites to bother with. There are whole areas of the map without data presence.'

'And I imagine your governments don't want every inch of the planet under surveillance. Where would they hide their own little secrets, hmm?'

Malady didn't look back at the Doctor. 'The CIA have looked for the RealWar factories, but we've not had much luck.'

'This isn't the only factory?'

'No one knows, but I doubt it.'

'Any idea why Baskerville is here? Could he be supplying the technology?'

'Possibly. It would explain how he pays his bills.'

'A time traveller could find other ways to make money,' the Doctor insisted. 'Instead of prophesying the results of football matches to convince investors, he could just bet on them.'

The Doctor hesitated, watched the production lines again for a moment, got caught up in the rhythm and movement.

'He could have a more sinister purpose for travelling to the past,' he muttered.

'Sinister?'

'Well, from this vantage point he looks remarkably like an arms dealer. With the Americans and Europeans on the verge of war, this could be the best possible time to come back to and sell weapons.'

'RealWar robots aren't that advanced.'

'They don't need to be. It's state of the art, but you only need to be a year or two ahead of your enemy, particularly with something that changes the rules. The development of the dreadnought made all existing navies irrelevant, the development of the atomic bomb shifted strategy towards attacking civilian targets. Or rather *not* attacking them. The whole emphasis shifted to preventing the start of a war no one could win. If you have teletroops and missile defence, it's a lot easier to fight a war.'

Malady looked at him, clearly disturbed. 'It looks like we have to stop him, whatever he's doing.'

'Agreed.'

They heard firing.

'The people on the Concorde are making a break for it.'

Relker was behind the hover tank, now, out of its sight. He edged back towards the main hangar. Once inside, he tucked himself behind a brick wall, and got his radio out. Three more class twos sat motionless here. They were always there – garaged along with the three helicopters and the two light planes. But Relker kept one eye on them, mindful now that they could come to life at any moment.

'Baskerville,' he hissed into the radio. 'Baskerville, what the hell is going on?'

Outside, the hover tank was concentrating on a group of four men who'd dug in and were covering the main door of the aircraft.

A grenade arced over, bounced off the armoured shell, then clattered away. It exploded a few seconds later, blowing a chunk out of the tarmac.

The tank was the only thing firing bullets.

Relker changed channel. 'Keep under cover!' he ordered his men. 'There's a malfunction. I'm going to the teletroop control room. Everyone just keep their heads down.'

Malfunction. The tank was functioning fine. Making short work of his men. And if they hadn't realised they should be keeping their heads down without him telling them, then they didn't deserve to have heads in the first place.

He hurried further inside the building, heading for Baskerville's office. It wasn't far. To get there faster, he could cut past the production lines.

Relker headed that way, swiped his way past two security doors. Once the second of those was closed again, he could no longer hear the gunfire, all the other sounds were drowned out by the clatter of the factory floor.

He cut across them by climbing the metal stairs to the gantry. Down on the factory floor, he saw someone moving. Not one of his men – Cosgrove, presumably. He'd have to be dealt with, but first things first.

Relker flung open the door to Baskerville's office, ready for anything.

What he found instead was nothing.

The RealWar booth in the corner, the only possible place in the complex from where the hover tank that was killing his men could be controlled. A cursory examination was enough to tell that it hadn't been on recently.

So what was controlling that tank? Was it just some malfunction, after all?

The office was empty. The light was on.

Baskerville and the Chinese girl, his assistant, weren't here.

So where were they?

No. First things first – stop the tank. He moved over the terminal, switched it on, and while he waited a few seconds for it to boot up, he went back to the door and barricaded it with the filing cabinet and desk.

The booth was running. He set it to the simplest control interface, found the rogue hovertank.

Then he was hoisted out of the chair and slammed against the wall.

Cosgrove.

'A word to the wise,' he said, in Russian with a thick Scots accent, 'if you lock a door, what's on the side you're on is far more important than what's on the side you aren't.'

'I saw you down on the factory floor.'

He looked puzzled. 'I didn't even know this was a factory; I came in through the window. Is that thing working?' he indicated the RealWar booth.

'Yes.'

Cosgrove knocked him out.

Baskerville sat in the cockpit of the Concorde, controlling the hovertank.

He paid for two dozen men to guard this facility. Which meant there were probably about fifteen. There were ten scientists, various assistants, a few support staff there to look after the autosecs, cleaning robots and food dispensers. He wouldn't expect any of those to put up a fight.

Even his mercenaries, who were meant to be there ready for the day the authorities discovered this place, were keeping down. They'd been hopeless against one class two tank. The whole point about the RealWar armies was that the robots were expendable, and dropped on to a battlefield in great numbers. A girls' hockey team should be able to immobilise *one* of them.

So he had no regrets in gunning the men down. They were incompetents.

He turned the tank about twenty degrees. Now he was facing a couple of them, huddled behind a crate.

Crosshairs appeared on the screen, and Baskerville decided to fire a couple of shots to the left with the secondary cannon, before strafing the right with machine gun fire. His guess was that they'd instinctively dive out of the way of the first volley... and into the second.

A competent soldier would know to stay where they were. So

this was simple Darwinism – if these people really were soldiers, they would survive.

He pressed the switch that fired the secondary cannon.

Nothing happened.

The signal was lost. They'd finally got around to jamming him.

Time to move out.

Anji and Mather sat still, waiting to see what happened next.

Dee was still by the front door, unable to move for fear of sniper fire. Outside, they could hear the hovertank moving, but it was a few minutes now since it had fired a shot.

Anji stood up.

Dee was whispering something into her radio – she sounded unhappy.

Anji strained to hear. 'It's not secure,' Dee insisted. 'We have twenty, thirty metres of runway, then a hangar then… well, who knows how far to the computer room?'

She paused, the radio hissed its response.

'We stay here,' she hissed.

Anji edged away.

Dee looked over. 'Where are you going?'

'Er… it was a long flight, and I had a lot of champagne and coffee.'

'OK. But be quick.'

Anji rolled her eyes. It was like being in primary school.

She headed down the plane, away from Dee, towards the loo, which was in a small section in the middle of the plane with the galley and some storage space. The whole area was curtained off. Anji slipped behind the curtain.

'Trouble?' the Doctor asked.

Anji almost jumped out of her skin. A beautiful young Chinese woman in black leather was standing alongside him.

'Anji Kapoor, Malady Chang. Malady Chang, Anji Kapoor. Good to see you again.'

'We met at the airport,' Malady said.

Anji shrugged. 'Which one? I've been to more airports in the last couple of days than...'

Anji shut up and hugged the Doctor.

The Doctor peeked around the curtain, over at Dee. 'She looks preoccupied.'

'How did you get on board?' Anji asked.

'There's a cargo hatch open at the rear.'

'Where Cosgrove got out...' Anji realised.

'He's here, is he?'

'He was.'

'Who's on the plane?' Malady asked.

'Baskerville, the pilot, Leo, and Dee. Oh, and the President.'

Malady looked surprised.

'No one else?'

'Well, not unless you count the dead alien in the rear compartment.'

The Doctor smiled. 'My, you have been busy.'

Twenty or so metres in front of them, Baskerville emerged from the cockpit, exchanged words with Dee, then headed towards the President. Leo was there, too. Both carried pistols, Baskerville was also carrying that carry case. The President was on his feet, arguing about something with Baskerville.

'What happened to the Fourth Prophecy?'

'There are forces acting against us,' Baskerville insisted. 'People that don't want humanity to get time travel. We have to hurry if we are going to defeat them.'

Baskerville and Leo were half-dragging the President to the door. Mather decided to co-operate. Dee recovered her rucksack. A moment later, all four had left the plane.

'We have to get after them,' Malady insisted.

Anji winced. 'Well, do you mind if I... if you just wait a minute or two? I won't be long.'

* * *

Five Onihrs in full armour stood in front of their deputy leader in a cavernous antechamber some way away from the control gallery of the space craft.

Fitz stood behind the deputy, smiling in a way that he hoped would be so winsomely charming that they wouldn't use him for target practice.

'The humans are resourceful,' the Deputy Leader barked. 'They have done the Onihr race a great harm. They have killed our leader, made us doubt our own manifest superiority. We could destroy them at a distance, but if we did so, we would never destroy that doubt.'

The Onihrs shifted around, looking uncomfortable. Their armour rattled like a car being dropped on to a scrapheap.

'We must avenge our leader's death in hand-to-hand combat. We must tear the human time machine from their mammal paws. Then we will return, and we will become the new Lords of Time.'

The Onihrs burst into spontaneous appreciation of this sentiment – banging gloved fists against the breastplate of their armour and hooting and growling their approval.

Fitz prided himself on his laissez-faire attitude to life, but that sound scared him almost witless.

The deputy leader clearly drew strength from this show of support. 'Let us go to the Earth – let us go to our destiny!'

And all six of the fully armed Onihrs faded into thin air.

It was suddenly very quiet.

Fitz fished in his pockets for his cigarettes, but could only find Anji's phone and Pad, the control box.

'How can I help?'

'You can generate smells, yeah?'

'The Onihr race's primary sense is that of smell. All displays configured for –'

'Can you copy smells? If so, could you copy the smell of leaf smoke. If not, could you shut up for a bit.'

To his intense relief, the smell of tobacco wafted up from the control box. Not the same as a smoke, of course, but the next best thing.

'Pad, old mate,' he said finally, 'how are you on noble self-sacrifice?'

'I am a control interface, sir, I have no sense of self. The Onihr race value the heroic loss of one life for many.'

'I don't think they'll be too hot on what I've got in mind. Could you teleport me to the Ee and Pee maintenance room, please?'

'Of course, sir.'

The Doctor examined the controls of the Concorde, Malady searched the rest of the small cockpit. Anji watched.

'The co-pilot's controls can be reconfigured,' he said. 'Look. Do either of you recognise this setting?'

Malady leaned over. 'It's been set up as a RealWar booth.'

'He was controlling the hovertank from in here,' Anji deduced.

'And the ones in Toronto,' the Doctor added. 'This place is well defended for a factory.'

That reminded Anji. 'The USAF is on its way. Mather was being tracked. But there are anti-aircraft defences here. We were going to try to deactivate them.'

The Doctor and Malady looked at each other. 'The tower,' they said together.

Malady peered out of the cockpit windows. 'Doesn't look that well defended. But we should really rescue the President first.'

The Doctor put his arm round Anji. 'Miss Kapoor and myself will do that. You sort out the tower and meet up with us inside.'

Malady clearly wasn't sure, but after a few seconds agreed to the plan.

She slipped away. A moment later, they saw her scurrying across the runway to the control tower.

The Doctor clapped his hands together. 'Right... What do you want to do first – rescue the President, negotiate a ceasefire with the remaining mercenaries, locate Baskerville's time machine, capture Baskerville himself or find Cosgrove and see what he's up to?'

Anji hesitated. 'Actually... I'd really like to find out what Baskerville wants access to ULTRA for. You wouldn't know what IFEC is, would you?'

Outside, the control tower exploded.

'Any sign of Fitz, by the way?' the Doctor asked.

Anji shook her head. 'Not since you dropped him off in America.'

'I'm sure he's out of harm's way.'

Cosgrove heard the explosion through the headphones of the RealWar goggles.

He turned his hovertank around. The runway control tower was now a pile of rubble. The cameras on RealWar robots were very low resolution, and couldn't pan without moving the whole unit.

He saw a dark shape on the edge of his vision, and instinctively fired at it with the robot's machine guns.

Malady Chang, he decided, a moment or two later.

He hadn't hit her. But she was here, which meant the Doctor almost certainly was, which meant that he needed more than one hovertank.

Cosgrove activated the other three class twos, the ones in the hangar.

After a moment, he decided to look around and see what other assets there were. It was a RealWar factory, after all.

He was pleasantly surprised to discover there were three dozen more class twos available, in a warehouse, earmarked for delivery to the EZ in the morning. It wasn't even stealing.

The twenty class threes in the same warehouse, bound for the American fleet in the Gulf... well, it would be treachery not to acquire those for the Eurozone, too.

He selected them all, and activated them.

Cosgrove had a couple of objectives - he had to clear the buildings of hostiles and potential hostiles, of course. But most of all, he wanted that time machine. It was here somewhere, he knew it. Baskerville had been panicked by the aliens, and he'd bolted here, to his stronghold. And this was the perfect place to build a time machine and defend it.

The RealWar booth had an extensive map of this complex.

Cosgrove preferred the tanks to the humanoid robots, but they were too big to operate indoors. He sent four class threes to the research labs. There were scientists there in white coats, half of them sitting at computers, the others standing around a class three which lay in bits on the floor. Eleven of them in total.

They looked up at the new arrivals, but didn't seem worried. Why would they, when they worked with RealWar robots all day?

Cosgrove flicked a switch, activated the loudhailer.

'I'm looking for the time machine,' he told them. The speaker was set a little more loudly than he'd anticipated, and the words echoed from the walls.

He used all four of the robots to look around the room at the scientists. Their expressions ranged from puzzled to bemused. It was obvious that none of them knew anything about it. This was a robotics lab, nothing more.

It only needed one of the class threes to finish them off. The other three robots gave him complete camera coverage of the room, as the men and women died.

He marked the research labs off the map. The time machine wasn't there.

The Doctor was about to charge into the hangar, but at the last moment he ducked behind a wall, keeping Anji from entering.

Something was moving around in there.

'One of those robots,' he explained. 'The tanks.'

'Class two,' Anji said. 'The humanoid ones are class threes.'

'What do the class ones look like?'

'No idea – I've not seen one so far. Who's controlling them?'

'Not Baskerville.' They'd seen Baskerville and his party scurry across the runway to one of the support buildings.

'Cosgrove?'

'That would be my guess. Right… it's facing the other way.'

They hurried through the hangar, to the door in the far wall.

'I went back to Baskerville's office in Athens,' the Doctor told Anji. 'Baskerville had removed the time machine – or the vital components from it, at any rate.'

'I think it's got something to do with his coffee machine.'

'Yes, he removed that, too. I was wondering about that.'

'It's in a silver case.'

'The one he was carrying just now?' The Doctor looked a little annoyed – he'd been almost within arm's reach of it.

'Uh-huh. I looked in it, but I only found the coffee machine. The time machine components must be in a hidden compartment.'

'We need that case.'

'Why does he need the President?' Anji asked. 'He's got a time machine, he's got enough money to buy a Concorde, he's got a robot army…'

'He said he wanted to get back to the future.'

Anji held up her hand. 'Right… you missed that bit. He's not from the future. He used to be in the Russian army.'

'So where did he get…?'

'I don't know, he wouldn't tell me that bit. He's ruthless, resourceful. I imagine he stumbled across the time machine somewhere, then killed its original owner.'

The Doctor winced. 'The damage he could do if he used the time machine without understanding it…'

Anji stopped, closed her eyes.

'Are you all right?' the Doctor asked.

It didn't add up. Baskerville had a time machine and no moral scruples. Or, more precisely – and more dangerously – a moral framework that meant he could justify just about anything in his self-interest. So why wasn't he using the time machine for himself?

'He could make a fortune,' Anji said. 'He could go back and sell weapons, he could play the stock market, he could set himself up as an adviser, an inventor, a brilliant medicine man... there are a million ways a time traveller could make money.'

'There are?' the Doctor asked.

'Hell... he could buy up old Batman comics for a cent a time, or get autographs, or go back and pretend he'd written Harry Potter.'

'I don't think he's really the –'

'He could bet on every horse race, raid the pyramids, take paying tourists to see the Crucifixion, buy up land...'

'Er, Anji...'

'Stake a claim for every oil field. He could clear up in the insurance market, buy up Van Gogh's unsold stock, he could put his money in an high-interest account two hundred years ago and –'

'I think you've made your point,' the Doctor said gently. 'Perhaps he lacks your business brain.'

'No. I've talked to him. Doctor, do you know the one thing I'd do if I had a time machine?'

The Doctor shook his head. 'Go home?' he said finally.

Anji bristled at that. 'No. The one thing I'd do, of all the things I could do, is simple: *I wouldn't sell it.*'

The Doctor took a deep breath. 'So he doesn't want money.'

'He does. He said he wanted money. Wait. IFEC... I have heard the word before.'

'It does ring a bell,' the Doctor admitted.

Something small whooshed over Anji's head, and exploded a few feet away.

Anji saw Baskerville and Leo, aiming chunky guns at them – they looked more like flare pistols than ordinary pistols.

'Gyrojet guns!' the Doctor said. 'Mini rocket launchers. Fascinating.'

Anji pulled him down behind a pile of steel oil drums. If they were empty, they'd provide perfect cover. If they were full of oil, then at least it would be quick.

'It's not a question of how interesting the bullets are, it's how hard they hit us,' she said.

Pad had given Fitz a running list of instructions.

The workings of the EMP cannon, the ones in this chamber at least, were vast machines, like the turbines of a power station. The Onihrs weren't big on miniaturisation.

One of the control panels was open, and the components inside were, variously, reconnected, disconnected or just lying in bits on the floor.

Pad had explained the exact functions of the bits of electronics. It all sounded fascinating, and Fitz harboured a degree of regret that he wouldn't be around to become a travelling EMP cannon repairman.

He connected the emitter power supply to the emergency buffer. Apparently. He stuck the big fat silver connector into the big green socket.

'Almost there?' he asked.

'Just four more connections,' Pad said cheerfully.

'You know what I'm planning to do here?'

'Of course, sir. The EMP cannon generates a vast amount of energy. You intend to channel that into the ship, rather than away from it. You want to attach the two yellow cables to that capacitor.'

'And?'

'Well, sir, the ship, everything on board, and everything else for a couple of light seconds around it will be annihilated. Now set that output level to maximum. And shut off that emergency override.'

'Is a light second like a light year?'

'The principal is the same, although it's a little less far.'

'Cool. You learn something every day. Er… you appreciate you'll be destroyed, Pad?'

215

'Well. Once you press that red button, sir, the one that's flashing there, then the ship will be destroyed in a chain reaction. It will start at the emitter at the front of the ship, then work its way back.'

Fitz took a deep breath. 'But the Onihrs will be stopped, the Earth will be saved, and there would be nothing they could do about it?'

'Not in the seven seconds the destruction of the ship would take, sir, no.'

Fitz pressed the button.

Pad squealed.

'Take it like a man,' Fitz suggested, a little weakly. He could hear the ship throwing itself apart. It sounded like the biggest china tea service in the world hitting the floor. Fitz was proud he'd come up with such a great simile under such pressure. It proved he was –

'Sir, I was rather hoping you'd use my teleport function to get us off the ship.'

The sound was deafening now. 'You can do that?'

'SIR!!!!!'

'Teleport now!' Fitz screamed, as the ship exploded around him.

Fitz appeared in what looked like an aircraft hangar. It was a bit chilly. And dark. But he felt like he was full of helium after several days on the Onihr ship, with its intense gravity.

He jumped up and down, enjoying his new-found freedom of movement.

'Well done,' Pad squeaked happily. 'I look forward to serving you again, sir.'

'I'm alive! I'm alive!' Fitz shouted, leaping for joy.

Anji grabbed his T-shirt and pulled him down, just as a streak of fire blew Pad out of his hand and smashed it against the back wall of the hangar.

The Doctor and Anji were squatting behind some oil drums.

'Hi,' Fitz said quietly.

'Where have you been?' Anji asked.

'Hey, I just saved the Earth from a race of invincible would-be time-travelling space rhinos.'

The Doctor smiled. 'In all of the history of the English language, I doubt that sentence has ever been spoken before. Well done. For the last few minutes, it's been nothing but "Doctor, help!", "Doctor, look out!", "Doctor, they've got us pinned down", "We're not going to make it". I'd begun to think I would never hear an original sentiment expressed again.'

Anji glared at the Doctor. 'Believe me, Doctor, I've thought of some great new words in the last couple of minutes. Swearwords, designed for unique circumstances like this, that ordinary swearing just doesn't cater for. Just before Fitz arrived, I was just thinking that you were a completely useless otterfuc–'

Another barrel exploded, drowning out Anji and showering them all in shrapnel.

'Who's the guy with the gun?' Fitz asked.

'Baskerville. He's a Russian arms dealer who's stolen a time machine.'

Fitz shrugged.

'A shrug?' Anji said, exasperated. 'Is that the best you can manage?'

'Look, I've just spent three days in space with a bunch of super-intelligent alien rhinos on a spaceship the size of Manhattan. This is normal by comparison. By the way, here's your phone back.'

Anji looked suitably impressed.

'Baskerville,' the Doctor called out. 'You can't possibly win.'

This was so clearly antithetical to the facts that Baskerville responded by increasing his rate of fire. The last few barrels were exploding, now.

'Er… what are those chaps?' Fitz asked.

Three chrome vehicles were taking up positions behind them. They were hovercraft, but with smooth, egg-shaped bodies. They looked a bit like tanks, an impression confirmed a moment later, when guns started emerging from hatches in their fronts.

'Class two RealWar robots,' the Doctor said.

Anji was lying flat on the floor. A moment later, the Doctor and Fitz realised that she was doing something rather sensible.

The tanks opened fire simultaneously, the bullets passing right over them, perforating the barrels. They were firing at Baskerville – the Doctor, Fitz and Anji just happened to be in the way.

A male scream. The mini-rockets had stopped. A moment later, the cannon fire had, too. Fitz kept his head down, though, and assumed the Doctor and Anji were doing the same.

'Baskerville!' the three tanks barked simultaneously, with a Scots accent.

Fitz was pleased to recognise the voice – it was the old man at the theme park who'd kicked his head in. Excellent – perhaps he'd get to see the really fit Korean bird again.

'Baskerville! This is Cosgrove. I have control of the RealWar robots here. All of them. I have control of this base. Nothing is going to arrive or leave unless I want it to. All your men are dead. It's just you and Dee. And you can walk away from this. I want the time machine. Now, you can tell me where it is, then leave, or I can kill everyone I haven't killed so far, and search this place at my leisure.'

Fitz sighed. 'Well, at least things can't get worse,' he suggested.

The air behind the tanks swirled, and six fully armed Onihr warriors stepped out of thin air and into the hangar.

'Eradicate all humans!' the deputy leader growled.

Fitz started banging his head against the concrete floor of the hangar. He couldn't think of anything better to do, and this way he'd save someone else the trouble.

Chapter Nineteen
Action

The Eurozone security service monitors in and around Istanbul were all starting to reach the same conclusion.

The President hadn't been seen since he'd entered the hotel, several hours before. The White House spokesmen had been waffling for most of that time – the President was being briefed, the President was unavailable. But something wasn't right. There were riots in Tripoli, now. The massacre of the children on the school bus might have been a rogue teletroop, but it was an American rogue teletroop and demanded a response at the highest level.

As soon as CNN and the EZBC had reported it, both the Americans and EZ got more troops on to the street and more planes in the air. They knew it was just the sort of incident that could start a whole cascade of other incidents.

The EZ President, the President Minister of England, the leaders and relevant secretaries of state and spokesmen from just about every country there was had made a statement about the Tripoli shootings by now.

But not the President of the United States.

The press corps knew the procedures, they knew what normally happened with this sort of incident. Most of all, they knew when the White House press office were trying to pull the wool over their eyes.

EZ monitors watched all this with interest.

They were also watching things the press corps had no idea about. Three squadrons of USAF hypersonic jets had shown up heading north from the Gulf into Russia. The Americans had gone out of their way to make sure the EZ didn't know about them. The natural conclusion was that they would swing back west, into eastern Europe. But why only three squadrons?

The tacticians concluded that the Americans were launching a pre-emptive strike, one that no battle plans had allowed for.

And the President wasn't available. Even on the hotline.

Whatever was going on in Istanbul, Washington seemed to know nothing about it. The Vice President wasn't in charge, they insisted, the President was still in charge.

Deliberate confusion, the EZ security chiefs advised their ministers. Deniability. The ability to claim that whatever was happening wasn't happening with presidential approval.

There were two American fleets in the Mediterranean. One in the Gulf, one in the Atlantic. The EZ navy were outnumbered, even on their own doorstep. The Americans had a ring of missile bases in the Med, too. Smart missiles that could hit any point in Europe, pretty well before they could scramble interceptors.

Meanwhile, the rumours were that the Americans had at least some sort of laser anti-missile defence. Conventional strategic thinking was that you told your enemy about your defences, to deter them from attacking. But the EZ weren't the enemy of the Americans, not conventionally. Conventionally, you wouldn't start your attack on Europe by flying three squadrons into Russia.

The political leaders of the Eurozone agreed that it was all adding up to a sneak attack by the Americans. A few junior White House and defence department staff were vehemently denying it, the ambassadors claimed not to know anything about it.

But the idea that the President had vanished was just ridiculous. Vanished where?

The situation now was critical.

For the Eurozone security advisers, it was simple. Either the Americans knew where the President was, and were launching a sneak attack, or there was confusion, possibly a critical power vacuum in the US chain of command.

Either way, there was only one sensible response for the Eurozone.

The Eurozone Council authorised an attack on United States forces in the Mediterranean and North Africa.

The deputy leader strode through the hangar, his warriors behind him.

In Terran gravity, they moved easily, almost skipping. This was a large chamber. The first location they had arrived at in the human structure had been appallingly cramped, and in the corridors they had had to move carefully, and in single file.

They had found a laboratory. There had only been room for two Onihrs, and a quick investigation revealed eleven dead human civilians.

'Killed by projectile weapons,' the scouts had told him. 'There is no evidence that these humans were armed.'

'There is more than one human faction at work here,' another had concluded.

'The only conclusion is that there is a rival group of humans who want the time machine.'

'This is a complex situation.'

The deputy leader nodded his agreement. 'Whoever killed these humans is clearly endeavouring to simplify matters.' He had studied his control box. 'We will teleport to the large hangar area, and –' they'd teleported then – 'eradicate all humans.'

Before they'd drawn breath, they were under attack.

The bullets bounced off the Onihr armour, but the momentum was enough to knock the deputy leader off his feet in this perilously thin gravity.

He struggled back on to his knees. Their attackers were primitive robots, little more than mobile artillery pieces. Behind the robots, two small groups of humans were running in opposite directions.

The bullets kept coming. For such ineffective weapons, they

were certainly efficient – hundreds of projectiles had reached their target. None had even dented or scratched the armour.

The Onihr was on his feet, now.

A single shot sliced the nearest robot in half. It fell to the floor, still firing for a couple more seconds.

The next robot launched itself at the Onihr, clumsily charging.

A couple of shots from his cohorts disabled the machine. It clattered to the floor in bits. The other warriors took their time, striding up to the machine, pulling the casing off, tearing out the vital components with their bare hands.

The Onihr kicked at the remains. There was a chance that a lucky shot could injure an Onihr. A slim chance.

Anji was attacking the foam insert of the case.

Baskerville had left it behind in his hurry to get out of the crossfire. The Doctor had grabbed it as he and his companions had also beat a retreat. They were back out on the runway now.

The inside of the hangar was lit by the tanks and the aliens firing their weapons at each other. Every so often, a stray shot would speed out of the hangar door.

The Doctor and Anji were bent over the coffee machine like it was the most important thing on Earth.

'I enjoy my coffee,' Fitz said. 'But this is silly.'

'The time machine must be in here,' Anji explained.

The Doctor was more interested in the coffee jug. He sloshed the coffee around experimentally.

'Anji… it's odd for Baskerville to pay so much attention to a coffee machine in the first place. But this jug is half-full. Or half-empty, of course, depending on your outlook. The point is that it's still got the coffee in it.'

Anji looked up. That was odd. 'The first thing you'd do would be to empty the jug.'

'Indeed.'

The Doctor sniffed the coffee.

'So what does that mean?'

'It means the coffee's the important thing.'

'It's time-travelling coffee?'

The Doctor frowned. 'I doubt it, somehow. Jaxa and Roja couldn't pick up any signs there had been time travel. They thought it was because Baskerville was using good shielding, but – have you still got that time detector?'

Anji handed it over. The Doctor waved it over the coffee machine, but there were no unusual readings.

'Doctor, I travelled in time. Cosgrove travelled in time.'

'But is there any physical evidence of that?'

Anji flashed her eyes at him triumphantly. 'What about the arrowhead?'

'Arrowhead?'

'In the case, there was that eleventh-century arrowhead. When Cosgrove went to the eleventh century, he picked up an arrowhead and brought it back.'

The Doctor thought for a moment. 'Simple enough to acquire – either it's a very well-preserved original, or a modern reconstruction. Because it's metal, it's impossible to carbon date. If I was going to plant evidence, I couldn't pick a better thing to use.'

Anji's head was spinning. 'But I was there. I was in Brussels.'

'You had those side effects,' the Doctor reminded her.

'Yeah… it was disorientating. But I was there.'

'You thought you were.'

'I was there.'

'They convinced you that you were.'

'In a bare room? They took me into a bare room, then I was in Brussels. I didn't move from the room, but I was in Brussels.'

'Which is easier? Making someone a time traveller, or conning someone to think they've time travelled?'

'How, though? You might be able to do it with, I don't know, holograms, or something. But that's hi-tech, too – they had a holographic TV on the plane to Athens and it was… well, it was rubbish. Blue and flickering. It's still future technology, so it's still evidence of time travel. I went into the sending chamber, then I was in Brussels.'

The Doctor tapped his lip. 'You've missed something.' He looked down at the coffee machine, just for a second.

'I had a cup of coffee.'

'You did.'

'OK… I've had plenty of cups of coffee in the past. None of them ever made me time travel.'

'No.'

'So why would this one?'

'Good question. What's the answer?'

Anji looked down at the coffee jug.

'There's something in the coffee that makes people who drink it travel in time?'

It seemed unlikely. But, frankly, running away from dinosaurs, talking to tigers and protecting the President of the United States from alien rhinoceroses seemed unlikely.

'No,' the Doctor said, 'time travelling coffee? That's utterly ridiculous. Think, Anji, think. What do you remember?'

'I was in Brussels. Right by the Mannkin Pis. I remember seeing the Atomium, and –'

'Wait. You were looking at the statue, but could also see the Atomium?'

'Er… yes.'

'Which isn't possible.'

'Well… no. And I sent my text message to Dave, and I was looking up at the Atomium, and thinking it looked like something out of Gerry Anderson, and suddenly the Atomium parted down the middle, the pavement was rolling slowly back, and there was a hangar below.'

The Doctor nodded. 'A hangar. Right. Then?'

'Hang on…' Anji said. 'There was a crack, like thunder, and then a rocket launched from the depths. That's… er… not possible, is it?'

'It's certainly a clue,' the Doctor said gently. 'Describe it.'

'It was about two hundred feet long, bright red, with a big white "3" on the side. It had stubby rocket pods at its base. None of the tourists even noticed. Perhaps it was an everyday occurrence there. That's what I thought.'

'Did you watch *Thunderbirds* as a child?' the Doctor asked. 'You must have done, you're the same age as… well, I remember watching children's TV in the eighties and –'

'*Thunderbirds*? It… it looked like Thunderbird Three.'

'Right down to the "3" on the side.'

'Yeah.'

'Didn't you find that a bit odd?'

'At the time… well… no, it all seemed to fit.'

'Because you were expecting it.'

'I wasn't expecting it. How could I?'

'You said it yourself: "it looked like something out of Gerry Anderson". You didn't travel back in time. You just thought you did.'

Anji looped a strand of hair back over her ear. 'It's not a time machine.'

'No.'

'But it makes people think it is.' She was stumped.

'It's a drug,' Fitz said offhandedly. 'There's something in the coffee that makes people think they're time-travelling. A hallucinogenic.'

The Doctor nodded. 'It has to be. Something that makes whoever drinks it very suggestible. Something that makes them see and hear things. Baskerville must be very skilled in directing that – making people see what they want to see. And it must metabolise quickly. If you remember back to what he said, I bet you'll see he was carefully directing events. That's why you only get ten minutes in the past. A clever precaution – it means that if anyone suspected they'd been drugged, there would be no sign of it in their system by the time they had a test.'

'It seemed so real.' But Anji was annoyed that Fitz got to the answer first, she wasn't arguing with the conclusion.

The Doctor nodded. 'By definition.'

'And it went wrong with me. Because I'm a time traveller – because I was experienced, and too open-minded about what might happen.'

The Doctor looked amused. 'Possibly. Either that, or you just had a bad reaction to he chemicals, or the conditioning went wrong.'

Anji preferred her explanation.

'So... Baskerville isn't a time traveller?'

'No.'

'He doesn't have a time machine?'

'No.'

'He's a local arms dealer on the verge of pulling off the biggest confidence trick in history?'

'Yes.'

Fitz looked back at the building. 'But there's an alien invasion force and a British secret agent in command of a robot army who are both after the time machine.'

'Yes.'

'They're not going to be happy when they find out there isn't one, are they?'

'No, they aren't.'

Baskerville bundled President Mather into a chair.

Dee tried to barricade the door, but couldn't find anything to use. This was a small first floor reception office – the place where the paperwork for the airstrip was stored.

'What is going on, Baskerville?' the President demanded. 'This is the "place of safety" you were talking about? It's a war zone. I have to get back to Istanbul.'

'With all due respect, Mr President, shut up.' He turned to Dee.

'The aliens have tracked us here. You said they couldn't do that.'

'I said they couldn't track the Concorde.

'This base is meant to be data-invisible. The whole point is that it doesn't have a data presence.'

'Perhaps the aliens can smell it,' Mather suggested.

Dee was switching on her laptop, checking its datanet connections.

'Come on, Baskerville. We can do what we came to do.' She turned to Mather. 'You remember your ULTRA codes?'

'I beg your –'

Baskerville rammed his gun into Mather's cheek. 'You heard. Now, please say "yes", or your country will go into a World War without its leader.'

'You don't scare me, Baskerville –'

Baskerville cocked his pistol.

'I don't care whether I scare you or not. Do you know the ULTRA code?'

'Yes. Some of it.'

'He'll know enough,' Dee assured him. The computer was up and running, connected to the datanet.

'Ready?'

Dee slipped a couple of VSCDs into the drive. 'Two seconds. Get the DNA scanner.'

Mather felt a jab at the back of his neck.

'Blood sample,' Leo said.

Baskerville held up what looked like a medical instrument to Mather's eye. There was a flash, which made Mather blink.

'Retinal scan. Say something, Mather. Say your name.'

'I am Felix Mather, President of the United States of America.'

'Voice pattern match,' Dee said. 'It's scanning to make sure it's not a recording or a sample.'

The screen flashed green.

Dee turned to Mather. 'Give me your ULTRA code.'

'There are safeguards.'

'Come on.'

He did, and a moment later, the screen showed a map of the world, with arrows of various sizes and colours swirling around the continents.

Mather looked Baskerville in the eye. 'Is this all this has been? A bank raid?'

Baskerville smiled. 'The IFEC. The International Financial Exchange Computer.'

'I know what the IFEC is. I was Vice President when the IFEC Accord was signed.'

'One protocol, one system that controls every single electronic financial transaction. Everywhere in the world. Everywhere that counts, anyway.'

Dee was tapping away, running programs from those discs of hers.

'You want to tap into it. Steal some money?'

'I have plenty of money, and the capacity to make plenty more. There's a World War brewing, Mr President. Your government has already paid me billions for RealWar hardware, and so have the Eurozone.'

Mather glanced back at the screen.

'The flow of capital,' Baskerville said, thumbing back at the screen. '*That* is capitalism. It's what made America great. Until IFEC, it was pretty difficult to see it spread out quite so boldly.'

'It's beautiful,' Mather said. It sounded silly, but it was. It was like looking at a living organism, and the closer he looked, the more and more details he saw.

'It is. And who owns it?'

'No one.'

'Exactly. And that's what I'm going to change. Miss Kapoor said it before – I'm going to steal money. All of it.'

Mather laughed out loud. 'All the money in the world?'

'Yes.'

'But that's mad. The authorities…'

'– won't know,' Dee finished for him.

'You intend to kill me?' Mather said, apparently resigned to it.

'No. I intend to cut you in.'

'You're mad.'

'You really should be careful what names you call your bank manager,' Dee chuckled.

Mather stood. 'I don't understand what I'm being offered here. You're still going to give the Americans time travel?'

The door exploded, and before the dust had settled, Malady Chang was in the room, an alien ray gun in each hand – both pointing at Baskerville.

'Don't move,' she said quietly. 'Mr President? You OK?'

'I'm fine, Malady.' He stepped behind her, towards the door.

Baskerville and Dee were both pointing guns at her.

'You won't make it through that door.'

Malady smiled, backing towards it.

She felt a gun in her back.

'Who are you?' Relker asked. 'What the hell is going on?'

Baskerville beamed. 'Finally. Relker, I presume? This is a CIA agent, that is the President of the United States, and I am your employer.'

'You're Baskerville?'

Baskerville sighed. 'Yes. Now, step out the way so I can kill these two.'

Malady lowered her guns, until they were pointing at the floor.

Baskerville chuckled. 'Not going down fighting, Lieutenant Commander Chang? How disappointing.'

Malady fired.

The floor beneath her feet, and the President's, disintegrated, and they dropped through the hole.

Relker fired, instinctively, almost hitting Baskerville.

Baskerville glared at him, then shot him with the gyrojet pistol. Relker exploded, a little messily.

'We really should get out of here,' Dee told him.

'Is it done?'

'Let's get to safety, then find out,' she suggested.

Cosgrove watched another sub-screen go blank as another robot was destroyed by the alien creatures.

There were six aliens in total, each in armour, each with those cutting beams. If he could just have one of his RealWar machines get one of the alien guns, he could even the odds a little.

Every RealWar machine in the factory was now active – he'd pulled them off the assembly lines, he'd pulled a couple from the repair shop.

The class twos could patrol outside, they could operate in the hangar and on the factory floor. But nowhere else. And they were slow and couldn't get adequate cover.

At one point he'd had twenty class threes. But they were big targets, a little too cumbersome to be practical indoors, they lost their balance too easily.

They were lasting longer than twenty human troops would have done, and putting up a better fight, but Cosgrove had less than ten of them left, and – as far as he could tell – hadn't even injured one of the aliens.

The aliens hadn't located him in his control centre – they hadn't come within a hundred feet of him. But they were keeping him from the main order of business: finding the time machine. Meanwhile, Mather and Malady Chang were loose, somewhere (it had been a while since they'd flitted past one of his cameras after escaping from Baskerville); Baskerville and Dee Gordon were still at large, and most worryingly, there was the Doctor. Not only was the resourceful Miss Kapoor with him, they'd been joined by the man Cosgrove had met in California. Cosgrove was worried that he couldn't even begin to work out how the lad had got here. It was possible to get from California to here in the time (he'd managed it, after all), but the lad must have been right on his tail the whole time – or known to head here.

All he had to do was find that time machine…

The Doctor sat in front of the laptop they'd found in a first floor reception room.

'An incredibly clever piece of programming.'

Anji was willing him on. 'Never mind that – can we find out what Baskerville's up to?'

'Or control those robots?' Fitz asked.

'The program's not about robots.'

Fitz looked disappointed. 'What is it about?'

'It looks like stock prices,' Anji told them. 'It's monitoring financial transactions. Perhaps he's waiting for a payment, looking for proof.'

Fitz was looking actively bored, now. 'We're looking at Baskerville's bank statement?'

The Doctor was staring at the data, trying to make sense of it all. 'More than that, I think. Anji, look: International Financial Exchange Computer.'

'IFEC. So… Baskerville has control of this?'

'I think so.'

'Then he's won. He's got control?'

'For what it's worth.'

'For what it's worth? He can charge commission on every financial transaction on the planet. He can stop business deals, shut down governments. If you control the flow of money, you control the planet.'

'A sad reflection on your species,' the Doctor said, in that irritating professorial voice he occasionally adopted. 'Hang on a mo…'

Anji saw what he was looking at. 'The transaction isn't complete until there's an IFEC number attached to it. He's not finished. He must have been interrupted.'

'There is a very large hole in the floor,' Fitz reminded them. 'And a rather nasty looking red streak on that wall.'

'Malady must have interrupted him before –'

'I understand, Doctor, I told you, remember? Now, quick, before they come back.'

'Quick, what?'

Anji held up a piece of paper. 'This is the IFEC number they were going to enter. The master account. Attach a different IFEC number.'

The Doctor floundered. 'Which one?'

'Any one.'

'*Any* one?'

Anji stared at the screen. 'Well, OK, not any one… er…'

The Doctor had a brainwave, and started rummaging around in his pocket.

'Hurry, Doctor.' She was looking around the room for another IFEC number, unsure why she thought she'd find one.

The Doctor had pulled out a bank card. 'I opened a bank account in Athens.'

'You had time to do that?'

'It was an accident. Look – let me enter the number.'

He tapped the fifteen digit code into the computer, winced as it scanned his retina.

'There.'

He tapped a few more controls.

'Now… the world's economy will be run through my bank account.'

Fitz was looking at the card. 'Hang on, you've got all the money in the world in your bank account?'

'Not exactly – for a millisecond or two, every financial transaction is channelled through my account, that's all.'

Anji stared down at the little piece of plastic. A hologram of Medusa stared back at her. 'Still, it's probably best that you don't forget your PIN number.'

The Onihr deputy leader sniffed the air.

Earth was cold, dark, insubstantial. The human structures were feeble. To prove the point to himself, he reached out, scooped a handful of brick from the wall, then crushed it.

'Report,' he barked into his nosepiece.

His warriors did just that – they were fanning out across the base, on full alert, but had come no nearer to finding the time machine.

The deputy leader leaned against a blue wooden structure. He sniffed it, peered at it. Its function was not immediately obvious. It was made of wood panels, with little windows towards the top, and a light on the roof. Primitive human writing adorned some of the uppermost panels. It would just, at a squeeze, be big enough for an Onihr to stand inside.

A useless human artefact.

The deputy leader was frustrated that his search for the human time machine was taking so long. He was irritated that the humans had a time machine in the first place. They must have stolen it, or had it fall on to their planet by chance. How dare these flimsy-skinned, insubstantial creatures have time travel when the Onihr race had strived so long to achieve it. What could the humans hope to do with the technology?

There was a time machine here, so close he could feel it. The ancient Onihr quest would finally reach its culmination.

He smelled the robot moments before it arrived.

A hydraulic arm clamped around the deputy leader's neck.

The deputy leader struggled, but the hold was tight. The other arm was tugging at his breastplate.

Another robot stomped slowly into the room, raised an arm. It was holding a projectile weapon. Its height and build had more in common with the Onihrs than its human creators. Not through any aesthetic sense, simply because human technical skills were inadequate to the task.

The deputy leader doubted that the human guns could harm him even if he wasn't wearing armour, but had no intention of finding out. These machines were crude, insulting.

He straightened up, pulling the robot that had hold of him off its feet. It strengthened its grip, constricting the deputy leader's throat a little, but not enough to block his breathing.

Its leg pedalled a little, trying to find the ground. The device was surprisingly light, even allowing for the low gravity.

The deputy leader slammed it against the structure behind them, heard a number of satisfying cracks and hisses. He slammed it again.

The other robot opened fire, and only succeeded in blowing the head off its comrade. Blinded, the machine tried to tighten its grip, but it had lost a lot of its balance. The deputy leader found it easy enough to extricate himself from its limbs.

He picked up the robot and swung it at the other. It broke the functioning robot's neck and shoulder, then fell apart.

The deputy leader had a hand free now to reach for his gun. It took three shots to damage the robot beyond repair, two more than the deputy leader would have liked.

He rubbed his neck. It hurt a little. There were hints of damage to his armour, too, and he was lucky they hadn't caught his gun, which wasn't as well protected. With the right combination of circumstances, the humans could harm Onihrs.

All the more reason to eliminate them as efficiently as possible.

Chapter Twenty
Endgame

Dee hurried through the robot factory.

The production lines were silent. At some point during the fighting, they must have been shut down. Rows and rows of half-completed robots stood there. It made the place look like a monumental gallery of statues.

Any robot that was complete, or near enough to complete had gone. They'd been sent to the front by Cosgrove. Dee could hear some of them, rumbling away deep inside the building, loosing off the occasional round of gunfire.

Baskerville had her laptop, and all her specialist software.

They'd got split up about ten minutes ago. Baskerville had run out of gyrojets, and they'd been forced to beat a retreat – straight into the path of the aliens. They'd both gone off their own ways.

Perhaps Baskerville was dead. He was certainly finished. He had hours at most – as soon as CIA or EZSS programmers got here, they'd be able to see what she'd done to get into IFEC, trace the software, trace the laptop. It would take them a little time, but only a little. She'd completed the transfer, at least she assumed she had, but she hadn't buried it deep enough. If you knew what you were looking for, if you asked the right questions, then you'd be able to trace it.

Dee realised, of course, that she could be dead long before that.

The radar tower was gone, so there was no anti-aircraft capacity here any more. Class twos and class threes were ground assault units – they could point their guns up and fire into the air, but they weren't designed for anti-aircraft operations.

She had to get to the hangar. It was tempting to steal the

Concorde, but it was too big to be useful – she'd need a big runway to land it, and wherever it landed in the world it would lead to a lot of awkward questions.

One of the light aircraft. They were easier to fly, would draw less attention, they'd be easier to sell on, maintain, get fuel for.

Dee reached the hangar.

One of the big freight helicopters was a burned-out shell. The hangar floor was littered with discarded bullet cases and bits of twisted metal.

It was dark by now, but there was a full moon, and the hangar door was wide open, so it wasn't too dark to see.

Outside, Dee could see two class twos moving around, the moonlight glinting off them. They were just on a standard patrol as far as she could see.

The Concorde was still there, golden light pouring from the doors and windows. Other than that, it was practically invisible in the dark. She was glad of the reminder it was there – it meant she would have to taxi her plane past it before powering up the runway. She'd hoped to be able to start her run from inside the hangar.

It would give the class twos a chance to shoot at her, of course.

First things first: she needed to find a plane.

There were two light aircraft, both relatively new jet-engined Pipers. She'd not flown the make before, but knew enough about them to feel confident she'd not have a problem.

There was nothing to choose between them, so she got into the nearest, closing the door carefully behind her, trying as hard as she could to make sure the cabin hadn't been punctured by stray gunfire.

She sat in the pilot's seat, strapped herself in, put the headset on.

Hotwiring it was easier than hotwiring a car would have been. The jet engines fired up, and the on-board computer began running the pre-flight checks. It chimed up at her when she started the plane moving before it had finished making sure it was

236

ready to go. But the engines were noisy, the noise would already have drawn attention to her, and the sooner she was away the better.

She used the pedals to steer it past the Concorde.

The two tanks had seen her, but they were too slow to react. She started her ascent run, powering up the engines and pointing the plane straight down the runway.

She was about to find out if the plane had been damaged.

The lights and other indicators all said it was fully fuelled, that the cabin had pressure. But, of course, one of the sensors might itself be damaged, in which case…

The plane lifted off the runway. Behind her, Dee thought she heard gunfire as one of the class twos got into a position to attack her plane.

But it was too late, she was already ten miles away from the base.

She'd lived to fight another day.

For the first time since she'd left his side, Dee wondered how Baskerville was managing.

Malady had hurt her leg a little in the fall, Mather was uninjured.

They were back outside, now. It was getting dark, but it was obvious that there weren't any people guarding the Concorde any more. A few bodies were strewn on the tarmac. A couple of class two hovertanks were patrolling the area – from the look of it, they were executing a routine search pattern – they were operating automatically, but would alert their operator if they came across anything of interest.

'I'm not sure the Concorde is safe, sir,' she said.

It had been their plan to head back there, use the radio to contact the authorities. But with the class twos there, it looked remarkably like a sitting duck. The plane hadn't been refuelled, so even if they could get it up into the air, they had no idea how long they could keep it there.

The best thing to do was sit tight and wait for the planes that would be heading for them.

Malady had handed Mather one of the ray guns. If it came to it, they could outgun the RealWar robots.

'There's a time machine somewhere on this base,' Mather said. 'We have to get it. The opportunities it would give us… well, I can hardly imagine them.'

Malady smiled, and pulled a short silver tube from her pocket. 'This isn't Baskerville's time machine, sir, but it's a time machine.'

Mather took it, and as he did, he must have touched something, because the controls swirled out and lit up.

'It's recharging,' she told him. 'I don't think it's fully charged, yet, but it's getting there. It's smart – it needs a lot of power, but it can tap into any energy source.'

Mather held it, amazed. 'Where did you get this?'

'We were attacked by time travellers in Athens.'

'Big creatures, like rhinoceroses?'

Malady frowned at him. 'No, sir. People. They looked like people, anyway. They wore purple uniforms. They were humans, from the future.'

Mather laughed. 'Did they have American accents, or did they sound European?'

Malady tried to remember. 'Honestly… I don't know. The boy sounded like a Dickens character. The woman…' What *had* her voice sounded like?

Mather put a hand on Malady's shoulder. 'I don't think it matters. You've done an excellent job, Malady.'

'What now?'

'We sit tight and wait for our airlift.'

A moment later, a light aircraft began taxiing down the runway. 'Someone's making a getaway,' Malady said.

Baskerville turned the corner, and ran straight into one of the aliens.

238

It growled at him, snarled. It was speaking to him.

'I don't speak your language,' he said, as calmly as he could manage. 'We need a translator.'

Baskerville backed away, into another of the creatures.

He was holding out his hands, acting as meekly as he could, speaking so softly they couldn't possibly interpret his intent as hostile.

One of the aliens produced a small, square box and held it over its snout.

It growled. A moment later, a pleasant male voice began: 'Where is the time machine? We have come for the time machine. Show us the time machine, or we will kill you.'

It was his own voice, Baskerville realised. Or at least a good synthesised version of it.

Baskerville straightened. 'I contacted you, remember?'

They glowered at him. He couldn't tell them apart, they almost certainly couldn't tell individual humans apart.

'I contacted your ship. I arranged this meeting.'

One of the creatures stepped forwards and grunted.

'Are you jamming our communications? We are unable to contact our ship.'

'No,' said Baskerville, genuinely puzzled. 'I wouldn't know how to…'

'You could communicate with our ship. Therefore you could block our signals.'

'It isn't me. My name is Baskerville, I have the time machine. You have technology that I am interested in. That translator alone would be worth… let us negotiate.'

The nearest creature sniffed the air. 'Where is the time machine?'

Baskerville was never one to miss an opportunity. 'My… headquarters here are under attack by rival human forces. This is a primitive, warlike planet. There are three human factions who are also after my time machine. One, I regret to say, has stolen vital components from the machine. They were in a silver case. He is

239

called the Doctor, and –'

The creature grabbed him, almost tearing him in two. 'The Doctor is here?'

'Yes.'

The creatures looked at each other, warily. 'The Doctor has tricked us and escaped from our ship. He will attempt to interfere with our plans. Our top priority must be to locate him and kill him.'

Baskerville dusted himself down, annoyed to find the creature had gashed the jacket of his suit with a claw. 'You took the words out of my mouth.'

The Doctor, Anji and Fitz were in the canteen.

It was small, fairly dismal. There was evidence the place had been cleaned recently – but only because there were swirls in the dirt, and some panels on the counter were a different coloured filth to the others.

The room was deserted – after the gun battles of the last hour or so, the whole complex was quiet, now.

One whole wall was taken up by a large plasma screen. It played images soundlessly, and there was no sign of the volume controls.

They didn't need to hear what was being said, or read the captions scrolling across the screen. The images of American ships under rocket attack didn't need any commentary.

One reporter, his head down, was shouting wordlessly into his microphone while behind him a fire was raging on the deck of a warship.

Aircraft streaked overhead – it wasn't clear if they were American or European planes.

There were gun battles raging in Cairo, but the pictures were fuzzy, because the soldiers were jamming, or trying to jam, RealWar control signals.

Every so often, maps would flash up, with reassuringly bold arrows.

They reminded Anji a little of the IFEC map.

'Hang on,' said Fitz, 'that's the news.'

Anji managed a smile. 'It's the news,' she said grimly.

The Doctor was pointing at the screen. 'It says there that there's no sign of the President. If we could get Mather to a radio, then –'

Cosgrove had arrived. He stood in one of the doorways, gun in his hand.

'It's good to see the three of you here, together at last,' he said coldly. 'And you've even managed to recover Baskerville's time machine.'

Anji glanced down at the case, which sat on one of the canteen tables. She and Fitz were a good four or five paces away from him. Cosgrove opened the case, looked in.

'I don't understand,' Cosgrove muttered.

'It's a coffee machine,' Anji explained helpfully.

'Shall I be mother?' the Doctor asked, taking the jug.

'Where's the time machine?'

'We were just wondering that,' the Doctor said cheerfully.

'Who do you work for?' Cosgrove asked.

'You first,' the Doctor replied flatly, sticking the jug in the ultrasonic oven.

'I'm a loyal servant of the Eurozone Council,' Cosgrove said, barely able to keep the smile off his face.

The Doctor thumbed back at the screen. 'So you'll be delighted by that, I take it.'

Cosgrove looked up at the screen. It took him a moment or two to register it.

'Idiots,' he said finally. 'They're all idiots.'

'I thought you were a soldier,' Fitz said. 'You should be relishing this.'

'I'm a spy,' Cosgrove said. 'That's quite a different thing. Still. Soon it won't matter.'

He'd been walking towards the case all the time they'd been speaking.

The Doctor watched him carefully. 'So what do you want time travel for, Cosgrove?'

The old man smiled. 'It's the ultimate weapon.'

The Doctor's shoulders sagged. 'It's so much more than that,' he said quietly.

'An ultimate weapon will do for starters,' Cosgrove said. 'Imagine being able to fight a war in four dimensions, when your opponent can't. Everything they do could be factored in and anticipated. If they launch an attack, you just go back and defend against it. Then you go back further and prevent it from happening in the first place. Then you launch surgical strikes into the past. Eliminate your opponents before they even are your opponents.'

'Endless war,' the Doctor said.

'Endless victory,' Cosgrove replied. He looked up at the screen. 'Endless prevention of politicians making idiotic decisions.'

The oven pinged to say it was done.

'Where do you draw the line?' the Doctor asked. He was also looking at the screen. 'How would you go back and stop that from happening? How far would you go back? A couple of days? Months? Or just cut out the middle man by making sure the EZ never formed. Better yet, you could go back and make sure the British win the War of Independence. No America in the first place.'

'If necessary.'

'You'd be playing with fire.'

'Playing with fire is how humanity left the caves, Doctor. I'm not out to make big changes. Just reverse a few decisions, give people the benefit of my hindsight. Make Britain great again, not just part of a superstate. Everyone knows it, Doctor, everyone knows that if our leaders had been a little bit braver, or cleverer or more imaginative, then we wouldn't be here. We'd still be a country. We'd still have a future. We wouldn't be about to fight a war against the greatest ally our country has had in its history.'

'And subverting democratic governments is part of that process?'

'Yes,' Cosgrove said quickly. 'It always has been. Since... since

242

Roman times, there have been people who've known what's really going on. People whose business it is to know. And they've advised their leaders, and their leaders have acted on that. Democracy is just a fancy name for mob rule.'

Anji stepped forward. 'So what's the fancy name for what you're planning? Dictatorship? Tyranny?'

'It'll be called whatever I want it to be called.'

The Doctor headed towards the canteen counter.

'What's first on the agenda?' the Doctor asked. 'Once you've got the time machine in your hand, what's the first item of business?'

'Eliminating opposition. Killing Baskerville, finding some way to kill those alien creatures. With time travel, I'll be invincible.'

The Doctor picked up a mug, looked into it thoughtfully. His eye was caught by a small black box. He slipped it into his pocket.

Cosgrove was rooting through the foam insert, just like Anji had done.

'It's a coffee machine,' she repeated. 'It's a con. There isn't a time machine.'

The Doctor handed Cosgrove the jug. Cosgrove examined it carefully, peering into the coffee as it sloshed around. The Doctor stepped over to him.

'I was there. I saw Macbeth.'

The Doctor chuckled. 'No you didn't. It's just coffee.'

Baskerville opened the jug, sniffed it.

'It's probably very nice coffee,' the Doctor added.

Cosgrove sat down. 'No time machine.'

'No,' said the Doctor gently. He handed Cosgrove the mug. 'All you get is the coffee.'

Cosgrove poured himself half a mug, watched the steam rise.

'I could have changed the world,' he said. 'I could have made it *work*.'

'You still can,' the Doctor assured him. 'But there's time for a coffee break first.'

Cosgrove sipped the coffee, wincing a little – it was piping hot, and a little sour.

The Doctor took the remote control from his pocket and tapped the 'mute' button.

It was almost deafening. The reporter was yelling over the sounds of fire, explosions and planes streaking overhead.

'This is the USS Delaware, forty miles off the Libyan coast, and we're under attack by EZ jet bombers!' the reporter screamed.

Cosgrove was on his feet. 'Civilians evacuate the area!' he shouted. 'Emergency fire teams to the main deck! Come on! Move!'

He was staring at the screen, fixed at it.

Fitz leaned over to Anji. 'Nutter,' he said knowledgeably.

'He's drunk the drugged coffee. He's taking his cues from the television.'

'He thinks he's on telly?'

The Doctor poured the rest of the coffee down the sink. 'He does. Conclusive proof of what Baskerville's been up to, wouldn't you say? Now, we've only got ten minutes before the drug wears off. I suggest we use the time to find those aliens, and get them back to their ship.'

Fitz looked a little sheepish. 'Er, yeah. About that...'

Baskerville jammed his pistol into the President's ribs.

'Tell her to drop her gun.'

'Malady...'

Malady circled for a moment. They were right at the edge of the runway, on the edge of the cliff. There weren't many places they could run to.

'I'll kill him,' Baskerville told her. He looked desperate. Malady thought about a headshot. She could probably do it.

Then six huge creatures lumbered out of the gloom.

One of them growled something. A moment later, it said it again, in Baskerville's voice. 'He has the time machine?'

She'd seen them before, she realised – back in Ibiza, the night that Cosgrove's boat had exploded. These were the things that had killed Garvin.

Baskerville was shaking his head. 'No – that's the most powerful man on Earth, the President of the United States.'

The creature was unsure whether Baskerville was pointing at Mather or at Malady.

Another one was snorting excitedly. The other turned to it, listened for a moment or two. Malady saw it was also getting excited.

The nearest creature swung its great head to face the President. 'You have the time machine.'

Baskerville looked bemused. 'There's some mistake…'

'No mistake. You have the time machine. Superior Onihr science has located it.'

The President hesitated, then held the silver cylinder out.

'Hand it over,' the translator voice said calmly. But all six creatures were aiming their weapons at the President, and shifting from foot to foot excitedly.

Mather passed the device to Baskerville, who held it up, triumphantly.

'This is my time machine,' he told the deputy leader.

The deputy leader leant in and sniffed it. '*That?*'

'Yes. It operates –' Baskerville tried twisting at it, looking for any hint of a control panel. He even tried *willing* it open, wondering if there was some sort of mental control involved. '– I will show you how it operates when we reach a deal,' he concluded.

'He doesn't know how it operates,' the Doctor said, stepping forwards. Fitz and Anji were right behind him.

A moment of silence.

The creature growled.

'That's right,' the Doctor replied. 'I'm afraid I have some bad news for you. This man has been trying to trick you. He's tried to trick a lot of people, and he almost succeeded.'

245

'Is this true, Doctor?'

The Doctor frowned.'I just said it is…'

After a moment's incomprehension, Fitz stepped forward. 'Yes, deputy leader, it's absolutely true. Everything he just said.'

The monster stepped over to Baskerville.

'They think you're me?' the Doctor asked.

'Yeah.'

'Why?' The Doctor looked deeply offended. 'I mean, how could they mistake you for me?'

'You've either got it or you haven't,' Fitz told him. An idea was clearly dawning. 'And… and I'm afraid Baskerville destroyed your ship,' he called to the creatures.'He used an impulse to set off your EMP cannon. That is why you can't signal it.'

The creature roared something.

'Destroyed your ship?' Baskerville whimpered. 'I wouldn't know how to do that…'

'He is a skilful and resourceful man,' the Doctor continued. 'Very dangerous. Probably the most dangerous human being alive.'

The alien was growling and snarling into its control box.

'You can teleport over such vast distances?'

A short grunt.

'I see… only at lightspeed. So it will be many centuries before you arrive? Then… yes… take Baskerville back to your planet for trial. Subject him to the full punishment of your law.'

'Wait!' Baskerville shrieked.'Wait!'

The Doctor reached out, snatched the time machine from Baskerville's hand.

Then the alien activated a control on the control box, and all six, and Baskerville, vanished.

The Doctor smiled.'There… safely packed off to another galaxy. Earth won't be bothered by the Onihrs for many more centuries to come.'He clapped his hands together.'I think that's all the loose ends neatly tied up.'

Cosgrove stepped out of the darkness.'All but one.'

He held the gun to the Doctor's head.

'I can't miss at this range, Doctor. I can kill you and take it, or you can hand it over. Those are the only two choices.'

'Choices…' the Doctor said, his voice trailing away. 'Is that really the last choice that anyone on this planet gets? Make you a dictator, or let you become one?'

'It certainly looks that way, doesn't it?'

The Doctor smiled. 'Here's a choice for you. You can catch it, or you can shoot me. You won't have time to do both.'

'I beg your pardon?'

'You can shoot me, or you can catch it.'

The Doctor tossed the time machine over the edge of the cliff.

Cosgrove leaped after it.

Fitz and Anji joined the Doctor at the edge of the cliff.

'He's mad,' Fitz said.

'Well, yes,' the Doctor replied.

'He can't possibly…' Anji began.

'He can,' said the Doctor, untroubled. 'Just. And he knew it. The slightest hesitation and he wouldn't have a chance.'

'But he has a chance?' Fitz asked.

'Yes.'

'And if he gets to the time machine, he'll get everything he wants? He'll be able to go back in time and kill his enemies? He'll be able to bring weapons and intelligence information from the future?'

'Yes.'

Cosgrove had his arms out, like a diver.

The wind was intense, freezing. He barely noticed it.

The fall was hundreds of feet, on to jagged rocks. There was not one chance he could survive this, unless he caught the time machine.

The silver cylinder tumbled down, ten or fifteen feet ahead of him. It looked like a cigar tube. It was that sort of size, that sort of burnished silver.

He was gaining on it. He was definitely gaining.

He had one chance. All he had to do was grab it, squeeze the controls at the end.

One chance.

He reached out, strained until his arm was almost out of its socket.

His fingertip tapped against the time machine. Just for a moment, as it spun, but he'd felt it.

Seconds.

He had seconds to do this.

His arm reached further. His hand brushed against the cylinder.

Cosgrove snatched the time machine, grabbed it.

This was his destiny.

He squeezed the controls, felt the machine powering up.

He hit the rocks.

Fitz looked away. 'Yuck.'

Anji and the Doctor were still looking over the edge.

'Why didn't it work?'

'It hadn't had time to recharge.' The Doctor sounded sad.

'You didn't mention that to him?'

'Cosgrove was the sort to follow orders, not to give them,' the Doctor said, not answering the question.

' "If the Doctor told you to jump off a cliff would you do it?" ' Anji said quietly.

'Pardon?'

'It's what they say at school, isn't it? When you say you did something because someone said you should.'

'I don't remember my schooldays.'

'Of course, I was forgetting.'

Malady and President Mather were running across the runway. They were, Anji realised with a start, the only five living beings still here.

'The USAF are on their way,' Malady said. 'There will be transport helicopters here in twenty minutes.'

Mather smiled, held out his hand. 'The least we can do is offer you a lift back to civilisation. Perhaps you could explain why you don't look a day older than you did in 1989.'

The Doctor looked away, a little embarrassed.

'We have our own way of getting back,' Anji told him.

'Don't tell me: a time machine.'

The Doctor looked offended. 'Time travel? My dear Mather, I know we've seen some extraordinary things in our time. In millions of years, perhaps time travel will be a possibility. But... well, for the moment, it's science *fiction*, isn't it? Don't get carried away – you just concentrate on making sure the Americans and Eurozone can share this planet without blowing it up.'

'The shooting's started,' Anji told them.

Mather looked panicked. 'How do we stop it?'

The Doctor took a deep breath. 'It's barely started at the moment. But this base is proof that you've had someone playing the EZ and USA off each other.'

'And that there were rogue elements operating in the EZ,' Malady reminded them.

'Use Cosgrove as the fall guy,' Fitz suggested. He glanced over the edge of the cliff. 'Er... you know what I mean.'

The Doctor smiled. 'Probably best not to mention any of that time travel and aliens stuff.'

Mather looked thoughtful. 'You're right, of course. Time travel? It's absurd.'

'That's how Baskerville operated, you see. The big lie. Time travel's such a ridiculous idea that he couldn't possibly be lying, could he? I mean... a time machine? Who'd believe that?' The Doctor clapped his hands on Fitz and Anji's back. 'OK, you two, let's get back to the TARDIS.'

HOPE by Mark Clapham ISBN 0 563 53846 5 ·
ANACHROPHOBIA by Jonathan Morris ISBN 0 563 53847 3

COMING SOON

THE BOOK OF THE STILL by Paul Ebbs ISBN 0 563 53851 1
(May 02)
THE CROOKED WORLD by Steve Lyons ISBN 0 563 53856 2
(June 02)
HISTORY 101 by Mags L Halliday ISBN 0 563 53854 6 (July 02)
CAMERA OBSCURA by Lloyd Rose ISBN 0 563 53857 0 (Aug 02)
TIME ZERO by Justin Richards ISBN 0 563 53866 X (Sept 02)

DOCTOR WHO BOOKS TELEPRESS
covers, reviews, news & interviews
http://www.bbc.co.uk/cult/doctorwho/books/telepress